Cooper

The work is a work of fiction. All of the characters, names, incidents, organizations, and dialogue in this novel are either the products of the author's imagination or are used fictitiously.

The views expressed in this work are solely those of the author and do not necessarily reflect the views of the publisher, and the publisher herby disclaims any responsibility for them.

Printed in the United States of America

Kirabaco Publishing

Sins of the Father

By
KR Bankston

In loving memory:

Mr. E. Lynn Harris,
Thank you for the wonderful advice
and great novels!

Sarah Jo Hurley -Thompson
Joe Bowman
Corrine Bowman
Arnette Simons
Alfred McCann

"Are you ready honey?" Mrs. Black asks Kayla. She is nervous and scared. She and Black are getting married today. She'd wanted a simple ceremony with close family and a few friends, but his parents wouldn't hear of it.

"We are going to share this happy occasion with all our family and friends," his mother told her, when they'd talked about it.

Kayla explained that she didn't have any family to speak of, and really didn't want all the fuss.

"Nonsense girl!" Mrs. Black chided her. "We're your family now, and trust me, we will fill up the entire church!" she'd laughed.

Kayla gave in and allowed her to plan the wedding. She had to admit she'd enjoyed the shopping, and trying on dresses. They finally found the perfect one, at a small boutique downtown.

It was a beautiful off white, t-strap dress, fitted around the bodice and waist. The bodice had been hand beaded, with beautiful iridescent pearls that shimmered in the light. Kayla had to admit, she loved the way she looked in it.

Mrs. Black and her sister, Aunt Leslie, complimented her again and again. She'd overheard Mrs. Black telling Leslie how proud she was of Donovan, for finding such a wonderful woman to marry. That made her feel loved and accepted. Something Kayla hadn't felt for a while, when it came to family.

"Yes," she answered softly, shaking her thoughts and confirming her readiness.

Mrs. Black smiled again and left her. Soon Mr. Black entered to walk Kayla down the isle. Black asked Maurice Collins, his ex partner, to be his best man. Kayla inhaled deeply, and took Mr. Blacks arm, as they headed for the sanctuary of the church.

She would never forget how handsome Black looked, standing at the altar waiting for her in his cream tuxedo. He'd smiled the entire time she'd walked down the aisle, never once taking his eyes off her. It was only when she got closer to him, that she noticed the tears in his eyes.

Kayla sighed softly, thanking God again and again, for sending this wonderful man and his family, her new family, and their beautiful daughter. Mariah was sitting happily in her grandmother's lap smiling at them. She was dressed in her own cream and pink dress, clapping happily.

They came together before the minister, as he began the ceremony. They repeated their vows to each other, and exchanged rings. Kayla's ring had been specially designed just for her. It was a three-carat solitaire diamond, surrounded by half carat emerald baguettes. The three-quarter inch band was inscribed, 'forever my heart'.

"By the power vested in me," the minister was saying, as they smiled lovingly into each other's eyes. "I now pronounce you husband and wife," he continued. "You may now kiss the bride," he finished, looking at Black, who took Kayla in his arms, and kissed her passionately.
She blushed, and the congregation laughed aloud.

"Ladies and Gentlemen, I present to you, Mr. and Mrs. Donovan Black," the minister said again.
They locked arms and walked out of the church, to the waiting limousine. That'd been the most wonderful day of her life, outside of Mariah's birth. They had a wonderful Caribbean honeymoon, after which, they returned to Chapel Hill to begin their life together.

Kayla and Black enjoyed marital bliss, and the years of watching Mariah grow. They watch her first step, turn into her first bike. They watched the joy Mariah had at Christmas and birthdays.

Black dotes on his little princess, spending every moment he can with her and Kayla. Black is a pillar in the local church, with both Kayla and Mariah attending regularly.

She basks in the love of her in-laws, who have welcomed her with open arms into their family. Kayla appreciates her mother in-law helping her to raise her daughter, giving her valuable advice and guidance. Mariah is a beautiful girl, who will soon grow into a beautiful woman.

She looks at the wonderful estate home Black has bought for her, taking in the hardwood floors and bay windows, looking out onto the majestic view of the forest beyond, watching the squirrels running across the lawn, as Mariah laughs and tries to chase them.

Her life is better than Kayla could have ever imagined it would be. Her husband comes in and kisses her, asking how her day was. She tells Black of her new clients, and the hustle and bustle of her day.

He smiles and tells her how much he loves her yet again. Fourteen years of togetherness with the man she loves more than anything. Her life is perfect and peaceful. Kayla can't imagine being any happier.

Still, there were times in the quiet stillness of full moonlit nights, when she would remember the city she'd lived in for so many years. The loss of her best friend, Taea. The memory was still painful, even after all the years that had passed. The place where she'd met one of the most intriguing men in her life; loved and lost him.

Remember a time and a place that was once magical for her. A place where she'd experienced the most wonderful fulfillment a woman could have. Kayla loved Black unconditionally. That was never an issue, but Dezi Gianni was a different breed altogether.

No other man had unequivocally made her feel like the queen that he did. No other man touched her soul as deeply as he had. She would close her eyes sometimes and feel his presence envelop her, bringing a deep sense of warmth and contentment. She could smell his cologne and hear him whisper his love in her ear.

Kayla knew she should let it go, but in the small inner sanctum of her heart there was still a burning ember, a deep unfulfilled love for him. A love that even after time and circumstance just wouldn't die.

Sadly, Kayla knew they were just memories, and seeing him again just wishful thinking. Dezi was dead and he wasn't coming back. Sighing deeply she returned her thoughts to the present rising from her comfortable rocking chair and going inside the beautiful majestic house she shared with her husband.

Entering the bedroom and showering, Kayla moments later, carefully climbed into bed, as Black reached over and pulled her close, absently kissing her forehead and drifting back off to sleep.

Kayla smiled softly to herself as she inhaled her husbands scent, and snuggled deeply into his arms, dismissing the memories of Dezi, as sleep found her.

1

The dream was replaying itself once again, as Kayla tossed and turned in her sleep before waking violently, tears flowing, as she continued to remember.
"Black, I don't think you should go," Kayla pleaded with him.
He'd smiled and hugged her tightly.
"I'll be fine baby, and I'll be home before you know it," Black told her calmly.
Even now, three years later, Kayla was still waiting for him to fulfill that promise.

Mariah heard her mother sobbing, and knew she was having another bad night. Agent Donovan Black had been killed in the line of duty trying to arrest a wanted felon. Mariah felt her mother's pain. She too, missed her father dearly.

She rose from bed to go and comfort her mother. Mariah often asked God to send her mother someone to share the rest of her life with, knowing her father wouldn't want her to be alone forever.
"Hi mommy," Mariah said softly, as she hugged her.

Kayla smiled and hugged her back. She was so thankful for Mariah. She was all she had, now that Black was gone. Kayla missed her husband so much and felt so alone. Everything in this room, and in the house, reminded her of Black.

"I'm sorry I woke you baby," she told her, still sniffling.
"It's okay mommy," Mariah replied. "Can I get you something to drink?"
Kayla smiled again and told her no, she would be fine.
"Go on back to bed baby," she told her again softly.
"Are you going back to bed?" Mariah questioned, looking at her closely.

She knew her mother didn't sleep well most times, and after this episode, she was sure Kayla wouldn't sleep at all.

"Yes, I'm going to lie back down," Kayla answered.
Mariah looked at her again. She really didn't want to leave her alone.
"Well then, I'll lay in here with you," she said and climbed into the huge, solid oak, king-sized bed.

Mariah loved the heavy, cream and gold, down filled comforter that adorned her mother's bed.
Kayla smiled again, thinking how much like her father Mariah was. Kayla climbed into the other side, and lay down. She closed her eyes, and drifted into a troubled sleep.

Mariah rolled over and looked at the clock. "Man, its already after 10?" she mumbled out loud.
She looked at the other side of the bed. Kayla was already up. She figured as much. Mariah thought about her father, and how it used to be when he was there.

Her mother was so much happier then. Mariah knew they'd had a great marriage. They very seldom disagreed, and they were always kissing and hugging each other. Mariah laughed to herself at how mortified they would have been to know she'd heard them on several occasions, making love to each other.

Mariah giggled at that thought. Most of her other friends had only one parent, or their parents were divorced. She'd felt so lucky to have them both. Now her daddy was gone, and Mariah had a hole she didn't know how to fill. She looked at the picture of him her mother kept on her dresser and sighed lightly.

She had a boyfriend, David Alston. Kayla liked him, and told her she had good taste. Mariah liked him well enough too. He was just starting to get on her nerves lately. David wanted to have sex, and she wasn't ready.

Mariah wanted a relationship like her mother and father had. She wanted magic. David told her he would wait and be patient, but lately, he'd been bugging her about it daily.

"Well, not gonna think about that anymore," Mariah said aloud, as she got out of bed.
"Mommy?" she called out, after she'd showered and dressed.
"I'm downstairs," Kayla returned.

Mariah headed down to try and talk her mother into going out with her today. They hadn't done that in a while, and she needed it as much as she knew her mother did.
"Come on mommy and go to the mall with me today," Mariah said cheerfully, looking her mother in the eye.

Kayla looked at her daughter. She really didn't like to go out much anymore, but the look on Mariah's face made her say yes.
"OK," she replied softly.
"Cool," Mariah replied excitedly. "Go get dressed so we can leave!" she rushed her mother.
Kayla laughed and told her okay.

Well here I am, Chris Lynch thought to himself, driving into the city, and taking in the view. It seemed like a very hospitable place. He liked the fragrant white fringe trees and fresh air he smelled as he drove admiring the tree lined highway he was traveling.

He would miss the climate and water he'd loved in Florida, but it was time for a change. He was moving here to serve as Assistant Pastor of the local church. Chapel Hill Church For Christ was a newer Christian fellowship, and they'd recently set a new pastor in place. So happens, it was one of his friends from the old church they both attended.

He'd called and asked Chris to come be his assistant. He was ready, so he accepted. Chris often thought about his life, and how differently it had turned out. He'd almost died all those years ago when he was shot, and thanked God everyday, that Brendan had come to check on him. He'd told Chris he saw the three men leaving his place, and his gut told him something was wrong. The doctors told Chris by rights, he should have been dead.

Chris later married a wonderful woman, and they'd had a happy life for at least the first three years. Then things went badly, and Chris decided the kindest thing he could do, was divorce her. They never had children, which Chris assumed, was God punishing him for what he had done to Kayla all those years ago.

Chris thought of her often. He wanted to find Kayla, and tell her how sorry he was. He needed to beg her forgiveness. Then maybe he could forgive himself, and be happy.

"Well, if it's in the plan," Chris said aloud. "I'll find her."

He looked up to see he'd arrived at the church. Getting out, he went in to find Rev. Thomas Bradford, the senior pastor, and one of his dearest friends.

"What do you think?" Mariah was asking her mother, modeling the dress she was thinking of buying for prom.

Kayla smiled to herself, thinking how much like Taea her daughter was, when it came to clothes and shopping.

"Its nice honey, but a little too suggestive don't you think?" she replied.

Mariah looked at herself, and thought about what her mother said. The dress was a brash shade of neon pink, and it dipped extremely low both front and back, leaving very little to the imagination. Mariah had to agree, she looked trashy.

"Yeah you're right," she replied, looking at herself again and frowning.

Mariah took the dress off, and went to find something else she would look, and feel, more like herself in. They finally found a beautiful raspberry halter dress, form fitting, with a beautifully sequined front, and sexy yet tasteful split on the side. Mariah looked gorgeous in it. She was truly her mother's daughter.

Kayla was still a very beautiful and shapely woman in her own right. She was approached every time she went out, today being no exception. Mariah had seen the man watching her mother.

He looked about her age, maybe a little older. He was one of the men from their church, Chapel Hill Church For Christ. Kayla didn't go very often anymore since her father died, but she and her grandmother still went regularly.

"Hi Sister Mariah," he said, when he walked up to her and her mother. "Hello to you too, Sister Kayla," he added, looking at her mother.

Mariah glanced at her mother, and saw the look. She knew he didn't have a chance.

"Hi Deacon Tolliver," Mariah said pleasantly.

"Hello," Kayla said, looking past the man standing in front of her.

"We haven't seen you at service for a while Kayla," he said softly, studying her and taking in the form fitting, diamond print, gold sundress she was wearing.

He smiled approvingly at what he saw. *What a stunning woman,* he thought to himself. Kayla absolutely hated these conversations. She knew this man was interested in her. He'd tried to make a move on her a year ago. She wasn't interested then, and she wasn't interested now.

"Well, I really don't have an excuse," Kayla told him matter-of-factly, exhaling deeply. "I just haven't felt like coming," she finished, with a tone of finality that the discussion was over.

"Well, I'm sure Mariah has told you about family and friends day," he went on, ignoring her tone. "We're welcoming our new Pastor and Assistant Pastor, so I know you'll want to be there," Deacon Tolliver finished, looking at her evenly now.

Kayla thought about it, and knew her daughter, and mother-in-law, would guilt her into going.

"Yes, I'll be there," she said simply, conceding defeat before the battle began.
Deacon Tolliver smiled and looked her over again. "Great! I'll be looking for you," he told Kayla, before saying goodbye to both her and Mariah.

Kayla was so irritated. Why couldn't they just leave her alone? She was still mourning her husband.
"Mommy?" Mariah said, interrupting her thought.
"Yes baby," Kayla answered, looking lovingly at her daughter.

"You know it's okay if you want to be with someone else, don't you?" she asked softly, looking at her mother intently. "Daddy wouldn't want you to be alone forever. You know that right?" Mariah finished, waiting for her mother to reply.

Kayla couldn't speak. The thought of someone else loving her, and touching her, was beyond her comprehension right now. She knew Mariah only wanted her to be happy, and not be lonely.

"I know baby," Kayla told Mariah, "I'm just not ready yet. Can you understand that?" Mariah looked at her mother. She saw all the pain and sadness in her eyes, and knew Kayla was telling her the truth.
"I know mommy," she said once more. "But at some point you have to live again."

"Hey man!" Thomas greeted his friend, as he and Chris embraced. "Glad to see you found the place okay," he joked.

"Let me give you the grand tour, then we'll sit down and talk," he finished, as he led Chris into the main sanctuary of the church.

Chris thought the main sanctuary was breathtaking. It was decorated in a majestic purple with gold accents. The draperies were a rich royal velvet shade with golden leaf accents. The baptismal pool was beautifully adorned with gold lettering and purple tapestry.

The hand painted portrait of Christ hung just above the pulpit, putting the final amen on the entire presentation.

They toured the entire church, and the annex buildings. Chris was completely impressed.

"So let me fill you in on what you're getting yourself into," Thomas began again, smiling at Chris.

At that moment there was a knock on his study door.

"Come in," Thomas called out.

"Hello, Pastor Bradford," the woman said. "I'm sorry to interrupt. I just wanted to let you know I was going out for lunch," she continued "Do you want anything back?" she finished, smiling sweetly at him before noticing Chris.

"Oh hello," she said finally acknowledging him. Chris returned her greeting as Thomas spoke, telling her he wouldn't need anything back. After she left, Chris gave Thomas a look.

"It's not even like that," he laughed when he saw Chris's face. "She's the church secretary, Rachelle Fields."

"Whatever you say man, whatever you say," Chris laughed, noting that Rachelle was an attractive woman, who obviously had a thing for Thomas.

She was about 5'7" or 5'8", he guessed. Looked to be in her mid thirties and was nicely built. *Guess he's just being careful.* Chris thought to himself, of Thomas's apparent lack of interest in the woman. They talked at length, and he told him about all the members he'd met so far.

He told him about the family and friends day Sunday, and that they would both meet more of the congregation than he originally had during his first Sundays.

"So, have you found a place?" Thomas asked Chris, looking at him evenly.

"No. Not yet," Chris replied. "I'll stay at the Inn for a couple weeks, while I look around."

Thomas told him he wouldn't hear of it. He had a house and had not one, but two extra rooms. So it was settled. Chris would come and stay with him until he found a place.

They both laughed about how being single, they knew the members were going to try and marry them off. "I have no objection to being married" Thomas laughed. "I just want to be able to choose my own wife."

They both burst into laughter all over again, recalling past experiences when women had been chosen for them by the church.

"Come on lets go," Thomas spoke again. "We'll stop and get something to eat on the way."

They'd had a wonderful day at the mall. Kayla was glad she'd gone. Even with the unpleasantness of running into Deacon Tolliver, her day hadn't been ruined.

She really should start getting out more often, Kayla thought to herself. Mariah was on her all the time about it. Even her mother-in-law chided her about it.

"Kayla, I know how much you loved my son," Mother told her. "I also know how much he loved you. But baby, Donovan is gone now. You have to still live your life."

Kayla really hadn't wanted to hear that. She just wasn't ready to let go of him yet, she couldn't.

"Mommy," she heard Mariah calling, snapping her out of her thoughts.

"Yes?" Kayla answered.

"I'm going out with David tonight okay," she told her mother.

"Where are you going?" Kayla asked.

"To dinner and the movies," Mariah replied back.

"Be home by midnight," Kayla told her, acknowledging that she had permission to go.

"OK," her daughter happily replied.

She was glad Mariah had David. He was a nice boy. Very respectable and he treated Mariah very well. David was almost six feet tall, and muscular. He was slim, as opposed to Mariah's other boyfriends, who were closer to her father's thick build. He had a very nice smile and a dimpled chin.

Kayla hoped that Mariah would never have to live through the pain she had been through with men in her life. Kayla wanted her to find that special one and be happy, like she had been with Black. She didn't want to continue to think about him, knowing it would make her sad and sulky. Kayla instead picked up the phone and called Jackie. She was one of the few people Kayla could call her friend. She'd been so busy being wife and mother when Black was alive, she didn't socialize much.

Jackie Pierce she'd met when she was active in church. They'd clicked right away. Jackie was divorced, and had a teen daughter too. She was a good-looking woman, who kept herself in shape. She had beautiful eyes, and a glowing smile, shoulder length hair, cut and shaped into a nice bob. Jasmine and Mariah were best friends, so it all meshed.

"Hello?" Jackie answered, thinking it was Mariah calling for Jasmine.

"Hey Jackie," Kayla said softly.

Jackie smiled. She was glad to hear from Kayla. She worried about her being alone so much, but didn't push. She knew her well enough to know Kayla would reach out when she got ready.

"Hey girl!" she said excitedly.

Kayla laughed in spite of herself, she was glad to hear Jackie's voice too.

"You want to get together and do something this evening?" Kayla asked.

Jackie couldn't believe her ears, but she was definitely going to take her up on it. "Sure. What'd you have in mind?" Jackie asked.

Kayla told her they could just play it by ear, and do whatever. Jackie replied that was fine, and she would see her in about an hour.

Kayla was happy to be going somewhere tonight. She just felt different today for some reason. Maybe it was what Mariah said to her about living again.

Her cell was ringing. "Hello?" Mariah answered without looking at the display.
"Hey boo," David greeted her. "I have to cancel tonight. Something has come up."
Mariah was hurt. He'd been doing this more and more lately. She knew it was because she wouldn't sleep with him, and David was trying to get back at her.
"What?" she asked him dryly.
"I've gotta help my dad and my uncle out," he replied. "They're helping one of the church members move tonight."
"OK. Whatever," Mariah sighed and told him.
David told Mariah he would make it up to her, and she told him goodnight.
"Well I guess it'll just be me and mommy tonight," She said to herself, as she went to find her mother.
Kayla was getting dressed when Mariah came into the room.
"Where are you going?" Mariah asked her mother, seeing her dressing.
"Oh, Jackie and I are going out for a little while," she replied, looking at Mariah intently.
"Are you okay?" Kayla asked, sensing something was a little off about her.
"I'm fine," Mariah answered quickly.
She didn't want anything to stop her mother from going out.
"So what time is David picking you up?" Kayla asked, as she fixed her hair.
"Later on," Mariah replied.
She never lied to her mother, but this was important. Mariah hadn't seen her happy like this in a long time.
"So? How do I look?" Kayla asked.

Mariah looked at her mother. She looked absolutely beautiful. She was wearing a soft aquamarine dress, asymmetrical cut, with white trim and matching butterfly stiletto sandals.

Her hair was pulled up in front leaving the length hanging in the back. The sterling silver butterfly jewelry ensemble matched perfectly, and she'd even put on a little makeup.

"You look wonderful mommy," Mariah told her smiling. "Have a good time and really enjoy yourself, OK?" she finished, looking at her mother evenly.

Kayla smiled back at her daughter and promised her she would. Just then the doorbell rang.

"Bye honey, have a great time with David. Love you," Kayla finished, heading down to the door.

Mariah watched her leave with Jackie.

Now Mariah had to find something to do herself. She picked up her cell, and called Jasmine.

"Hey girl!" Jaz greeted Mariah as she answered. "What's up?"

"Not much," Mariah replied. "What're you doing?"

"Just hanging out with my cousins and a few friends," she replied. "If you're not doing nothin', come on over."

Jaz knew her mom and Kayla were out together, so unless Mariah was going out with David, she should be free.

"Sounds like a great idea," Mariah told her. "I'll be there in about thirty minutes."

Mariah loved hanging out with Jaz. They had great fun when they were together. She'd been neglecting her lately because of David, but Jaz hadn't tripped. She still treated her like they hadn't missed a beat.

Jaz was loud, and Mariah loved that about her. Jaz was a petite little thing, and you expected her to be mousy, but she wasn't. She kept her hair short and changed the color often, wearing matching contacts to fit her mood. She was an attractive girl, with a great figure, and always had her share of guys who were trying to get close to her.

Maybe tonight would be okay after all, Mariah thought to herself smiling, as she got dressed. She arrived at Jaz's house about forty-five minutes later.

"Hey girl!" Jaz greeted Mariah, opening the door for her to come in. Jaz was going through her red phase today, as Mariah took in the scarlet hair, and emerald green contacts.

"Let me introduce you to everybody you don't know," Jaz said laughing.

There were about fifteen people, most of which Mariah knew. "These are my cousins DeSean Guthrie, and Aidan Preston," she said, pointing to the two young men standing in front of them.

"You guys, this is Mariah," Jaz introduced Mariah to her cousins.

They all said hello and began to mingle with the other guests.

"So that's the best friend she was talking about," DeSean was saying to his brother.

"Guess so," Aidan replied, as he looked Mariah over. *She's definitely a dime, probably stuck up though,* he thought to himself. Most of the girls he knew back in Virginia Beach that looked like her were.

"I might hafta see what's up before the night is over," DeSean laughed to himself.

He was the more outgoing of the two, even though Aidan was the older.

"She has a boyfriend," Aidan told his younger brother.

"How you know?" DeSean asked his sibling.

"I heard Jaz talking about him with the girls," he replied.

Aidan didn't tell DeSean that he heard Jaz say how much she disliked him, and hoped Mariah would find someone else. Aidan watched her for a while. He loved the way the cotton candy pink Capri's fit her trim waist and accentuated her thighs and butt. The pink, multi-color, spaghetti strap tank Mariah wore with them lay very nicely on her breasts. She seemed nice. Maybe he was wrong about her.

"One way to find out," Aidan mumbled to himself, as he headed over to ask Mariah to dance.

"Hey," Aidan said, once he reached her.

"Hi," Mariah replied, smiling at him.

He has the most beautiful gray eyes I've ever seen, and the body to match, Mariah thought to herself as she looked at him in the burnt sienna tank and relaxed fit jeans Aidan was wearing. He had a sexy, developed chest and muscular arms. Aidan was fine in every sense of the word.

"How about we dance?" he asked her.

"OK," she replied, as they went out into the great room.

Aidan loved looking at her. She was pretty, and she'd turned out to be really nice. *Maybe he would reconsider his aunt's invitation, to stay and complete his senior year here. He needed a change anyway and she was definitely another great incentive,* Aidan thought as they danced. He also remembered Mariah had a boyfriend.

"A little competition never hurt anyone," he mumbled half aloud.

"Did you say something?" Mariah asked him, still smiling.

"No, just singing along with the music," Aidan told her, smiling back.

After they'd spent themselves on the dance floor, Aidan asked Mariah if she wanted to go cool off. She told him sure, and they'd ended up here on the porch, sitting on the swing. The night air was a perfect blend of coolness and serenity. The aromatic citrus like fragrance from the sweet shrub planted in the window boxes, added the perfect romantic touch.

"Where are you from?" she asked him.

"Virginia Beach," Aidan replied, still looking intently at Mariah.

"My mom used to live there for awhile. It's where I was born," she told him.

He told her that was interesting, and asked had she ever been back. Mariah told him no. Aidan only remarked

that it was odd, but it made Mariah think too. Why hadn't they ever gone back to her birthplace? Why wouldn't her mother even entertain the idea of a trip there?
"Hey, what's got you so deep in thought?" he asked her softly.

Mariah shook the thoughts she was having, and smiled at him. He saw the dimples up close and fell in love with them. *She is absolutely beautiful,* Aidan thought to himself, taking her in fully.
"Sorry, my mind just kinda drifted there," Mariah laughed.
"My aunt asked me to come here and finish my senior year," Aidan told her, trying to see her reaction.
"Really?" Mariah asked, seemingly interested. "That would be nice."

"Would I have the pleasure of seeing you more if I did?" Aidan asked, looking at her very intently.
Mariah liked him, and he was fine as hell, but she still had a boyfriend to consider.
"I'm seeing someone," she told Aidan honestly.
"I know that," he said simply, "but there's nothing wrong with having a friend is there?"

Mariah smiled again and told him no, there wasn't and they could definitely hang out, if he moved here. Aidan leaned over and kissed her. It happened so quickly Mariah didn't have time to prepare, or think about it.
"That shouldn't have happened," she said quietly afterwards, secretly relishing the feel of his lips on hers. Instead of answering her, Aidan lifted her chin and kissed her again, gently exploring her mouth with his tongue. This time Mariah kissed him back. Jasmine smiled, as she saw her cousin, and her best friend, on the porch.
"Good," she said softly to herself. "Now she can finally dump that dog David, and get herself a good man."

2

Mariah was up early. Normally the alarm clock had to scream at her to get up so she could get dressed for church, but this morning she had awakened on her own. Mariah thought about last night, Aidan, and him kissing her.

"What was I thinking?" she said aloud.

She was with David. Mariah had to be honest with herself though, and admit she'd really enjoyed it. Aidan was a really nice guy. They'd talked at length after the kiss and she'd found out they had a lot in common. *So what am I going to do if he actually moves here?* Mariah asked herself. David was still very much her boyfriend. *If he moves here, then I'll be forced too. Not right now though,* she thought to herself, heading for the shower.

Mariah thought of him again while she was rinsing. Aidan was taller than David. He had to be at least 6'2", if not taller. He had a toned muscular body, thick like her father was, with a great smile, and those beautiful gray eyes. *He was one serious kisser too!* Mariah thought again, and found herself getting turned on.

"Whew, I better think of something else quick," she chided herself. "It's Sunday and I'm getting ready to go to church."

"I saw you two last night," Jaz said slyly to her cousin, as they headed downstairs to breakfast.

Aidan smiled, and looked at her.

"Is that a problem?" he asked.

Jaz laughed. "Of course not," she replied looking at him evenly. "I think its great, and I hope you two hook up," she went on. "Of course, you can't do that living in Virginia Beach though, now can you."

"No, I guess you can't," he replied, smiling slyly. Jaz knew then he would come back to live, and she was thrilled. Not only was Aidan her favorite cousin, he was interested in her best friend.

Aidan thought about Mariah as he walked down the stairs. He'd never met anyone like her. She was warm and open, loving and friendly. Aidan was seeing a girl in Virginia Beach, but he wasn't serious about her. They slept together and had decent sex, but that's all it was to him, a friendly bounce.

Aidan wasn't interested in a loveless relationship like his mother had with Wallace. He had plans for his life and Mariah was going to fit into them very nicely. Aidan wondered if she were still a virgin. He reminisced about the kiss again. He'd really taken a chance, since she could have slapped him, or told him to back off, and he would have lost any chance with her.

Mariah felt good in his arms, and he'd really enjoyed kissing her. He would see her again today. Jaz told him she went to the same church they were going to, and that she sang in the choir. Aidan would also get a chance to size up his competition. Mariah's boyfriend went to the church too.

Aidan wasn't bothered at all by her having a boyfriend. From what Jaz said about him, he wasn't any good, and Aidan already knew Mariah was attracted to him. Aidan chuckled to himself, thinking he actually owed the guy a thank-you for standing Mariah up last night. If he hadn't, he would never have met her.

Kayla rolled over and looked at the clock. She needed to get up so she could get ready for church. She wasn't looking forward to it. It wasn't that she didn't believe in God, she just wasn't feeling him lately. He'd let Black get taken away, and Kayla was still angry. They'd had a wonderful life, and a wonderful marriage. She wasn't ready for it to be over.

"Now what am I supposed to do?" Kayla asked God quietly.

She missed Black so much. Last night she dreamed they were making love, and it was wonderful like it used to be. It had been so real and vivid that Kayla could actually feel his lips on hers, and feel his touch as he caressed her body. This morning she awakened, to find herself still very much alone.

Suddenly, a revelation hit her, and as much as she didn't want to admit it, she had too. She was lonely. Kayla wanted a man in her life. She began to cry softly. Was she being unfaithful to her husband's memory? Would Black really want her to find someone else? Kayla got up, and tried to pull herself together. She pushed the thoughts away and instead started thinking about last night, and what a good time she and Jackie had, when she heard Mariah knock.

"Come in," Kayla called out pleasantly.

"Good morning mommy," Mariah said smiling, looking at her mother. "And how was your evening last night?" she giggled, with an emphasis on your evening.

"My evening was great," Kayla laughingly replied. "And yours?"

Mariah laughed. "Oh, no you don't. You will not change the subject. I want to hear all about your evening!"

Kayla told her about going to Champions Green, one of the more exclusive restaurants there, and then to The Blue Note, a popular jazz nightspot.

"Did you dance with anyone?" her daughter asked, looking her in the eye.

"Yes, I danced with a couple of guys," Kayla told Mariah softly.

Mariah was so proud of her mother. She knew that was a really big step for her.

"Good mommy," she told her, hugging her. "I'm glad you had a good time." Mariah finished, pulling back and looking at Kayla again. "Now come on, and get dressed. We're going to be late."

Kayla smiled and told her okay, then headed to the shower. They were dressed and ready to go by 10:45.

"I don't know why I let you and your grandmother, talk me into this," Kayla was grousing.

"Come on mommy," Mariah giggled "Don't be like that. You know God is always glad to see you."
Kayla had to laugh in spite of herself. She knew Black had been responsible for Mariah's deep faith, and for that she was grateful. It kept Mariah very grounded, and Kayla experienced none of the trauma she heard other parents of teenagers say they went through.

She looked at the church once they'd driven up. It was a beautiful edifice. The windows were stained with various biblical figures. The sign, majestic in its own right, with large purple lettering, trimmed with gold. She hadn't been here since mother's day of last year. She'd felt guilty, and went for her mother-in-law's sake. Kayla wanted to get back into the church though. She felt drawn to it, for some reason she couldn't understand

"Well God," Kayla began, getting out of the car to go inside. "I'm here. Let's see what you have to tell me today."

Chris was nervous. This was his first Sunday in his new position. Thomas told him the congregation was friendly, and the people enjoyed their worship. Chris couldn't shake the feeling that something was going to happen today. It wasn't a bad feeling, just one that wouldn't go away.

Chris looked at himself again in the mirror and adjusted his robe. He'd had it tailor-made for today. It matched the churches colors, majestic purple with white, and the facing, sleeves, and collar were trimmed in gold.

At that moment, Thomas walked in, dressed in his robe too. His was solid black and trimmed in gold, his initials on the upper right breast pocket. Chris thought they both looked splendid.
"Well man," Thomas began, smiling at him. "This is it. You ready?
Chris smiled back. "Yeah, I'm ready," he replied. "Let's go have church."

They both laughed. Then becoming serious again, they talked together before leaving the office.

Thomas was speaking to some of the choir members, when Chris saw the girl. He had to look at her twice. She was almost the spitting image of Kayla, twenty years ago.

"My god," he said quietly to himself, looking at the young woman.

The hair, the features, everything, reminded him of a time and place long ago. She came over to them.

"Hi, Pastor Bradford," Mariah said pleasantly, smiling at Thomas.

"Hello Mariah," Thomas returned to the girl before continuing. "This is Assistant Pastor Lynch."

The girl extended her hand, and Chris took it, never looking away from her face.

"Hi Pastor Lynch," she said pleasantly.

Chris had to shake himself. "Hello, Mariah?"

She smiled again, and told him that was correct.

"I have to go now Pastors," Mariah said, smiling at them both.

"Bye Mariah," Thomas told her. "Sing well today," he added, still smiling at the young woman.

"Wonderful girl," Thomas remarked to Chris, once she walked away. "If only we could get her mother back into the church," he finished, almost wistfully, to himself.

Thomas was thinking of what Mother Black told him about her daughter-in-law, and her withdrawal from God when her husband, Mother Black's son, was killed. Thomas told Chris they would enter as soon as the choir got up to sing. In the meantime, they would just wait here in the wing.

Kayla was seated on the third row beside her mother-in-law.

"Our new pastor is wonderful Kayla," Mother Black remarked to her.

Kayla simply smiled as she thought to herself how out of place she felt. The choir began to file in and she saw Mariah. Kayla exhaled and made an effort to relax, and actually enjoy herself.

She soon found herself enjoying the music, and watching her daughter sing, made her feel even more at home. Kayla was so engrossed in watching the choir that she never saw the two ministers walk in.

Mariah spotted Aidan sitting beside Jaz, and smiled. He smiled back. Jaz had been kind enough to point out her boyfriend, David, to him. He'd looked back to find the guy glaring at him. *I guess he saw her smile at me*, Aidan thought to himself, chuckling. He'd already made up his mind that Mariah was for him.

Aidan didn't see this guy as a threat at all, a familiar coldness coming over him, as his mind wandered and he thought back three months earlier.

He watched Bobby flirting with Cheryl. He'd already warned him to stay away from her. Bobby was obviously stupid.

Aidan didn't act immediately; he continued to stand in the shadows and watch. Cheryl tried to walk away, but Bobby grabbed her arm and pulled her back.

She pushed him away and he became angry. "You need to stop trippin," he told her. "You know you need a real man."

"You must be kidding," Cheryl laughed as she answered him. "Aidan is hella more man than you could ever hope to be."

Bobby lost it then, slapping her hard across the face. Aidan had seen enough. He stepped out of the shadow and began to walk toward them. Cheryl was in tears as Mina tried to comfort her. Aidan told her to take Cheryl and leave right now. She complied immediately without question, too scared to argue. Bobby stood his ground as Aidan approached. Bobby didn't like Aidan and him taking Cheryl away only added fuel to the fire.

"So what you wanna do fool?" Bobby asked defiantly. Aidan didn't utter a word, his expression saying all that needed to be said. Bobby never saw Aidan move or flinch, but the blow to his midsection dropped Bobby to his knees. Aidan hit him with an overhand right, knocking him completely down.

He kicked him in the face, drawing blood from his mouth and nose. He stepped back and allowed him to get up. Bobby charged straight at Aidan, trying to tackle him. Aidan deftly sidestepped him, and took his legs out from under him. He stomped him in the chest as he lay on the ground.

Bobby gasped for air and tried in vain to remove himself from Aidan's assault. He probably would have killed Bobby, the way he was banging his head on the cement, if his friend Jeff hadn't arrived with a couple of other friends and pulled him off.

The choir began to sing again, shaking Aidan out of his thoughts and back to the present. This guy had no idea of the depth of trouble he would find himself in, if he crossed him and tried to get in his way. Aidan turned around to look at Mariah again, her beautiful face made him forget all about old what's his name and return to his normal self.

3

Chris was taking in the congregation, and enjoying the choir. He looked over at Thomas, and saw him doing the same. There were as usual, several ladies sitting on the front row, giving them both looks, and sly smiles, wearing skirts that were far too short for the row they sat on. A couple of them were brazenly sitting with their legs apart, to afford them both a view of their inner most parts. They'd talked about this yesterday, and both knew well enough, not to be drawn into it.

Thomas was looking at the beautiful woman standing next to Mother Black. That had to be her daughter-in-law, Kayla. He loved the royal blue silk dress she was wearing. The jewelry was collection of sapphires and silver, which he saw matched perfectly, without overshadowing the outfit. He also noted that she still wore her wedding rings.

Mariah looked very much like her mother, Thomas thought to himself. He'd hoped to see her finally, taking the time to look her over admiringly. She was smiling now, and seemed to really be feeling the service. He smiled to himself, and returned his attention to the service.

Chris was looking at the floor, deep in thought. The young woman had made such an impact on him. She looked so much like Kayla, that he couldn't believe it. Chris wanted so much to find her and apologize for what he'd done. Thomas's voice brought him back to the present.

"Welcome, all our brothers and sisters in Christ," he was saying. "We are so glad that you're here with us, on this Family and Friends day."
Kayla looked up at the man talking. He was the new pastor her mother-in-law told her about. She almost chuckled out loud, thinking of what Jackie said about him last night, while they were out.

"Girl, I definitely could have a little bible study with him," she'd laughed, while telling Kayla what an attractive man he was.

Studying him now, Kayla saw that she was right. Thomas was a very attractive man, standing about 6'2", beautiful brown eyes, nice smile, manicured mustache that accentuated his features. Kayla glanced at the other minister, but he was looking down at the floor. *Praying perhaps,* she thought to herself, returning her attention to Thomas.

"For those of you who haven't been home in a while," Thomas went on, looking directly at Kayla now. "I pray you will take this opportunity to come back."
Kayla bowed her head. She knew Mariah and Mother wanted her to come back. She guessed Mother had told her pastor that too.
"Now I would like to introduce to everyone, our new assistant Pastor," he was speaking again.

Kayla looked up once more, to find Thomas still looking directly at her as he spoke. "Brothers and Sisters, Visitors and Friends," he went on, still never taking his eyes off her. "Our Assistant Pastor, Christopher Lynch."
Who?!! Kayla gasped. Chris took the pulpit, and smiled at the congregation.

Kayla couldn't breathe. She could not believe her eyes. The man standing in that pulpit was the same man that raped her, twenty years ago. Thomas was watching Kayla intently. She looked like she'd seen a ghost. *Did she know Chris?* He wondered, intrigued with her now.

He'd watched her the whole time he was talking, taking in every inch of her, thoroughly approving of what he saw. Thomas didn't want anything to happen that would keep her from coming back. He wanted very much a chance to get to know her.

Kayla knew she had to get herself together quickly. Neither Mariah, nor her mother-in-law knew about her past. Even Black, had never known about the rape. Kayla lowered her head, and tried to get her breathing back to normal. Chris was finished, and getting ready to take his seat again.

Thomas stood up and returned to the pulpit, asking the ushers to receive the offering. He was looking at Kayla again. She was still visibly upset. *I have to find out what is going with her, and how Chris is involved,* Thomas continued thinking. Chris was in his seat, thinking to himself how well that went, when he saw her.
"Oh my God," he gasped quietly.

Thomas, who had been watching him now as well, saw the recognition. At that precise moment, Kayla looked up at Chris and their eyes met. She glared at him, and turned away. Chris could only hang his head in shame. Thomas saw the exchange, and was even more determined to find out just what history they had between them.

Mariah was looking at Jaz, who was smiling, and cutting her eyes at Aidan, then back at her. It took all her energy not to laugh. *He must have told her about the kiss*, Mariah thought to herself. She looked at David. He was smiling and blew her a kiss when she looked his way.

Mariah smiled back, and turned toward the Pastor, who asked them to sing another selection. As she was singing, Mariah looked at Aidan. He was looking at her intently, those gray eyes trained right on her. She wondered what he was thinking at that moment.

Aidan looked really good in the periwinkle shirt he was wearing. She'd seen him standing earlier, and taken in his form in the midnight blue pants that completed his outfit. He had the most wonderful thighs, and butt. Mariah could only imagine what he carried in the front. Aidan smiled and she had to look away. She felt herself feeling things she really shouldn't be, in the middle of church service.

Aidan looked back at David again. He was still fuming. He'd seen the looks they'd exchanged. Aidan gave him a look. One that said, watch your back. David gave him one back, as if to say, give it your best shot. Aidan turned around again, looked at the beautiful young woman singing, and smiled.

Kayla wanted out of here, and she wanted out now. How could she sit here and listen to this man. The same man who had violated her in the worst way. The scene was trying to play itself again in her mind, and she was struggling to keep it at bay.

Kayla knew that God could change people, and she supposed she was glad Chris had gotten his life together, but she still had so much hurt. Kayla closed her eyes and began to pray. Something she hadn't done in earnest, for a long time.

Thomas hadn't taken his eyes off her. He had to talk to her. He tried to justify it, by saying it was because of Chris's status in the church that he needed to know, but he knew the real reason was because of his growing attraction to her.

Finally, Kayla thought to herself, the service was over, and she could get out of here. Unfortunately, Mother had other ideas.

"Come on," she told her, taking her hand. "I want to introduce you to Pastor Bradford."

Kayla sighed softly, but followed dutifully.

"Pastor Bradford?" she called to him, once they were behind him.

"Hello there, Mother Black," Thomas said pleasantly.

"This is my daughter Kayla," she told him, stepping aside so Kayla was directly in front of him.

"Hello Kayla," Thomas said smiling at her, as he took her in again. "I'm so glad you came today. Do you think you'll be coming back?" he asked, looking at Kayla intently.

What was she supposed to say? Hell no, and let God strike her down? Kayla thought to herself.

"Yes, I'll be back," was all she could manage.

"Good. I really look forward to seeing you again," Thomas told her, the meaning very evident.
Kayla blushed, and Mother Black chuckled, as they walked away.
"I think Pastor may have his eye on his first lady," her mother-in-law teased her, as they walked outside.
"Mother!" Kayla said, exasperated.
Her mother-in-law looked at her hard.

"Kayla I've told you before, now you listen to me this time," she began, still looking at her. "Donovan is dead. He's not coming back. I loved my son and I know you loved my son, but its time for you to move on, to let someone else be as fortunate in the love you have to give, as my son was," she finished gently, seeing that Kayla was crying softly. She hugged her daughter-in-law, and walked her to her car.

Thomas watched them outside. He didn't know what Mother Black said, but Kayla had been crying, which bothered him.

"Thomas," Chris said, bringing him back to the present. "I'm going to take off now. I need to be alone for awhile."
Thomas looked at him evenly. "How do you know Kayla Black?" Thomas asked point blank.
Chris was a little surprised, but then he knew Thomas had always been very observant. He'd probably seen them in service. He had to talk to Kayla first.
"I can't answer that for you yet Thomas," Chris told his friend honestly.
Thomas sighed evenly.

"OK. I'll accept that for now," Thomas returned, still looking at him hard.
"But I do want an answer eventually," he finished, and left Chris standing there lost in thought.
Thomas was attracted to Kayla, he could tell. Chris needed to think, and figure out how to deal with this situation.

Aidan was waiting for Mariah after service. Jaz was standing with him, and of course, Mariah came straight to her after service. Aidan liked the mauve, paisley patterned, thigh length dress she was wearing. It was very flattering; square neck cut, simple, but elegant. It brought out her eyes, not to mention her beautiful figure.

"Hey girl," they both giggled to each other.

"Hey Aidan," Mariah said sweetly.

He smiled, and she thought she would melt.

"Hey beautiful," Aidan replied, as he looked her over again. "I hope your boy over there doesn't explode."

Mariah looked at David. He was angry, and it was all over his face. Something clicked inside her, and she didn't care.

"So? Let him explode," she said simply.

"I didn't know you had it in you girl!" Jaz laughed.

Aidan was still looking at Mariah intently.

"So, can we spend some time together today?" he asked her softly.

Mariah looked at Aidan again, and realized she really liked him, and the thought of being with him, in fact pleased her.

"Yeah, that would be nice," she said back. "Let me go over here, and deal with him first."

"I'll be here," Aidan told her, as she began to walk toward her boyfriend.

David was livid. Who was this guy? And what was Mariah doing with him?

"Hi David," she said flatly.

He recognized her tone. She was mad at him about last night. Now it made sense. Mariah was trying to make him jealous.

"Hey boo," he spoke back, trying to kiss her.

Mariah turned her head, which made Aidan smile as he watched them intently.

"It's like that baby?" David asked her, feeling hurt.

"Yep, just like that," she replied calmly. "Look, you've been doggin' me really badly these last few months, because I won't let you inside me."
David was looking at her now like he didn't know her. Mariah never talked to him this way.
"I'm sick of it, and I deserve better," she finished.
"So you think this clown you're looking at is gonna treat you better?" David asked, angry again. "You think he doesn't want to sex you too?" he asked getting angrier, and louder.

Aidan began paying closer attention, as did Jaz. She knew Aidan would beat the hell out of David if he touched Mariah.
"Look David," Mariah went on coolly. "I want my space, and I want you to leave me alone. You and I are done," she finished, and turned to walk away.
David grabbed her arm, and spun her around.
"It ain't goin' down like that! You're mine! Do you hear what I'm saying?!" he had Mariah by both arms, shaking her as he screamed at her.
Mariah was looking at David like he was crazy.
"Do you hear me Mariah?!" David was still screaming at her.

Kayla saw the commotion, and walked over to see what was going on. She arrived just as Aidan pulled David off Mariah and hit him hard, sending him to the ground.
"What's going on?" Kayla asked Jaz who was holding Mariah.
Jasmine explained what'd happened. David was on his feet now, ready to fight with Aidan, when Kayla stepped between them looking at him hard.
"I expected better from you concerning my daughter David," she said frigidly.
"She wants to leave me, Mrs. Black," he was trying to explain.
"I don't care. You had no right to touch her," she replied again.

"I know. I'm sorry," David said quietly to Kayla and Mariah simultaneously.
"I'm not going to get in the middle of whatever relationship issues you two are having," Kayla responded. "But you will never put your hands on my daughter again. "Am I making myself abundantly clear?" she asked him, with a tone of conclusiveness.
David shook his head yes, and looked down at the ground.

Kayla turned to Aidan. "Thank you, young man," she said gently having to catch herself as she looked at him. *My god,* Kayla thought to herself, *he looks almost exactly like Dezi.*
"I'm glad to know Mariah has a friend like you, to protect her," she smiled, still taking in the gray eyes and uncanny resemblance.
Aidan smiled back and told her she was welcome.
"Come on Mariah, we're leaving," Kayla spoke aloud shaking the thoughts from her mind.
"Mommy, I promised Aidan I'd spend some time with him. And I'm fine, really," Mariah said, looking at her mother.
"You're sure?" Kayla questioned as Mariah nodded she was. "Alright sweetheart, have a good time," she finished, headed for her car.

Aidan gave David a look, as he stepped toe to toe with him again, speaking so only David could hear. "That shit was foul. Don't ever put your hands on her again, or I will take your ass out," he said flatly, without emotion, his gray eyes cold and hard.

4

Jackie was talking to her sister on the phone. "He said he wanted to come and stay Liv, so let him," Jackie told her.
This was her younger sister, Olivia Preston Guthrie, Aidan and DeSean's mother. Jackie knew her sister and her husband, Wallace, fought constantly.
"Are you sure its going to be okay Jackie?" Olivia asked her hesitantly.

She only wanted what was best for her son. Olivia knew his home life there with her was terrible. Aidan really was a good boy. He got good grades and had plans for his life. DeSean was just like Wallace. He didn't really care about school, only about running the streets and picking up different women. He already had some girl saying she was pregnant by him, and he was only 16.
"Yes girl, its fine," Jackie said, bringing her back to the present. "He has a room, and all I need from you is guardianship papers for school and stuff."
"Well okay then," Liv finally acquiesced. "He can get all his stuff when he comes back, and I'll drive him back up," she went on. "It will give us a chance to visit too."
Jackie smiled and told her she was very much looking forward to that. The two hadn't seen each other in almost a year.
"Girl, let me go and finish dinner before the kids get back from church." Jackie told her sister.
"You didn't go?" Liv asked surprised, because she knew her sister always went.
"Yeah girl I went," she replied. "I just left early," Jackie finished, as Liv acknowledged her statement and they said goodbye.

After the conversation with her sister, Liv thought about her oldest son, and how different he was from her youngest.

"I guess he would be," she said softly aloud as she headed for her room.

Liv pulled the box out of her closet, and began to go through the items inside.

"I wish things could have been different," she said aloud, looking at the newspaper article she'd saved. Her mind began to wander back almost 19 years to a long ago love.

"What the fuck?" he said angrily.

"I'm sorry baby, it broke. It wasn't my fault," Liv pleaded with him.

The look he gave her was ice. "If you fucking get pregnant, kill it," he told her flatly, handing her five one-hundred dollar bills. "I already have a child with the woman I love, and I'm not trying to have one with a piece of ass I was just fucking."

That had crushed Liv. She'd fallen for him during their daily sessions when she worked at the hotel. She thought he had some kind of feeling for her too. She was young and stupid then. By the time Liv found out she was pregnant, he was dead, and she'd spent the money. She looked again at the clipping, with the photo of Dezi Gianni, Aidan's natural father.

She shook herself and got up, putting away the box. Liv would never let Wallace see the things she kept in there. He knew Aidan wasn't his, but he just assumed she didn't know who his father was either. Liv let him believe that, as it was simpler than the truth. She'd made up her mind that when Aidan turned eighteen, she would tell him who his father was. Liv was starting to see Dezi more and more in Aidan. The looks, the temper, that coldness he would get at times.

She prayed silently, that whatever made Dezi the sadistic killer he was didn't pass on to her son. Liv hoped with everything in her that his going to live with Jackie, would keep the evil of Dezi at bay in his life, and he could live without the long shadow of his father's sin on his head.

Aidan was enjoying his time with Mariah. He hadn't told her yet that he was definitely coming to stay. He wanted to surprise her.

"Let me see your arms," Aidan told her softly.

Mariah looked at him quizzically, but complied. He looked at each arm, finding a bruise on one, which made him frown deeply.

"It's OK," Mariah told him. "I bruise easily. It will go away in a couple days."

Aidan was looking at her intently.

"It's never okay for some fool to put his hands on you," he said simply.

"I've never seen David like that," Mariah replied, staring into space.

"Maybe he really loves you," Aidan told her, still looking at her intently.

"Hmph, maybe," Mariah answered. "Or maybe he's just pissed, because he figures he won't get what he wants now."

"You don't love him?" Aidan probed.

"I care for him, but I don't love him enough to sleep with him, if that's what you mean," Mariah finished, looking him in the eye.

"So is it over between you two?" Aidan asked, really wanting an answer to that question.

Mariah thought for a moment.

"Yeah," she answered. "I think it has been for a while, I just didn't want to see it."

Aidan looked at Mariah again, and moved very close to her face as he spoke.

"I won't lie and say I'm sorry to hear that," Aidan told her. "I'm looking very forward to having a long, wonderful, relationship with you," he added as he pulled Mariah to him, and began kissing her.

Jaz came to get them for dinner, and saw them kissing again. She chuckled to herself, deciding she would come back in a few minutes.

Mariah pulled away from Aidan and looked at him. He made her feel feelings she'd never felt before. He intrigued her and she liked being with him. Mariah loved what he'd just said to her, and she prayed he was sincere.

Jaz made her way back to them now.

"If you two are done sucking face," she began, laughing. "Dinner is ready."

Mariah blushed, which made Jaz laugh even harder. Aidan just smiled, and took her hand to go inside.

Kayla was still blown away with having seen Chris today at church. *What am I going to do now?* She thought to herself. She'd promised to come back to church, and Kayla knew her daughter and mother-in-law would hold her to it.

She hadn't thought about the attack for years now. Now Chris was here in front of her, forcing her to relive it. Kayla decided she would pull Chris aside next Sunday, and ask if they could talk.

Seeing Chris made her think of her past again and meeting Aidan made her think of Dezi. Kayla sighed deeply. She hadn't seriously thought about Dezi for a number of years now since before Black's death. She'd loved him deeply at one time, that is, until he went off the deep end and filled her heart with fear.

Still, truth be told, there was that very tender spot even now deep inside that continually longed for his touch. Dismissing the thoughts Kayla rose and headed downstairs to her kitchen, thoughts of hot tea on her mind.

Chris was sitting in his room at the inn, replaying the grievous act he committed twenty years ago in his mind. *"No Chris," Kayla was screaming. "I don't want this," she repeated as she continued to fight him. "Stop," she screamed once more as she bit him hard drawing blood. Chris hit her hard then, closed fist, and knocked her out. He saw himself stripping her clothes off and touching her body. He saw himself putting on the condom.*

How could he have done that? Hurt her like that? He'd loved Kayla. How could he face her again? He had to though. Chris had to apologize to Kayla, and pray that she could find it in her heart to forgive him.

Then he thought of Thomas. He was his friend. They'd known each other for years and had been through a lot together. How would Thomas react when he found out? Especially now that Chris knew Thomas was attracted to Kayla. Chris needed a miracle, and he needed it now.

Thomas had been thinking about Kayla, and about Chris, all afternoon. He'd gone to the gym to work off some of the tension of the day.

Thomas was in good shape at forty-four, and tried to keep it that way. He thought about Kayla, and how much he wanted to get to know her. She was a beautiful woman who'd kept herself very well from what Thomas could tell. Kayla still had a great figure, beautiful smile, and great legs.

He began to reflect on his own life. Thomas was single, and had been for a number of years, after his first marriage failed. They were young when they married. He was twenty-one, and she just a year younger. They were both partying and clubbing when they met, so that was the lifestyle she loved.

Once Thomas found God and answered his call to the ministry, things fell apart for them. She wanted no part of church, or God. She'd told him as much, during one of their many arguments. They'd divorced five years later.

Thomas was still a young man, and he'd occasionally slipped and slept with various women. He'd even had a serious relationship with one, almost marrying her, but that didn't work out well at all.

He hadn't been with anyone in the last year though, and he certainly hadn't tried to be with any of the women here at the church. Thomas knew his secretary, Rachelle, was more than willing. She'd made no secret about that with what she wore to work, or the way she was always looking at him.

Thomas wanted a wife now, not just sex. First, he needed to clear up whatever the drama was between Kayla and Chris. Thomas didn't need anything to keep her from fully giving herself to him. He went back to his weights, deciding to call Kayla after he was finished with his workout.

David was still fuming. *She is not breaking up with me,* he thought angrily to himself. He cared deeply for Mariah.

She was the perfect girl. He knew he'd been really pestering her about the sex thing lately, but he was a guy, and he had needs. He shouldn't have pushed so hard though. Mariah was special.

That's what made him love her so much. She wasn't like most of the girls he'd dated. He'd easily gotten inside their panties, and the flame quickly went out. *I've got a lot of apologizing, and making up to do,* David sighed heavily to himself, picking up his cell.

Mariah didn't answer her cell, so he had to leave a message. David was frustrated. He hoped she wouldn't stay mad at him. She couldn't possibly be serious about breaking up with him, could she? The two of them had been together, as a couple, a year and a half almost. They'd been friends for as long as he could remember. It was that guy's fault, whatever his name was. That joker had threatened him.

David had to admit that Aidan's cold look and demeanor sent a chill through him. He couldn't explain it, but he saw something else when he looked into his eyes. David knew in his heart, it wasn't just an empty threat he'd issued. Aidan seemed fully capable of completing the promise he'd made.

David shook himself and called Sherice Collins. Sherice was a pretty girl. She was taller than Mariah, standing about five foot nine inches with nice breasts and hips. She had almond shaped eyes, with a nice smile, and full pouty lips. She was also the girl he was getting sex from.

Sherice thought he really liked her, and David wasn't going to tell her any differently. He laughed to himself, thinking how stupid Sherice was every time she believed that same old lie that David was going to leave Mariah to be with her.

"Well, a man's gotta do what a man's gotta do," he laughed to himself, picking up his keys, and heading over to her house.

David arrived and rang the bell. Sherice came and opened the door. She was home alone, as usual, with her younger brother and sister, who were in the den watching TV.

"Hey David," she greeted him warmly.

He smiled, and returned her greeting.

"Do you want something to drink?" Sherice asked, looking at him amiably.

"Nope," David returned, reaching out to pull her close. She giggled as he kissed her.

"I'm glad to see you too," Sherice returned, as he began to nibble her neck.

"Wait," she told David, pushing him gently. "Let me go get them settled," she told him, referring to her siblings.

David smiled and kissed her again, as he headed to her room. He walked in and began to undress. David looked around. It was nothing like the room he had at home. Of course it wouldn't be, since they lived in the lower end of town, but he thought it was nice enough.

Sherice had her dolls and stuffed animals, on shelves. The computer was in another corner, on the desk. Her books and book-bag were on the floor. Her bed was neatly made with her favorite green comforter on it. She'd told him that, the last time he was here.

David chuckled softly at how gullible she was again, as he heard her enter the room.

"I've missed you so much David," Sherice told him, looking into his eyes.
He told her he'd missed her too, which was true. David always missed their sexual encounters.
"When are you going to leave her?" she asked him, whining.

David hated this part of the act. He had to lie to her again, and tell her what she wanted to hear.
"It's not that easy Sherice," he said. "You know how emotional Mariah is," David went on. "Then theres my parents and that whole trip."

Sherice sighed gently, and told David she understood. They began kissing passionately, and he undressed her. Sherice pushed him back onto the bed, took him in her mouth, as he moaned with pleasure. *Damn this girl gives good head,* David thought to himself, as Sherice continued to pleasure him. She brought him almost to orgasm, then stopped, and mounted him.
"Mm, you feel wonderful," David mumbled aloud, as she rode him.

Sherice looked down at his face, watching David enjoy their lovemaking. *I love him so much, why won't Mariah just let go?* She thought to herself almost angrily. Sherice pushed it out of her mind, and focused on David again. She rode him harder, feeling herself ready to explode.

He was moaning loudly at this point, as was she, they both exploded together, her body trembling from the force of the orgasm. David lay there, trying to catch his breath as Sherice rolled off him, and lay beside him.
"That was the shit right there," he told her breathlessly. She giggled, and told him she'd enjoyed it too. He dozed gently, and Sherice went to check on her siblings. David was getting dressed when she came back.
"Why you gotta zoom?" she asked quietly.

Sherice hated how he had to always leave immediately when they were together.
"You know I have to be at home when she calls, or I get the third degree," David lied, referring to Mariah.

Sherice sighed again, and told him ok. David kissed her softly, and said goodnight, as she watched him walk to his car.

Soon he'll be mine, and he won't have to endure her foolishness anymore, Sherice thought to herself, heading into the den to watch TV.Sherice picked up the phone, and called her best friend, Elaine Harris.

5

Sherice went on to tell Elaine about David's visit, and that he'd just left. Elaine was quiet. She really didn't care much for David. She felt that he was using Sherice and lying to her, but she didn't have proof yet.
"I just wish Mariah would get the message and step off, damn," her friend continued, oblivious to the silence on the other end.
Elaine sighed deeply.
"Have you ever thought that maybe it's not Mariah that's holding on?" she asked softly.

Sherice frowned. She knew Elaine didn't like David, but she figured it was because Elaine wanted to be with her.
"He wouldn't lie to me like that Elaine," Sherice replied. "David really cares for me."
Elaine wondered who she was trying to convince.
"OK, well I guess you would know better than me," she replied tiredly.
She didn't want to talk about David anymore.
"What's up with Jaz?" Elaine asked. She'd seen her at school, and even hung out with her and some other friends a couple times.
"I don't know. Why?" Sherice asked.
Elaine thought Jaz was attractive, and she wanted to approach her, she just didn't know if she would be receptive. She'd been trying to get a feel of that by asking Sherice about her.
"I just thought she was kinda nice," Elaine replied.
"Yeah Jaz is cool, with her crazy self!" Sherice laughed out loud. "She is killing me with the different hair and eyes every week!"
That's what Elaine liked about her. She was unique and individual.
"They always look tight though," Elaine replied, chuckling lightly herself.
Sherice caught what Elaine wasn't saying.

"You like her?" she asked softly, more than a little disturbed by the thought.
"I think she's nice, that's all," Elaine replied evasively.
Sherice didn't push, uncomfortable with how upset Elaine's attraction to Jaz made her.
"Well, okay then I guess," Sherice replied and Elaine let the conversation go.

They chatted on a few moments more about school, and their weekend plans, and then disconnected. Elaine sat back and reflected on her friend. She was crazy about Sherice, but Elaine knew she would never entertain the idea of them being together that way. Jaz on the other hand, she might be down for whatever, being the adventurous person she seemed to be. Elaine made up her mind to seek Jaz out at school, and try to feel her out.
"Who knows, might make a love connection," Elaine said softly, as she rose and headed for the kitchen.

The phone was ringing. Kayla looked at the ID.
"Hello?" she answered.
"Hi, Sister Kayla," Thomas said pleasantly. "I wanted to call and tell you personally, how much I enjoyed meeting you today after service."

Kayla smiled to herself. He was trying to hit on her, that much she was sure of, finding herself actually pleased a little at the thought.
"Well Pastor Bradford," she began. "I honestly did have a good time today. It was also a pleasure meeting you as well."

Thomas was glad she was talking to him. He knew Kayla was still closed to dating. Mother Black told him that when they'd talked, expressing her own desire that Kayla start dating again.
"I hope you remember the promise you made to me today," Thomas said softly.
Kayla smiled again, remembering how he'd looked at her, when he'd asked her to come back.

"Yes, I remember," she told him. "I'll be there," Kayla finished, chuckling lightly.

Thomas heard her laugh, and smiled to himself, remembering how beautiful she was when she smiled. "Well I won't keep you," he told her, hating to end the call. "I'll be looking for you Sunday," he continued. "Good night Sister Kayla, and sleep well."
"Thank You Pastor," Kayla began. "Good night and you do the same."

As she walked back to her room, Kayla heard the car drive up, and peered out the window. Aidan walked Mariah to the door, and kissed her goodnight. Kayla smiled to herself knowing how embarrassed Mariah would be if she knew she saw them.

She'd found out this young man was Jackie's nephew. He seemed nice enough, and Kayla could tell he really liked Mariah. What was going on with her and David, Kayla wondered, making a mental note to ask her about it soon.

Mariah let herself in, and headed up to her room. She was floating from spending the afternoon with Aidan. He was wonderful. She'd meant to ask him if he were moving here, hating the thought of the week being over, and him leaving. She pushed the thought out of her mind, as she headed for her mother's room, to talk to her about church today.

Liv was dreading the conversation she was getting ready to have. Wallace wouldn't want Aidan to leave. He always accused her of treating him better than DeSean, which of course wasn't true. They were two different children, and that's how Liv treated them. Secretly, she thought Wallace was jealous of Aidan. He was a tall, good-looking young man, whereas DeSean was shorter, and average, like his father.

Wallace had been going through his midlife crisis Liv supposed, which was why he'd dreaded his hair. It was in short locks now, which she hated, but didn't comment on. Liv had to let her son leave, his future depended on it. DeSean had already started hanging around the local hoods and pimps, marveling at their lifestyle. She knew no matter much she tried to steer him the right way, he was determined to do the opposite. Liv still had a chance with Aidan.

She heard Wallace come in, and rose to go meet him.

"Hi baby," Liv said pleasantly.

She needed to keep him a relatively good mood.

"Hey girl," Wallace said back, smiling at her.

So far so good, she thought to herself.

"I made your favorite for dinner," Liv told him again.

"Sounds good, I'm starved," he told her, giving her a quick hug before heading off to wash up.

She fixed their plates, and they sat down to eat. They enjoyed pleasant conversation about his day at work, and people he'd seen on the way home. Liv carefully brought up the subject she wanted to discuss.

"Baby," she began. "My sister Jackie has asked if Aidan can come and finish school there with her," she finished cautiously.

Wallace finished chewing his food, and looked at Liv evenly. He took a long drink of his beer then spoke.

"We gotta send her money?" he questioned.

Liv breathed a little sigh of relief. Maybe he wouldn't put up a fight after all.

"No baby," she went on. "Jackie is cool with taking him in, and he's old enough to get a part-time job."

Wallace sat back and thought about it. He really didn't like his stepson very much. He'd always resented the way Liv treated Aidan better than his own son.

Maybe with him away, DeSean could get the attention he deserved, and needed. Not to mention Wallace was afraid of him. He'd never admit it to anyone else, but Aidan made him very uncomfortable.

His mind went to an evening last month when he and Liv had fought and he'd hit her. Wallace had come into the living room and had a couple of beers. He lay on the couch and was soon asleep.

He remembered waking with a start feeling uneasy, only to find Aidan sitting in the chair across from him staring intently. The boy never said anything but the look he gave Wallace was deadly. He'd risen shortly afterward and headed to his own room. Wallace shook himself and began talking to Liv again.

"Sure. He can go," Wallace told her calmly.

Liv smiled, and got up to hug him.

"Thank you so much baby," she told him squeezing him tightly.

Her touch aroused him and Wallace wanted to make love. He began kissing Liv, and stroking her body. She knew what he wanted, and after what he had just done for Aidan, she would definitely give it to him.

Liv normally hated sex with Wallace. He was rough, and had no imagination. She spent a lot of time fantasizing when they did have sex, and usually it was about Dezi.

Even now, almost eighteen years later, she still thought about the wonderful sex they had. Wallace saw that Liv was responding to him, took her hand, and led her to their bedroom.

6

Big D was hanging out at his sister's house, waiting on his nephew to get home. He'd been teaching him about pimping, and the boy was a natural. Big D was trying to get things flowing for himself again.

He'd spent the last five years in prison, and all his girls had gotten away from him. He thought about the good old days when he was running with The Clique. He thought about Dirty, and Devastator.

"Them was two cool brotha's," Big D said aloud.

He'd heard about Devastator getting killed by that FBI agent. *Wonder what ever happened to that kid he had,* he thought to himself.

"Wassup unk?" his nephew Cameron asked him.

"Nothing boy," he replied. "Been waiting on you all day."

Cameron laughed. He loved his uncle, and Big D was gonna teach him to make that fast money. Cameron had no interest in school, college, or any of that other nonsense.

He wanted to live large, and enjoy life. Cameron knew his uncle had been a serious player in his day, and that was the experience he needed. He was going to introduce Big D to his boy DeSean, as soon as he came back from North Carolina.

"Well I'm here now," The boy replied again, laughing.

"Let's go. I got a couple of girls that are looking to get paid," Cameron finished, peaking Big D's interest.

He knew the younger they were, the more he would get for them. Old men loved young booty, and that was just that. Besides, Big D needed some sex himself. Five years is a long time to be jacking off. He got up, and followed the boy to their destination.

Wallace was sleeping now, as he normally did after they had sex. Liv was lying awake unfulfilled as usual. She just could never seem to get an orgasm when she was with him.

Even when she got close, Wallace would always finish before she did. Liv thought about her son again, and how happy she was that Aidan was escaping this dismal existence.

She'd thought about leaving herself, but knew Wallace would kill her if she did. He beat her still. Not as often as he used too, but often enough. Liv had to always be careful not to set Wallace off. It only took the smallest things. She'd seen him take out his frustration on both of the boys. Wallace still bullied DeSean, but left Aidan alone once he outgrew him in height.

She'd seen the look in Aidan's eyes the last time Wallace beat her. Liv knew then she had to get him away from here. Aidan looked the spitting image of Dezi when he was angry; cold and distant.

She didn't want him to do anything crazy. She didn't have to worry about that now though. Liv would have him packed, and ready to go back to Jackie, as soon as he got-back. She didn't even want Aidan to spend the rest of the summer here.

Wallace stirred, and his hand fell on her breast. He began to rub and squeeze it. She knew what that meant. Liv rolled over, allowing him to climb on top of her again. Hopefully he would finish quickly, and she could go shower. Liv felt extremely dirty at that moment.

Big D looked the girls over. They were cute, had nice bodies. They would do for starters. He talked to Cameron, and told him what needed to be done. Cameron told the girls what was up. They agreed, as they all headed off to his mom's house.

Big D's sister worked in the evening, so she left Cameron with him. To keep an eye on him, he remembered her saying, as Big D laughed to himself. "Well, what she don't know, won't hurt her," he said aloud.

Big D chose the older of the two girls, Shay, who was 18. She was slender but shapely, cute face and street smart. "You ever been with a grown man before?" he asked the girl, when they got to his room. Shay looked at him evenly.

"A dick is a dick, ain't it?" the girl replied, as she was getting undressed.

He gave her a little instruction but Shay was pretty damned skilled all on her own. She'd given him head that had his toes curling, before they had sex and Shay once again surprised him with her skill.

"So, do I pass the test?" Shay asked slyly.

Big D smiled at her, and began to tell her how the game was going to go. After the girls left, he and Cameron discussed business, and how they would split the money.

"Unk," Cameron began. "I got a partner I want to introduce you too," he went on. "He's the one who came up with the idea, and I want to include him."

Big D told him it was cool, and they would need about four or five more girls, to begin to make that big money he wanted. Cameron smiled, and told him no problem. The high school was full of ho's. They both laughed, and went to his room to smoke weed.

DeSean was bored. He hadn't met any girl that was willing to have sex since he'd been here. He missed home, and the girls there. DeSean had at least three that he could get with at any given time.

He was mad at Angel though; talking about she was pregnant from him. She was lying. DeSean had only slept with her once without a condom. He was going to make her take another test when he got back.

DeSean liked the pretty one that had come over that night, but Aidan beat him to her.

"That dirty dog," he said aloud.

DeSean hated how his brother always seemed to get everything he wanted. He loved Aidan, don't get it twisted, but DeSean always felt like he was competing with him. Even for their mother's attention, and affection.

"Guess that'll change now though," he said aloud again, to himself. DeSean knew Aidan was going to move here with Auntie Jackie and Jaz. That was cool with him. Maybe he could enjoy being an only child for a while.

He wondered if Aidan slept with Mariah yet. DeSean knew his brother had a girl of his own back home he was hitting regularly. He laughed to himself, thinking that Aidan better get all he could when he got back. He might be in for quite a dry spell.

Aidan was thinking of his earlier conversation with his mother.

"I've already talked to your Aunt Jackie," she told him. "I gave her my permission, but you know I have to talk to Wallace too."

Aidan was angry. Why did she have to ask him? He wasn't his father, so her word should have been good enough. He knew she was afraid of Wallace. Aidan knew Wallace beat her still, and he hated him for it.

The last time he'd hit her, Aidan wanted to kill him. *Something's wrong with me,* he thought. *I don't know who I am sometimes when I get angry,* he continued thinking.

He'd seen his mother look at him with a faraway look in her eye sometimes, like she was remembering. She'd never told him anything about his father, although Wallace had hatefully told him she didn't even know who his father was. Aidan didn't believe that. He believed it was something worse.

Maybe his father had raped Liv, and gotten her pregnant. Maybe he'd left her before Aidan was born. He didn't know, but he was sure of one thing, Liv knew exactly who he was.

"Maybe she'll tell me one day," Aidan sighed to himself, getting up and pushing the thoughts away.

Mariah promised to come by, and he wanted to take her to the movies. Aidan smiled when he thought of her.

He'd found out that Mariah was indeed still a virgin. He promised himself he wouldn't pressure her about that right off the bat. Aidan just loved being with her and for now that was more than enough.

Once Mariah arrived, they'd come to the theatre. He'd just discovered something new about her. She was one of the few girls Aidan knew that actually loved horror movies. When he'd asked what she wanted to see, he'd steeled himself for some chick flick. She'd instead chosen the slasher flick, and his mouth dropped.

"You wouldn't be scared would you?" Mariah teased, seeing Aidan's reaction. He'd laughed and told her of course not.

"Mm, well don't be screaming and grabbing me in the movie either," she continued to tease him.

They were enjoying the film now, sharing the popcorn they'd purchased. Mariah was leaning close to him, and Aidan inhaled her scent. He loved the outfit she was wearing.

The jean skirt hugged her perfect butt and thighs, and the baby blue tank lay beautifully on her ample breasts. Aidan found himself very aroused sitting with Mariah like this. He kissed her gently on the ear. She smiled, and sighed softly. He put his arm around her, and enjoyed her presence.

"You wanna go grab something to eat afterwards?" Aidan whispered.

Mariah looked back at him, and told him that would be nice.

After they'd left the movies he headed to a pizza place she'd told him about.

"Did you enjoy yourself?" Aidan asked Mariah.

"Yeah, I had a great time," she replied.

Aidan chuckled.

"What's so funny?" Mariah asked, looking at him quizzically.

"You, and the portion of the movie you saw, when you weren't hiding your eyes," Aidan replied, laughing harder now.

Mariah rolled her eyes at him, and laughed.
"Whatever, Aidan Gianni Preston," she told him playfully. Mariah loved his middle name. It was unusual. She asked him where his mother had gotten it, and he'd replied he honestly didn't know.

They arrived at the restaurant, and went inside. "It always smells so good in here," she told him inhaling deeply the aroma of fresh baked dough and cheese. Aidan noticed the looks he was getting from some of the other guys in the place. *They must go to her school, and know about her and David,* he surmised. One of the guys spoke to Mariah.
"Hey Mariah," Bruce addressed her.
"Hey Bruce," she replied smiling.
"Where's David?" he made a point of asking, and looking at Aidan.

Mariah frowned, and sighed deeply before answering.
"Bruce, I don't know where David is," she went on, looking at the young man evenly, her jaw clenched. "We're not kickin' it anymore, but this is Aidan, my new boyfriend."
Aidan smiled at Bruce, and said hello. Bruce was taken aback, and mumbled a brief hello, before wandering off to join his friends. Aidan looked at Mariah.
"You have quite a temper there missy," he said playfully. She smiled, and told him it was her father's.
"Well, remind me never to get on your bad side," Aidan chuckled.
"That's your best bet," she told him, full of false macho bravado.

They both burst into laughter, drawing looks from others in the restaurant. Aidan loved looking at Mariah. *I've finally found what I've been looking for and no one is gonna take her away from me,* he thought calmly to himself, as their pizza arrived, and they began to devour it.

7

Thomas had a busy day today. He looked at his calendar and called Rachelle in.
"Has Pastor Lynch called?" he asked her.
Rachelle told him he hadn't, and Thomas thanked her. He gave her directions for the rest of the day, since he would be out.

"Would you like me to accompany you on your visits Pastor?" Rachelle asked him hopefully.
Thomas looked at her, knowing what she was trying to accomplish. She'd worn an exceptionally short, and tight, black dress today.
"No Rachelle," he said gently. "I'll be fine. I'll be back after 5:00," he finished, and left his office.

He smiled to himself as he entered his car. Rachelle definitely was letting him know she was interested. Normally, Thomas probably would have taken her up on her offer and had sex with her, but he wasn't trying to go there this time.

He'd seen what, or should he say whom, he wanted. Now he just had to work on getting Kayla to see it. Thomas smiled again, thinking about the dress she was wearing yesterday that flattered every curve she had, started his car, and began his day.

Chris had spent all last night searching himself. He knew he had to go and talk to Kayla. He didn't want to go to her home, and make her feel uncomfortable. Plus there was her daughter to consider.

Chris was fairly sure she hadn't shared this part of her past with the girl. He would call her, and ask her to meet him. It had to be somewhere public, yet private, where Kayla would feel safe, and they could actually talk.

Chris thought about the church. Thomas would be out most of the day doing follow-up visits from the visitors they'd had at service Sunday.

"Lord, I need you to help me through this," Chris began. "And I need you to allow Kayla to understand, and forgive me," he finished, heading for the shower.

After finishing his shower and dressing, Chris dialed her number. He'd gotten it from the church directory. Actually it was a listing for her daughter, Mariah. He hoped it was the home number, and not the girl's cellular number.

"Hello?" Kayla answered.

Chris was terrified. He knew he had to talk to her. He just wasn't sure how she would react.

"Hi Kayla," he said gently.

Her mind was spinning. *Oh my God!* Kayla thought, hearing his voice.

"I know it's been a long time," Chris went on. "I also know we need to talk."

Kayla had to try and gather herself. She was angry and frustrated all at once.

"You're right," she began. "It has been a long time, and yes, we really do need to talk."

Chris asked her to meet him at the church. They could talk there and have privacy. Kayla was all right with that. She didn't think he would try and hurt her again, but you never knew.

"So I'll meet you there in an hour?" Chris asked her.

"That's fine," she replied and disconnected.

Chris sunk back onto the bed. It had been so good to hear her voice. Now he had to actually face her. Chris gathered his things, and headed out to the front desk.

Kayla was grabbing her bag, having showered and dressed, to go and meet Chris. She checked it, and decided to put the gun Black had given her, inside. He'd insisted on her having it and had taken her to the range to teach her how to use it.

Kayla didn't think Chris would try to do anything to her again. She had the gun just in case. She wasn't going to be a victim ever again.

Chris arrived at the church a few moments earlier. He'd asked Kayla to meet him here in the annex. He figured it would give them more privacy, and he wouldn't have to explain to Rachelle why Kayla was there.

Chris was nervous. He wondered how he was going to even begin to talk to her, or explain his actions, all those years ago. Kayla's tone had been rather ambiguous. Chris couldn't really gauge her mood, or what she may have been thinking.

"Well," he began, talking aloud to himself. "You'll find out soon enough."

Kayla pulled into the parking lot and saw his car. She looked at the annex where she was supposed to meet Chris. Kayla took a deep breath, marveling in the beauty of the day, the vibrant sun and blue skies, and got out of the car, headed toward the building to face a dark specter from her past.

Thomas watched her from his office window. Kayla was wearing wide leg jeans, with a brown leather belt, and matching heels. The top was a fire orange, t-strap fitted tank. Her hair was pulled back into a ponytail.

Thomas could see it was extremely thick, hanging almost to the middle of her back. Even in causal clothes Kayla looked stunning. He'd left his car at the shop, when it had suddenly broken down on him. Neither Rachelle nor Chris knew he'd returned. He'd seen Chris earlier, and knew he was in the annex.

Now, with her arriving, Thomas had to find out what was going on. He'd give them a few moments, and then he would go over and get some answers to his questions.

Chris heard her come in, and got nervous all over again. She pushed the door to the office open and entered.

"Hi Kayla," Chris said gently "Thank you so much for coming."

"Hi Chris," Kayla replied quietly.

"Please sit down," Chris told Kayla, motioning her to the chair across from him.

She sat down and looked at him. He was still a very attractive man, 6'1" with a creamy caramel complexion, beautiful dreamy brown eyes, and that tilted smile she'd grown to love when they were together. Chris was as usual, impeccably dressed. The shirt was a soft azure, tailor fit, and the black slacks complimented both the shirt and his body, as he wore them.

It had been twenty years, but Kayla still felt the hurt like it was yesterday.

"Kayla," he began again, his voice wavering. "I've been praying for this moment for a long time," he went on. "And now that its here, I'm not sure how to begin."

Kayla understood. She felt the same way. She took a deep breath, and tried to start.

"I'm so angry with you," she told him. "I've been carrying this pain, shame, and guilt with me for all these years," she went on. "I was never anything but good to you Chris. Why, why, would you hurt me like that?" Kayla continued, crying now.

She was sobbing deeply and Chris thought his heart would explode he was hurting so much. Thomas was standing at the door. He'd heard her questions. He heard Kayla sobbing now. *What the hell happened between them?* Thomas thought to himself.

He felt terrible standing there eavesdropping, but he had to know. He wanted this woman to be in his life, and Chris was one of his dearest, friends. Thomas heard Chris begin to speak, and returned his attention to their conversation.

"Kayla," he began. "You didn't do anything wrong that day. Not one thing," Chris told her. "I should never have hurt you like I did. I was an animal that day."

Chris was quiet for a moment.

Thomas's mouth was hanging open. *Is he saying what I think he is?* He thought to himself, getting angrier by the moment.

"I raped you Kayla," he said plainly. "I hit you, hurt you, and took away your dignity that day," Chris went on. "I cannot begin to tell you, how much I regret what I did to you that day," he was still speaking. "And believe it or not, I did suffer and pay for that."

Thomas was beside himself. He heard Kayla speaking, and hurriedly gathered himself again.

"How did you suffer Chris?" she asked, more hurt than angry now. "I'm the one who had to see that every night in my sleep," Kayla went on. "So tell me. How did you suffer?"

Chris took a deep breath, and unbuttoned his shirt. Kayla watched him guardedly, her hand on her bag, and the gun inside.

"This is how I suffered," he told her simply, showing Kayla the scars still on his chest from the gunshots.

"Your boyfriend, and his friends, tried to kill me," Chris said quietly. "They would have succeeded, if God hadn't sent Brendan by to see me that day," he finished, buttoning his shirt back.

Kayla was stunned. She hadn't thought about the deeply violent side of Dezi in years. He'd lied to her. *Figures,* Kayla thought to herself the disappointment of the realization startling her. "He told me he didn't kill you," she said simply.

"Well, technically, he told the truth," Chris said plainly. "His friend actually shot me. He just beat the hell out of me."

Thomas wanted to burst in. He wanted to hurt Chris for what he'd done to Kayla. He wanted to hold her, and tell her it was all right.

He couldn't though. He wasn't even supposed to know. *How the hell was he going to pretend not to know when he saw Chris or her for that matter?* Thomas thought to himself.

"Chris," Kayla started again. "I'm glad to see God has changed your life. Believe it or not, I'm actually proud of you becoming a minister," she went on.

"I needed closure, and you've given me that today," she continued. "I just want to go on with my life. I forgive you," she finished softly, looking at him, tears streaming down her face.

Chris broke down and Kayla knew he had been tormented all these years, just like she had been. She got up, went to Chris, and embraced him.

He hugged Kayla back, still sobbing, and told her thank you. They held each other until they were both spent. Chris told her thank you again, and Kayla gathered her purse to leave.

Thomas left when he heard Kayla say her goodbye to Chris. He was sitting in his office now, trying to absorb all that he'd heard. *Why would he do that to her?* Thomas thought to himself. He still needed more answers. Thomas saw Kayla leave, and Chris shortly after. He called the repair shop, and they told him his car was ready. He would go see Chris after he picked it up. This time Thomas wasn't leaving, until he got the whole story.

"Well, well now," Rachelle mumbled to herself, as she watched Kayla leave the annex and get into her car. *What in the world is she doing here?* She thought to herself, as she saw Chris exit a few moments later.

"Ahhh," she said, smiling knowingly. "I guess Pastor Lynch has decided to make a move on the widow Black, hmm?" Rachelle chuckled.

She was glad that he'd chosen to pursue Kayla. She'd seen Thomas watching her closely in church Sunday. *That would never do,* she'd thought to herself. She'd been trying hard to get Thomas to pay attention to her, but he'd so far managed to resist her temptation.

I don't know what's wrong with that man, Rachelle thought to herself. She'd worn her sexiest dress today, and practically put herself in his lap, and Thomas hadn't responded.

Maybe he's gay, she wondered, dismissing the thought just as quickly. She'd seen how he was looking at Kayla, Sunday, and Thomas definitely wasn't gay.

He's gonna be pissed that Pastor Lynch beat him to the punch though, Rachelle thought again, chuckling. She picked up the phone, and called her girlfriend Gina. She had to tell her about this.

"Girl are you sure?" Gina asked.

"Pretty sure, I mean, they were coming from the annex, and no one even knew he was meeting her," Rachelle replied, still watching the window, in case Thomas came back early.

"Mmm, I guess Thomas missed out huh?" Gina said laughing.

Rachelle joined her.

"Yep, now he can stop tripping, and come on and get him some of this honey right here," she replied, and they both pealed into laughter.

"Do you think he'll get rid of Chris now?" Gina asked.

"Girl who knows" Rachelle replied. "We'll just have to wait and see." She went on "Of course, I'll be there to help him ease the pain of not getting with Kayla," she finished, and they once again, burst into laughter.

"I gotta go girl, my next appointment is here" Gina told her.

Her best friend was also her hairdresser.

"Ok girl, I'll call you later with more details as they develop," Rachelle finished and hung up.

Thomas arrived at his house shortly after retrieving his car from the repair shop. He saw Chris's car, and knew he was home.

"Hey Chris?" Thomas called out, as he entered the house.

"Yeah man. I'm in the den," Chris replied.

Thomas took a deep breath as he went in to talk to him. Chris looked at him when he entered the room. He knew Thomas wanted an answer to his question yesterday.

"I was worried about you last night when you didn't show," Thomas said simply, looking at Chris levelly.

"I'm sorry about that man," Chris answered.

"So, are you ready to answer my question now?" he asked. Chris looked at his friend, nodded his head, and began to speak.

He told Thomas about meeting Kayla when they were in college. That they dated. That he was her first lover. Chris told Thomas about his cheating ways, and how he'd broken Kayla's heart.

"I found her again a year later, but she was already dating someone else," Chris told him.

Thomas was looking at him intently, taking in every word that he said.

"I went to her office that Saturday morning, with the intention of getting her back," Chris told him, remembering it in his mind. "She and I argued. Then things got violent."

Chris went on, taking another deep breath.

"I hit Kayla, and knocked her out," Chris told him.

Thomas was trying hard to control the anger he felt right now. He had to remember, this was years ago.

"After she was unconscious," Chris stopped, and looked Thomas in the eye. "I took her clothes off, and I raped her."

After he finished talking, Chris looked to his friend for a reaction. Thomas was silent. He knew Kayla had forgiven Chris, but Thomas was still furious with him right now.

"Why did you keep this from me?" Thomas asked, harsher than he intended.

"What would you have said Thomas?" Chris countered. "Would you still have offered me an Assistant Pastors position?" he continued. "Hell, would you have even spoken to me again?"

Thomas had to admit Chris was right. It bothered him even more, because it was Kayla.

"Listen, Thomas," Chris began again. "I know you're attracted to Kayla," he continued. "What happened with me and her was a lifetime ago. Please don't use that to judge me, or her, now," Chris finished.

Thomas thought about that statement. Chris was right again.
"You're right Chris," Thomas told his friend. "I just need to go and think," he finished, sighing deeply.
"I still want you to stay on at the church," Thomas told Chris simply, as he left the room.
Chris was glad to hear that. He liked Chapel Hill, and he liked the church. Chris hoped Thomas could forgive him, and that he and Kayla would actually connect.

8

Kayla's meeting with Chris had done wonders for her. She could actually put the incident in proper prospective. Chris had changed a lot since then she had to admit.

He'd also made her think again about a time she'd tried hard to forget. To think about a person, Kayla wished sometimes she'd never met. She was still thinking about Dezi, even now.

"My god that turned into such a nightmare," she said aloud.

Kayla had to stop lying to herself and admit it wasn't always bad. Dezi had been fantastic when they first met. Even during the turmoil, he'd always been protective of her. She believed him when he said he loved her. Dezi was just so twisted by that time he didn't know love from obsession. Kayla thought about his smile, and those wonderful dimples. Those beautiful gray eyes.

"Well, no need reminiscing on the past," she said aloud to herself, once again feeling a deep sense of loss. "I've got to live in the here and now," she finished, just as her cell rang.

"Hello?" she answered.

"Hi Kayla," Thomas said quietly.

Kayla was taken aback. He hadn't called her Sister Kayla this time, and he sounded strange.

"Hi Pastor Bradford," Kayla said guardedly.

"I need to see you please," Thomas told her.

Kayla wondered what in the world Pastor Bradford could possibly want with her. What was going on with him, he sounded so very unusual.

"Well, when did you want to see me?" she probed.

"Can I come by your house in a few minutes?" Thomas asked again.

Kayla thought about it. Mariah wouldn't be home yet. She was at Jaz's.

"Well alright. That'll be fine," she answered. "Pastor?" Kayla probed again "Could you tell me what this is about?"

Thomas didn't want to get into it on the phone. "I'd prefer to tell you when I get there," he replied. Kayla told him that was fine, and she'd see him in a few minutes. *That was totally odd.* She thought to herself turning into her driveway.

Thomas's nerves were on edge. He knew he had to talk to Kayla and tell her that he knew. He just hoped she wouldn't run away once he did. "Well," he began, speaking quietly aloud to himself. "Here we go. Sink or swim," he finished, turning on Kayla's street.

Thomas arrived moments later as Kayla graciously invited him inside. They were now seated in her sunroom. It was her favorite place in the house she told him. Here the light came naturally and filled the house with a glorious warmth and serenity.

Kayla was seated on the loveseat and Thomas on one of the single chairs. She'd offered him something to drink when he arrived. Kayla was watching him intently now, sipping her tea. Pastor Bradford hadn't said anything yet, and she was worried.

Thomas looked back at Kayla, finding her looking at him expectantly. He knew he had to say something. He just didn't know where, or how, to begin.

"Kayla," Thomas said slowly, choosing his words cautiously. "There are some things I need to say to you," he went on. "But I'm not sure how. So, please be patient with me, while I try to get them all out."
Kayla wondered what was so pressing on his mind. "Sure Pastor," she replied gently. "Take your time."

Thomas took a deep breath, and looked right at her. "Chris told me about the past you both shared," he said delicately, never taking his eyes off her.
Kayla gasped slightly, and her eyes immediately began to tear.

"Kayla, please don't be embarrassed," Thomas said, getting up to go sit beside her. "I know what happened to you wasn't your fault, and it was a long time ago," he went on. "I just wanted you to know, I'm sorry it ever happened."

Kayla was crying softly. Thomas reached out for her, and Kayla allowed him to hold her in his arms. Thomas loved the way she felt.

"Are you going to make him leave now?" Kayla asked Thomas quietly, as he still held her.

"No," he told her. "I know he's not the same man he was then, and if you and God can forgive him," Thomas continued. "I certainly can."

Kayla pulled away, and looked at him.

"Thank you so much for understanding," she told Thomas. "I'm actually proud of how he's gotten his life together," Kayla finished, looking at Pastor Bradford closely now.

Thomas was looking in her eyes, noticing how beautiful they were, and how beautiful she was. He smiled. "Everything's going to be fine," he told Kayla. "You're still coming back on Sunday, right?"

Kayla smiled, and told him yes.

"Kayla," Thomas began anew. "I know all about you and Donovan," he said simply. "I know you loved him very much, and he loved you too," he went on. "I don't want you to ever forget the love the two of you shared; but I'd like to be able to give you the same loving memories in the future."

The intent of his statement evident in the adoring look Thomas was giving her now.

Kayla studied him. Pastor Bradford was indeed an attractive man. He reminded Kayla a lot of Black, physically. He was very well built, she could see now. The gray polo shirt was bulging from the well-structured chest beneath it, and the jeans she'd noticed earlier, clung to his well-defined thighs and butt.

Kayla was ashamed to admit, she'd even glanced at his crotch, and took note of the sizeable bulge fashioned. His arms were huge, and she'd enjoyed being encompassed in them, as he held her earlier. Pastor Bradford took very good care of himself Kayla could tell. Still, she wasn't totally sure she could move on yet.
"Pastor," Kayla began, before he cut her off.
"Please, call me Thomas," he said tenderly, still looking at her.

Kayla smiled and corrected herself.
"OK, Thomas," she continued. "I'm not sure if I'm ready to move on yet honestly," she went on. "I can't make you any promises," Kayla said, and then stopped talking.
Thomas was crushed. He wanted so much to be with this woman. He wouldn't give up though. Kayla was speaking again, which broke his thought.
"I'm willing to try," she was saying. "I just ask that you be patient with me."
Thomas was elated! She wasn't saying no. He would definitely be patient.
"I can do that Kayla," he said gently, looking at her again.

Thomas reached out, and softly kissed her. Kayla didn't push him away, so he kissed her again, more insistent this time. Kayla was torn. Thomas, seeing that she was really trying, pulled Kayla to him, took her into his arms, kissing her deeply.

Mariah arrived home, and saw his car. She wondered what he was doing here. She'd found them in the sunroom, but didn't interrupt. Mariah smiled to herself, as she saw her Pastor, and her mother, deeply embraced in the passionate kiss they were sharing.

Mariah thought about what she'd just witnessed. She smiled softly, thinking that her mother had finally come out of her time of mourning, and was going to live her life. She hoped her mother didn't feel guilty about what she felt for Pastor Bradford. Her father wouldn't want her to be unhappy and miserable forever.

Mariah wondered how they would handle dating each other. If the members at the church found out, they would have no privacy. She definitely wouldn't tell anyone, and if she knew her mother, she wouldn't either. She chuckled, thinking how fiercely private her mother was. *There are probably things about mommy I don't even know,* Mariah thought to herself.

Her mother would seldom discuss her romantic life before her father. Kayla told her all about her great grandmother, and her best friend, for whom Mariah was named, but never about old boyfriends. Mariah thought it was a little odd, but it wasn't a big deal. She laughed to herself again, and began to get ready for choir rehearsal.

Thomas was on top of the world as he drove. He couldn't believe how wonderful it had felt kissing Kayla. He was happier than he'd been in a long time. Thomas chuckled to himself thinking of the three or four women he knew of, that would be upset when they found out he was no longer on the market. *He would probably have to get another secretary once Rachelle found out,* Thomas thought to himself, causing another chuckle. He wouldn't tell anyone though.

Thomas wanted them to have their privacy. He would announce it when they were engaged, and about to be married. That couldn't happen soon enough for Thomas. He knew Kayla was the one. He wanted to see her smile everyday. Thomas wanted to know what it felt like to lay beside her at night, and feel her warmth next to him. He wanted to know the joy of making love to her. He had to think of something else quickly.

Thomas found himself becoming very aroused at that last thought. *She is nowhere near ready for that yet,* he thought to himself as he arrived at the church. Tonight was choir rehearsal, and Thomas liked to hear them rehearse. It helped him write his sermons. Thomas gathered his briefcase and went inside to his office.

"Mariah?" her mother called to her.
"Yes Mommy?" she answered.
"Can I speak with you a moment please?" Kayla asked.
Mariah came downstairs to the sunroom, where her mother was still sitting. Kayla smiled at her daughter, as Mariah came in and sat down.
"What's going on?" Mariah asked.

Kayla looked at her daughter, and thought again of her husband. She wasn't sure how Mariah would really react to her seeing someone else.
"I need to talk to you about something important," Kayla began.
Mariah looked at her mother evenly. She already knew what Kayla was going to tell her. She could hardly contain her excitement.
"What is it mommy?" Mariah replied.
Kayla took deep breath before she spoke.
"I'm going to be seeing someone," she said simply.

Mariah looked at her for a moment to see if she would say anything else, before asking her, "A man?"
Kayla looked at her to see what she may be thinking, but Mariah had no particular expression.
"Yes," she said softly, never taking her eyes from her daughter.
"Who is it?" Mariah probed.
She didn't know why her mother was being so guarded. *Maybe she thinks I'll be upset.* Mariah thought to herself.
Kayla took another breath.
"Pastor Bradford," she replied, still looking intently at her daughter.
Mariah smiled.

"Mommy!" she cried. "I'm so happy for you!" she finished, as she jumped up to come and hug her mother.
Kayla was surprised. She was glad Mariah wasn't upset, but she had to make sure she wasn't just trying to fool her either.
"Are you sure you're okay with this baby?" she asked Mariah, looking her in the eye.

"Mommy, I couldn't be happier," Mariah told her. "He reminds me alot of daddy," she finished, still smiling happily.

Kayla had to admit she was right. That was one of the biggest things that had caught her attention the first time she saw Thomas.

"I have to be honest though" Mariah began, looking sheepishly at her mother.

What in the world? Kayla was thinking to herself.

"I saw the two of you kissing earlier," Mariah replied.

Kayla blushed deeply, and Mariah laughed.

"Aww mommy," she said, still laughing. "It's okay. I know people your age still kiss," she teased, as she got up to leave for choir rehearsal.

Kayla laughed herself, and told her daughter to be careful. Mariah replied that she would, and left.

Kayla smiled to herself at how fortunate she was to have Mariah, and now she had Thomas. Kayla thought back to their kiss, and how good it felt to have a man's arms around her again. She smiled again, as she headed to the kitchen to make herself something to eat.

9

Mariah was still smiling to herself thinking of her mother and Pastor Bradford.
"I'm so happy she has someone now," she mused aloud. Mariah was surprised to see David waiting for her outside, when she drove up. Her good mood immediately went south.

"Hello David," Mariah said cynically, as David walked up to her.
David knew she was still angry. He was prepared for that. He didn't let it stop him from his mission here tonight, and that was to win Mariah back.
"Hey Boo," he replied carefully, smiling at her.

Mariah really didn't want to deal with him now. She was truly over David. He'd treated her badly for the last time. She'd been hearing rumors for months now that he was sleeping with someone else.
"What do you want David?" Mariah asked bluntly.

David plunged ahead, ignoring her tone and mannerisms.
"I want to apologize again for Sunday," he told her. "I was wrong for ever hurting you like that," he continued. "I was just hurt when you told me we were over. Baby, I can't lose you."

Mariah took a deep breath, and sighed. "David, you and I have been headed toward the end for a long time now," she went on. "I just finally made the move, that's all."
Damn, he was thinking. *She's still on this leaving me kick.*
"Boo, what can I do for you to forgive me, and come back to me?" David asked her, pleading.
Mariah looked at him again. She liked him well enough that they could probably be friends, but she didn't want him in her life romantically anymore at all. Not this David.
"Nothing David, Absolutely nothing at all," she replied, with a tone of irrevocability. Mariah walked away, leaving him hurt and angry.

"It's not even going down like that," David angrily said aloud to himself, as he watched her walk into the church. He turned to go to his car vowing to get Mariah back, and rid of Aidan once and for all.

"So what do you know about him?" David asked Jared, one of his friends, after he met him at one of the local hang out spots.

Jared dated one of Jaz's friends, and he generally knew the scoop on what was going on.

"Not a lot," he replied. "He's from Virginia Beach, and he's supposed to be moving here to go to school."

David was livid. This guy had come in and stolen Mariah from him. He loved her. He was a normal guy, so why shouldn't he want to sleep with her. Mariah was gorgeous. David shouldn't have stood her up.

He was being an ass. He only did it to get back at her for telling him no again when he wanted to have sex. Now he was losing her.

David refused to say lost. Mariah wasn't going to leave him. She was just mad. He had to get through to her, but he needed this guy out of the way.

"So you talk to Elaine?" David asked Jared again.

They'd come up with a scheme to get Aidan out of the picture.

"Yeah, she says she's down for whatever," Jared replied.

David smiled. *No matter how good he pretends to be, he's still a man,* he thought to himself.

"Good," David spoke again. "Tell her it's on, at the spot."

Jared told him okay, and they went their separate ways. David knew the one thing Mariah would never forgive was infidelity. She'd never caught him, but he would make sure Mariah caught Aidan, right in the act.

David laughed again, and snapped his fingers.

"That ass will be history," David laughed. "And I'll be right there, to pick up the pieces and love Mariah all the way back to me," he finished, as he got in his car and sped away.

Elaine finally had what she needed to prove to Sherice that David was a lying dog. She reflected on the call she'd gotten from Jared, and what he'd wanted her to do.

Elaine guessed she should have been offended by the inference she was that easy, but she didn't care what the hell those little boys thought of her.

Elaine was trying to decide when she was going to tell Sherice, when her cell rang. "Hello?" Elaine answered.
"May I speak to Elaine please?" the female voice asked.
"Speaking," Elaine replied, still trying to figure out who she was talking to.
"Oh, hey girl, I didn't recognize your voice. This is Jaz," she replied.
Elaine smiled widely. *What are the odds?* she thought to herself happily.

Mariah entered the sanctuary, and ran into Pastor Bradford. "Hi Pastor," she said cheerfully.
Thomas smiled at Mariah, and returned her greeting.
"Everything okay with you and David?" he asked her, after witnessing them in the parking lot.

Mariah frowned. "There is no David and I anymore, Pastor," she said plainly. "He just doesn't want to accept it."
Thomas smiled at her.
"It will be alright Mariah," he told her. "Keep the faith that David will understand, and you two can at least be friends."
Mariah nodded, but she didn't think it would be quite that easy.
"I'd better go now," she told him, hearing the musicians begin to play.

Thomas smiled, and told her to go ahead. Mariah looked back at him before she entered.
"I'm happy that God sent you to my mother," she said gently, looking him in the eye before going inside to rehearse.

Thomas smiled. He should have known Kayla would tell her. They didn't seem to keep secrets from each other. He was also pleased she was happy about it. Thomas knew if she hadn't approved, Kayla wouldn't have continued to see him. He headed back to his office to call her.

Kayla answered on the third ring.

"Hello?" she spoke.

"Hi Kayla," Thomas said cheerfully.

"Hi Thomas," Kayla returned pleasantly. She smiled at the sound of his voice. *It was very nice of him to call again,* she thought to herself.

"I just wanted to call, and check on you," Thomas said again.

Kayla smiled again before replying.

"I'm fine. I'm about to go out for a little while," she told Thomas.

"Really?" he replied. "Where are you going?" he asked, and then caught himself. "I mean, if you don't mind my asking?"

Kayla chuckled lightly, and he heard her. Thomas had to smile himself. Kayla made him feel like a teenager all over again.

"I'm actually going to visit my friend Jackie for a little while," she replied.

"Well, have a great time," he told her.

Kayla told Thomas she would, and she would call him when she returned.

"That'll be wonderful," he replied.

They said their goodbyes, and hung up. Kayla was still smiling, when she got in her car headed to Jackie's.

"Hey Jaz," she returned. "What's going on?"

Jaz giggled, and Elaine felt herself getting turned on again.

"Nothing much, I was wondering if you had Desiree's number?" she asked. "I'm trying to get some help with this stupid project we have for class," Jaz giggled again. Elaine laughed with her.

"Yeah I got it around her somewhere. Can you hang on for a sec?" she asked.

Jaz told her sure. Elaine put her cell down, and took several deep breaths. She knew Desiree's number by heart. She just needed to gather herself. Elaine wasn't going to let this opportunity pass her by. She needed to feel Jaz out. *But how,* she asked herself. She picked the phone up.

"Hey sorry it took so long," she replied.

Jaz told her it was okay. Elaine gave her the number, and Jaz told her thanks.

"Are you guys getting together this weekend?" Elaine asked, trying to prolong their conversation.

"Yeah, we'll probably go hit the spot or something," Jaz replied.

"Hmm, ya'll doing the couple thing?" Elaine asked.

Jaz giggled again before she answered.

"I dunno. They'll probably bring their men," she replied, still chuckling lightly.

"Oh, so you don't have a man?" Elaine replied, fishing.

Jaz laughed, and told her not this week.

"You don't sound too upset about it," Elaine replied softly.

Jaz chuckled again. "Not really. I mean, it's not the end of the world to not have man you know," she continued still laughing. "I don't see you with one either, miss thang!"

Elaine chuckled lightly. "That's because I prefer women," she replied softly.

Jaz was quiet for a moment, and Elaine was scared. She hoped she hadn't run Jaz off, and she would stop talking to her.

"Really?" Jaz returned. "Wow, I didn't know."

Elaine was glad she hadn't hung up.

"Well, it's not something I broadcast. I just figure it's my own business," she replied calmly.

"Yeah I guess you're right," Jaz said, "I mean that it's your own business."

Jaz didn't know why, but she found herself very intrigued with what Elaine was telling her.

Big D had the operation flowing pretty smoothly now. They had six girls, ranging in age from seventeen, to twenty-two. He and Cameron were making good money. Cameron told him his boy DeSean would be home today, and they could meet.

Big D hoped the boy was as good as Cameron in the game. He wanted to shift into more of a consultant type role. *He was getting too old to be on the street, chasing bitches and johns, and shit,* Big D thought to himself. He would leave that to the younger crew.

"Hey Sweet Daddy," Shay said seductively, to Big D. She was the same one he'd broken in their first day. He liked her style, so he kept her around, mostly for himself. She was too damn young though.

He wanted a more mature woman. Not that he was complaining, because the sex was great. Big D just wanted something more. For now, he would sex her and not complain.

"What you want sugar?" Big D said sweetly to the girl, knowing already what she had in mind.

"I wanna give my sweet daddy some loving," Shay purred, as she mounted him.

He closed his eyes, and let the girl's warmth envelope him. *Yeah man, this girl can definitely get down!* Big D thought to himself again, as he enjoyed her.

Cameron's cell went off. He saw it was DeSean. *About damned time!* He thought to himself.

"Yo man! What's up?!" Cameron asked his friend cheerfully.

DeSean smiled. It was good to be home.

"Shit man. Not a damned thing!" he replied.

"Well playa, come on over then, and I'll catch yo' ass up to date on thangs!" Cameron replied.

"I'm on my way man!" DeSean laughed, and hung up.

Cameron knew Big D was busy. He'd seen the girl go in, so he knew exactly what they were doing. He laughed at the thought, and headed off to the kitchen to get himself something to drink.

"Where are you going DeSean?" his mother asked, watching him get dressed.

He didn't feel like the third degree today. Why didn't she just leave him alone?

"I'm going over to Cameron's for a little while," DeSean replied testily.

Liv sighed deeply. She knew Cameron was nothing but trouble. He and DeSean had already gotten picked up for stealing. God only knows what else they'd done, and not gotten caught for.

"You just got home," she replied. "Your father hasn't even seen you yet," Liv finished, hoping it might make some impact.

DeSean knew his dad would be cool with it. He and his dad got along great. They saw eye to eye on most things.

"Yeah, but he'll be alright with it," DeSean told her.

Liv knew he was right, and she didn't feel like arguing with him anymore.

"Well could you at least try to be home at a decent hour?" she asked him.

He thought about that too. He was glad she was taking Aidan back to Aunt Jackie's in the morning. DeSean needed a break from her, and he had just gotten here.

"I'll try and do that mama," he told her plainly, as he darted out the door.

She just shook her head. DeSean was a lost cause and Liv knew it. She turned her attention to her eldest son, who was coming out of the bathroom.

"Hey Mama," Aidan greeted her with a smile.

Liv smiled then herself. He was a wonderful child.

"So? Tell me all about your visit," she prodded him.

Aidan laughed and sat down at the worn kitchen table to tell her about his trip.

Once they'd finished talking, Liv looked at him long and hard.
"What's wrong mama?" he asked her, concerned with the look on her face.
"Nothing baby, I'm just glad you're going to stay with Jackie, and finish school," she said quietly.

Aidan knew what she meant. He knew DeSean gave her nothing but grief, and was failing everything in school. He also knew she was glad he was getting away from Wallace. Aidan hated his stepfather, and he was sure Wallace didn't like him much either.
"Mama?" Aidan began, looking at her seriously "Are you going to be alright here with him?"
Liv smiled. She knew Aidan was worried about Wallace hitting her all the time.
"I'll be fine baby," she told him, as she caressed his face. "As long as I know you're OK, I'm OK," she continued. "Now, tell me about this girl you met," she teased.
Aidan laughed, and began to tell her about Mariah.

"'Sup man?" Cameron greeted him at the door. "Come on in!"
DeSean was sitting on the couch, with his drink and a joint, when Big D walked into the room with Shay. DeSean almost choked.
"What's up youngblood?" Big D greeted him, smiling at the boy's expression.
Cameron laughed too. Cameron went on to explain to DeSean who Big D was, and what was up. DeSean was smiling himself now, after hearing all the exciting things they had going on.
"So, we expanding into the dope business too," Cameron was saying.

Big D had talked to one of the leading suppliers, and he was looking for another way to get his dope on the street.
"Man, sex and dope go together, like hand and glove," Big D told the youngsters.

DeSean was down for whatever. He wanted to be paid. Cameron told them he had two girls coming over tonight, who were looking for pimps.
"You ready young blood?" Big D asked DeSean.
He thought he had to be dreaming!
"Hell yeah!" DeSean replied, already thinking ahead.
"Good then!" Big D replied, laughing.
"Oh yeah," he said, looking at both of them hard. "Secret to pimpin' is not to get attached, and don't never hit it without a rubber," he went on. "You get soft, and some other pimp got yo' money and yo' bitches. You hit that shit without a rubber, and they burying yo' ass with AIDS!" he continued; looking at them, until they told him they understood.
"I'm going down to the corner store," Big D told them "I need me a beer, and yo' mama sho' ain't gonna let me have one here."

Cameron and DeSean talked more after he left.
"Man, this has been the shit!" Cameron exclaimed, telling DeSean how many women he had been with as he laughed.

DeSean joined him. It looked like he was going to finally get the respect and recognition he'd always desired. He liked Big D. *He was true old school pimpin'*, he thought to himself. He was going to help him and Cameron go real far. DeSean could feel that.
"So what time the booty getting here man?" he asked Cameron, as they both burst into laughter all over again.

10

"I'll go for you mama," Aidan was telling his mother.
"No baby," she told him, grabbing her change purse. "You keep packing. I'll be right back," she finished, closing the door behind her.
Liv needed to get Wallace some cigarettes, and a beer. She knew if they weren't there when he got home, Wallace would hit the roof. Liv didn't need anything to go wrong when she was so close to getting her son the hell out of there.

Big D saw the woman walk in the store. It was a familiar neighborhood dive, with the usual outdated, overpriced, merchandise and the typical foreign owner behind the glass, watching everyone who came in with suspicion.

She was pretty, big bright brown eyes, nice teeth without any gold. She had a nice body. Her breasts were firm and full, her waist narrow, and she had nice hips and thighs. Big D watched her for a minute to see what she was buying.

Liv got herself and Aidan, a coke. She got a sprite for DeSean, and the beer for Wallace. She asked for his cigarettes at the front counter, as she paid. Big D knew she had a man, from the smokes and beer. He could tell by looking at her, she didn't do either, or if she did it wasn't often.
"How you doing today?" he asked her nonchalantly.

Liv looked at the man speaking to her. She'd never seen him before. He was good looking, tall and very sexy, with great features, all proportion to his face, and a body that wouldn't quit. *Damn!* Liv thought to herself *he looks good as hell to be my age!* She could see the years in his face. Not that it took away from his overall appearance.
"I'm fine," she replied pleasantly, "how about yourself?"
Big D smiled, and she saw he had gorgeous teeth.
"I'm doing very well, thanks," he replied smoothly.

He liked her, liked what he saw. He needed to find out about her man though.
"So, how long you been with your man?" Big D asked Liv, watching her reaction.
Dag! she thought again, *he doesn't waste any time does he?*
"About 17 years," Liv said plainly.
Big D knew from her answer she wasn't happy, and that was what he wanted to hear.
"So, what you wanna do?" he asked her again, point blank.
I can't believe I'm standing here having this conversation, Liv was thinking again.
"Honestly?" she asked, looking at him evenly.
"Definitely," Big D replied smoothly.
Liv thought a moment before she answered.
"I'd like to actually have an orgasm, while I'm being screwed," she said bluntly.

Big D smiled, he liked her for real now.

"I can make that happen for you baby," he answered confidently.
Liv looked him over again, and thought to herself that he probably could do just that.
"So when you wanna get that big O?" Big D asked, looking at her again.
I wouldn't really screw him would I? Liv thought to herself.
Then she began to think about all the unfilled nights with Wallace. All the beatings, and arguments, and decided yes she would.

"How can I reach you?" Liv asked him.

Big D didn't miss a beat. He gave her his cell, and told her to call him when she was ready to be completely, and totally, satisfied.

"I will most definitely do that," she said smiling, as she took the number, and her purchases, leaving the store.

Big D leaned back on the cooler, and smiled again. He hoped she would call soon. He wanted to see just what her body felt like.

Wallace came home in his usual sour mood. Liv was careful not to say, or do, anything to set him off. Aidan just stayed out of his way.
"Where the hell is DeSean?" he yelled.
"He went over to Cameron's," Liv told him quietly.
He grunted and told her to get his dinner, he was hungry.
"Where's the other one?" Wallace asked again testily.
"He's in the room," she said again.

He grunted again, but said nothing else. Wallace ate in silence, only taking time to occasionally give Liv an evil look. He wasn't mad at her. She was just easiest to take it out on. They'd been giving him grief all day at that lousy job he had. Marie didn't want to sex him during lunch today.

Marie King was the woman Wallace was having an affair with. Said she was mad at him. He knew why, but there was nothing he could do about that right now. He'd been stringing Marie along for the last three or four years, telling her he would leave Liv, and be with her.

Wallace didn't know why he didn't leave. He guessed some part of him actually did still love Liv a little. Although unlike Liv, Marie liked to have sex with him. Liv was cold and unfeeling. She acted like she hated him touching her. He'd do her today though. Wallace looked at Liv and spoke.

"I want some," he said simply.

Liv knew what he meant and got up headed for the bedroom. He followed, and they had passionless sex. Afterwards, Wallace went to shower.
Liv lay in bed, thinking about her earlier conversation with the sexy stranger.
It dawned on her then, that she hadn't even asked his name. *Guess it doesn't matter,* Liv thought to herself. *As long as the sex is good, I don't care what his name is.*

Wallace came back into the room now interrupting her thoughts.
"What time you leaving tomorrow?" he asked her plainly.
"Early in the morning," Liv replied quietly, and simply.

She just wanted to get through this night without a beating.
"I'm going out for awhile," Wallace told her, as he dressed.
"OK," she said simply, silently thankful he would be gone.

Aidan sat on his bed fuming. He'd heard Wallace come home. Heard him yelling at his mother, even heard them having sex. He knew Liv hated Wallace touching her, but she did it to keep the peace.
Why won't she just leave him? Aidan thought to himself. *Hell, why don't I just kill him for her?* He thought again, and scared himself at how calmly he could imagine himself doing just that.

Aidan was glad to be leaving tomorrow. He couldn't wait to get away from all the turmoil here. Just thinking about Mariah made him smile. Aidan couldn't deny he was horny though. He picked up the phone to call Cheryl. He would force himself to be bothered with her long enough to get some. Aidan thought about what would happen once he got back to Aunt Jackie's. *Might have to learn the true meaning of abstinence for real,* Aidan thought to himself, chuckling lightly.

Cheryl answered on the second ring, purring in his ear about how good it was to hear from him.
"Can I come over?" Aidan asked her.
"Of course baby," Cheryl returned. He told her okay, he was on his way and hung up.

"Girl, he is on his way now," Cheryl told her friend Mina.
"So you got everything ready?" Mina asked.
They had been discussing how Cheryl was going to get Aidan to stay with her.
"Girl yes, I took care of the condoms already," she said laughing.
"Are you sure he won't do you raw?" Mina asked.

That was the best chance of her actually getting pregnant, like she wanted.
"No," Cheryl replied. "Believe me, I've tried," she finished sulkily.

Cheryl Johnston was in love with Aidan. She wanted him to marry her. She wanted to have beautiful gray-eyed babies with him. Aidan wanted to leave her and go off to law school. *Well he might still do that, but I'll be right there with him,* Cheryl thought to herself.
"Well, let me get outta here girl, before Aidan catches me," Mina laughed, as she left.

Forty-five minutes later Aidan rang the bell, and her sister answered.
"Cheryl's in her room," she replied, stepping out of the way.
Aidan entered the concrete walled fortress. They lived in the projects, and the house was boorishly decorated with various throw covers, and run down furniture.

The kitchen smelled of burnt chicken, and he saw the all too familiar cockroach, running around the walls. They all knew he and Cheryl were having sex. They just didn't care.

Aidan hated that about her family. They had with no goals or ambitions except living off the government. Aidan knew Cheryl was trying to trap him and get out of her poor existence. That's why he was always careful when he had sex with her. She'd tried to get him to go raw a couple times, but he wasn't hearing that. No sir. When Aidan left here, he wasn't leaving any little surprises behind or taking any extra baggage with him.

Aidan knocked on her door and Cheryl told him to come in. She was already naked, and under the covers waiting for him. He sat down on the bed beside her, and she reached up to kiss him.
"I missed you baby," Cheryl said softly, reaching down to stroke his erection.

He was horny as hell and Cheryl did have one banging body, and a cute face. Her figure was what had attracted him in the first place. Aidan undressed, and slid in beside Cheryl.

They began to kiss, and touch each other.

"I want you now baby," she said, softly in his ear.

"OK, hold on," Aidan replied, as he reached for his jeans to get the condoms he'd brought.

"I have some condoms baby," Cheryl said again, handing him one.

Aidan knew better than to fall for that old trick. She'd probably put all kinds of holes in them, or they were outdated. Aidan kissed Cheryl again, and told her he wanted to use his own. He was allergic to certain ones, and didn't want to take any chances.

Cheryl didn't know he was lying, so she didn't get upset. Aidan put on the condom, and began to kiss her once more. She quickly found herself aroused all over again. He pulled her on top of him, and they began having sex.

Aidan still didn't remember saying it, but she'd slapped him, and was yelling at him now, tears streaming down her face.

"Who the hell is Mariah?!!" Cheryl demanded.

She couldn't believe it. Here they were making love, and he cries out another woman's name. Aidan didn't answer her as he continued to dress. He just wanted to get the hell out of there.

"Who is she Aidan?!" Cheryl was still screaming, demanding an answer.

She blocked the door, standing in front of it.

"Cheryl," he said tiredly. "Please move."

She leaned against the door.

"Not until you tell me who the hell Mariah is?!" Cheryl said angrily.

Aidan sighed deeply, and asked Cheryl to move again. She stood her ground. He was getting angry, that all too familiar coldness beginning to creep in.

He would be gone tomorrow, and he would never have to see her again. Aidan just wanted to leave without a big production.

"Cheryl," he said again, calmly. "Please move out of the way," Aidan finished, and looked up at her.

"No!" she screamed again, still looking at him hard.

Aidan snapped, jumping up and grabbing her by the throat. "Bitch, you are really beginning to work my fucking nerves," he told her coldly.

Cheryl was terrified. Aidan had never touched her, and he'd never talked to her the way he was talking now.

"I'm so sick of dealing with your hood ass," he went on still choking her.

Cheryl was desperately trying to get Aidan's hands away from her throat. Finally after what seemed an eternity, Aidan flung her back onto her bed.

"Do you know why I mess with you Cheryl?" he asked acidly still looking at her hard. "Because you're an easy piece of ass."

Cheryl began to cry again, crouching against the corner of the wall closest to her bed.

"Hell, you screwed me the first night I met you," Aidan went on coldly, feeling his anger come full force.

"What guy you think gonna respect a ho that has his dick in her mouth thirty minutes after meeting him," he continued, laughing meanly. "Shit, you didn't even know my name good," he told her as he grabbed his keys from the nightstand.

"We were never a couple Cheryl," he told her still glaring hatefully at her, "You were someone I screwed and got my nut with," he continued, hand on the doorknob.

"The shit is done, forget you knew me, forget my number," he told her. "And don't ever damn cross my path again, ever," he finished calmly, opened the door and walked out, leaving Cheryl sobbing uncontrollably.

"He's messing around on me girl," Cheryl said sadly, still sniffling.

"Girl, how do you know?" Mina probed.
Cheryl recounted the evening for her, minus the violence, and what Aidan said while they were having sex.
"Wow!" Mina replied. "He actually called her name?"
Cheryl told her Aidan had indeed called it.
"Then he wouldn't tell me who she was!" she said angrily. "I know she's not at our school. I've never heard that name, and I know just about everyone there."
Mina told her maybe the girl went to one of their rival high schools.
"We don't know what she looks like, so we can't even ask around," Mina replied.
"I need to find out who this bitch is!" Cheryl said venomously. "She is messing with my man, and I don't appreciate it."
Mina sighed as she thought. Cheryl was trying to hang on to Aidan as a meal ticket, and Mina already knew he wasn't trying to hear that. She was surprised Aidan hadn't left Cheryl alone a long time ago.
"So, what are you going to do about it?" Mina asked, shaking the thoughts from her head.
Cheryl sighed, and told her she didn't know right now.
"I guess I'll call him tomorrow, and try to smooth this thing over," she told Mina. "I still love Aidan, and I'm not giving him up without a fight," Cheryl vowed, unmindful to the warnings Aidan had already given her.
Mina sighed again and told her good luck.
"Thanks girl," Cheryl replied. "I don't know what I'd do without you around."
Mina told her she was welcome. *She's going to find out what she'll do when I leave for Texas,* Mina thought, of the impending move her family was about to make. She hadn't told Cheryl yet because she wanted to avoid the scene, and the guilt trip, Mina knew she would lay on her.
"Call me tomorrow after you talk to Aidan" Mina told her instead.
"I will girl, have a good night" Cheryl replied, as they hung up.

Please don't get caught up in Cheryl's trap Aidan, Mina thought to herself, the old feelings she carried for him coming to the surface again. Mina got up, and sighed deeply, heading to the shower to try and cool off.

11

Liv had been lying in bed thinking about her encounter earlier. She knew Wallace wouldn't be home until well after four or five in the morning.
Liv pulled the number out of her change purse, and called. Big D answered on the second ring.
"Wassup baby?" he said smoothly into the receiver.
Liv smiled.
"How'd you know it was me?" she asked.

Big D laughed, thinking to himself women were the only people who called him, so baby worked on all of them.
"Lucky guess," he said aloud to her. "So you ready for that big O now?" he asked huskily.
Big D really did want to see what she felt like. He liked her. She was an attractive woman. Who knows? Maybe they could get something going.
"Yeah I'm definitely ready," Liv replied.
"So you wanna get a room?" he went on.

Big D had a standing arrangement at the local hotel. He and the owner worked out a lucrative arrangement for them both.
"Yeah that sounds good," she replied. "I can't stay all night though."
Big D chuckled lightly. "Its okay baby," he said, "I'm just there to please you."
They discussed the hotel, and Liv told him she'd meet him in an hour.

The walk was short, and Liv found the place with ease. They were in the room now, looking at each other. She'd worn a cute little tangerine mini dress that showed off her figure.
"You know," Liv began. "I didn't even get your name?" she finished, looking at him as he took off his clothes.
He looked up at her and smiled.
"Big D," he said, as he took off his pants.

Liv immediately saw what the D stood for. Big D walked over to Liv, and began kissing her, taking her clothes off as he did. After he had her completely naked, Big D stepped back and looked at her. Liv had a nice body and he definitely was ready to touch it.
"Now, you come on over here, and tell Big D what you want him to do," he said, as he led her to the bed.
Liv looked at this gorgeous specimen towering over her, and spoke.
"I want you to make me come," she said simply.
"As you wish," he said still smiling, as he began to touch her.

Aidan crept in the house, careful not to make noise and wake his mother. He went to his room. He knew DeSean wasn't there. He was probably staying at Cameron's. Aidan reflected on the argument with Cheryl, and what'd happened. He'd been thinking about Mariah, when he was with Cheryl. He wanted it to be her he was making love to.

Aidan couldn't believe he'd done that. He usually never cried out during his orgasm. *Oh well,* Aidan thought to himself. *Nothing I can do about it now.* He lay back on his bed, and let sleep take him. Aidan wanted nothing more, than to forget about tonight, forget about Cheryl, and see Mariah tomorrow.

Liv was still trying to recover from the wonderful sex she'd just had. Big D brought her to three orgasms, before he'd even had one. She had never been with a man who made her feel like he did, except Dezi of course. Liv didn't want to think about him now. Big D had done things to her body, she hadn't had done in over 17 years.

Wallace was very boring in bed, no foreplay or anything, straight in, straight out. Liv was dressing now, and Big D was watching her.
"Is this the last time I'm going to get to feel that beautiful body of yours?" he asked, eyeing her lustfully again.

Liv laughed.
"Hell no!" she told him emphatically "I will definitely be calling you again."

Big D leaned back on his pillow.
"So, you wanna tell me your name now?" he asked smiling.
Liv laughed again, realizing she never did tell him.
"My name is Liv," she said.

Big D repeated it, and smiled again. She walked over to him, and leaned down to kiss him goodnight. He pulled Liv into the bed as they kissed, and began to use his fingers to pleasure her again. She came hard, and Big D whispered in her ear
"Just a little something to keep you interested," Big D kissed her ear gently, and let her go.
Liv was floating on air when she got home. Wallace still wasn't home, thankfully. She saw that DeSean wasn't either, which made her frown, but Aidan was.
"Such a good boy," Liv remarked to herself, as she went to her own room to shower.

DeSean was looking at the girl lying in bed with him. He smiled at his good fortune. *This is the life!* DeSean thought to himself. He thought about calling home, but decided against it. His dad wouldn't say anything, and his mom and Aidan would be gone by the time he got back.

It wasn't that he didn't want to say goodbye to his brother. He just didn't feel like the whole scene thing. DeSean would never admit it to anyone else, but he secretly envied Aidan.

Things were different now though. He and Cameron were big time pimping, and soon they would be big time dope slinging too. DeSean was already picturing what he was going to buy with all the money he would be making.

"I'll show him," DeSean said aloud, thinking about his older brother. He looked down at the girl, and began to get aroused again. DeSean woke her up, and told her to make him happy. She readily complied. DeSean forgot all about Aidan, as he felt the girl's warmth envelope him.

Big D dozed for a while then got up to leave the room. He thought about Liv. *What the fuck has her old man been doing all these years?* Big D thought to himself.
"Well it doesn't matter now," he said aloud "She's had a taste of Big D," he laughed to himself, knowing he and Liv would enjoy many more days of sexual bliss.

Big D ran right into Shay as he opened the door, to leave the motel.
"Who was you giving my candy to Sweet Daddy?" Shay asked him.
Big D could see she was angry. He didn't need this drama. That was the only problem about messing with them young. They fell in love.

"Baby girl," he began. "It wasn't like that."
Shay looked him up and down. She didn't like the thought of him being with anybody else. She was sprung, and she knew it, but she didn't care.
"I saw that bitch leaving," Shay said angry still.

Big D didn't want this to escalate. He didn't want to have to go back to his old ways. He hadn't beaten one of his girls in a long time.
"Shay," Big D said, with a tone that he meant business. "You know the deal. I'm free to screw whoever I want to," he went on. "You work for me, remember?"

Shay was hurt. She had tears in her eyes. Big D hoped that would end the drama, so he didn't have to get violent with her.
"I'm sorry Sweet Daddy," she said quietly. "I just get so jealous sometimes," Shay finished her eyes still on the ground.

Big D sighed softly, and kissed the girl. He pulled her into the room, and proceeded to give her what she wanted. Afterwards, Big D kissed her and told her to go on home.

"OK Sweet Daddy," Shay giggled, as she walked out the door.

Big D sighed again, and thought to himself, *pimpin' ain't easy.*

12

Mariah was excited. She knew Aidan was coming back today, and she couldn't wait to see him. He'd only been gone a little while, but Mariah really missed him.
Kayla questioned her about him after he'd left. She was only curious. Kayla didn't think Aidan was a bad person. She'd said she thought he was a nice young man.

Mariah's cell rang. It was David.
"Why won't he leave me alone?" Mariah said aloud.
"Hello?" she answered.
"Hey Boo," David said pleasantly.
"David, would you please stop calling me that?" she said plainly.

He was really trying to be patient with her. Mariah was still on this breaking up kick, and he was frankly growing tired of it.
"I'm sorry Mariah," David corrected himself. "It's habit."
"So why are you calling me?" Mariah asked him.
David still couldn't believe how cold she was being to him.
"I want to see you Mariah. Please," he added quickly.
"Why?" she asked plainly.
"We need to at least talk, don't you think?" David pleaded, hoping she would agree.
"I mean, can't you do that much for me?"

Mariah thought about it for a moment. Maybe that was all he wanted, and he would leave her alone.
"Yeah, okay," Mariah told him hesitantly. "When do you want to talk?"
David smiled. He knew exactly when, and exactly where.
"How about tonight, around eight?" he asked. "Meet me at the spot."

Mariah didn't see anything wrong with that. The spot was a small diner many of the kids like to hang out in. It was public, and she wouldn't be alone with him.
"OK, that's fine," Mariah told David. "I'll see you there."

David was elated. His plan was going to work out just fine. Now he had to call Jared, and tell him to get

Elaine in place. David knew Aidan was coming back today. Nina, Jared's girlfriend, and Jaz's friend, told him after she heard it from Jaz.

"This is your last night with my girl fool, believe that," David fumed to himself as he dialed Jared's number.

"So he wants you to do what?" Sherice asked Elaine, as she sat on her bed.

"He wants me to seduce this new guy Mariah is seeing, so she'll catch us, and break up with the guy," she told her friend.

Elaine knew David was playing Sherice, now armed with proof, she told her.

"So what time are you supposed to be there?" Sherice asked her friend.

"Eight," Elaine replied.

Sherice was livid. She'd been sleeping with David for months now. He'd always promised he would leave Mariah for her. Then she found out Mariah had broken up with David weeks ago, and he was still lying to her. To make matters worse, Sherice found out three days ago, she was pregnant.

"I got a little something for that ass, Elaine," she said coldly.

Elaine agreed. Neither of them disliked Mariah. This really had nothing to do with her. It was David they were after.

"So, what you gonna do about the baby?" Elaine asked her.

Sherice really hadn't thought much about it. She thought she and David would be together, and they could raise their child together. They would both be eighteen soon. Now Sherice was just mad and wanted to hurt David, like he'd hurt her. She knew he adored Mariah, and that was the one thing she had to power to take away from him.

"OK, here's how this is gonna go down," Sherice began, as Elaine gave her full attention. They talked for the next half hour. This would be a night, Mr. David Maurice Alston II, would never forget.

Aidan was unpacking when Jaz knocked.
"Come in," he called out.
"Hey you!" Jaz said cheerfully, as she entered.
"What's up?" he smiled back.
"I'm glad you're here Aidan," she said sincerely.
He was too. He loved his Aunt Jackie, and Jasmine was his favorite big head cousin.
"We're going to the spot tonight, to hang out," Jaz began. "You want to come?"
Aidan thought about it, and decided he wanted to stay in tonight.
"Nah, maybe next time," he replied. "I think I just wanna chill tonight," he finished, just as the phone rang.

Jaz answered the extension that was in his room.
"Hey girl," she quipped into the phone.
Aidan rolled his eyes. *One of her girlfriends no doubt,* he thought to himself.
"Yes, he is as a matter of fact," Jaz said, looking at him slyly. "Hold on."
She handed him the phone. It was Mariah.
"Hi," she said cheerfully.

Aidan smiled at the sound of her voice, and Jaz started making kissing noises. He laughed and told her to get out. "I wanted to tell you about my evening, before you heard it from someone else," she told him.
His curiosity was peaked. Mariah told him she was going to meet David tonight, because he wanted to talk. Aidan asked her where, and when. Mariah told him, and Aidan told her that was fine.
"I'll let you go now," she said, as she prepared to hang up.
"Hit me up me later?" Aidan asked.
"Sure," Mariah replied, as they hung up.

"Jaz!" Aidan called out.
She stuck her head in the door.
"I think I'll be heading out with you after all," he said.

Jaz smiled, and told Aidan she figured as much, after that call. He laughed, and told her whatever.

Aidan was thinking about David, and his wanting to talk. *That joker just doesn't know how to take no for an answer does he?* He thought angrily, to himself. Aidan just wanted him and Mariah to be able to get to know each other and date, without all this interference.

Aidan supposed he couldn't blame the guy for trying. Mariah was a fantastic girl. *He had his chance,* Aidan thought again trying to keep the coldness at bay. Mariah told him about all the times David stood her up, and treated her badly, all because he was too immature to wait on her for sex.

Aidan wouldn't push her like that. *Stupid ass, don't know shit about shit,* Aidan thought to himself. A girl like Mariah wasn't just going to put out because you said so, you had to work at it, and Aidan fancied himself the master craftsman.

David was looking forward to tonight. He was going to get rid of this clown once and for all. Mariah was his. He sat thinking about her, and how they had been together all this time. She was perfect and both his parents loved her. She was going to law school. He was going to medical school.

They would be the perfect power couple. *Now along comes this low life from Virginia Beach, and he thinks he can just walk in, and take what's mine?* David thought venomously. He headed out to the mall. He wanted to get something really nice for tonight.

"Yep," David said aloud. "This is going to be a night to remember," he finished, chuckling as he got into his car.

He met up with Jared once he got there.

"Everything set with Elaine?" he asked.

Jared shook his head yes, not wanting to stop devouring the cinnamon roll he was eating. David just laughed. His friend loved sweets.

"What if he doesn't come?" Jared asked.
"I'm sure he will," David said. "He'll come with Jaz. He probably figures Mariah will be there too," he went on. "Which she will, but with me," he finished, laughing loudly.
Jared laughed too. "She's gonna be all yours, once she catches him with Elaine," Jared commented, which was exactly what David had in mind.

He found a nice body molding shirt in one of the sport pro shops. It was blue, Mariah's favorite color. *This will do very nicely.* David thought to himself, as he paid for the shirt.

"Now let's get some shoes, and we're out," he told Jared, as they headed for the athletic footwear store in the mall.

"Mommy, I'm going out to the spot tonight," Mariah called to her mother.
Kayla was downstairs in the kitchen, with Mariah's grandmother.
"OK honey. Have a good time," Kayla yelled back.
"Hi Grandma," Mariah yelled.
She heard her grandmother laugh then yell back her hello.

Mariah went to shower. She was meeting David in an hour. She really wasn't looking forward to it at all. Mariah was glad she told Aidan about it though. She didn't want to start their relationship by keeping secrets from him. He'd been very understanding, and she liked that. Mariah made a mental note to call him when she got back.

The shower was refreshing, and she felt much better. Mariah looked over her outfit. She was wearing a canary yellow tank, and jean Capri's, nothing special. Mariah wasn't trying to give David any ideas. She was only coming to talk to him. She pulled her hair back into a ponytail, and put a ribbon on it, started down the stairs, grabbing her keys as she reached the bottom.
"Bye you two!" Mariah called to her mother and grandmother again.

They both told her goodbye, and she was out the door.

Jaz yelled at Aidan to come on. He checked his reflection once more in the mirror. He had on a simple jersey and jeans with his boots. Aidan wanted to be loose, in case anything went down tonight with David. He knew what the joker was up to. *Talk my ass!* He thought to himself.

He was already thinking of them being married, and he'd just started dating Mariah. He'd been messing around with Cheryl for almost a year, and had never given a thought to marrying her.

He'd actually wanted to talk to Mina the night he met Cheryl. His friend Jeff set up the evening, and Aidan was supposed to talk to her. Mina was a petite little thing, with beautiful hazel eyes, and Aidan loved her demur personality. She was bright and fun, when she had a mind to be.

Cheryl however, had seen him and took over. Mina was quiet and non-imposing, so she hadn't objected. Cheryl slept with him that first night. Aidan had to be honest, and admit the sex was good, and it kept him coming back.

He and Mina settled for being friends, though at times, Aidan thought he saw something more in her eyes when she looked at him. *Water under the bridge now,* he thought again. Aidan was happy with Mariah. She was absolutely perfect to him.

"Except for that fiery temper she has," Aidan said aloud, chuckling. He never wanted to see her completely angry, he had a feeling it could get very ugly. Aidan chuckled again.

This fool is gonna make me whip his ass before its over, Aidan thought to himself seriously as he headed down the stairs, to where Jaz was waiting impatiently for him. He laughed when he saw her standing there, hands on her hips, tapping her foot.

"I'm ready girl," Aidan laughed.

"'bout time!" Jaz playfully fumed.

Elaine and Sherice were ready too.
"So do you think the guy will go for it? Sherice asked Elaine.
"Yeah, why wouldn't he?" Elaine returned. "He wants David out of Mariah's life, so he can be in it," she went on. "It's a win, win situation for him."

Sherice was already thinking ahead to what she would say to David, when she confronted him. She had nothing against Mariah. Sherice thought David really cared for her.

She knew his parents wouldn't have approved of her. Sherice wasn't what they thought their son should have been with. Her mom worked three jobs, to take care of her, and her two siblings. They didn't have much, but they weren't trash either.

The Alston's always looked down their nose at her. Sherice felt she was doing Mariah a favor. David was no good. She'd found that out the hard way. Now, she had a child to consider.

If Sherice could spare Mariah the pain she felt right now, plus get even with David, for all the lies and treachery, so much the better.
"OK girl," Elaine said, bringing her back to the present. "We're here."
Sherice smiled, an evil, vengeful smile, and snapped her fingers.
"Showtime!" she announced, getting out of the car, heading for the meeting spot.

David was waiting for Mariah. He'd double-checked with Jared, and everything was still a go. He needed this to work. David saw her drive up, and get out. Mariah looked great he thought still watching her.

He had to win her back tonight, David sighed to himself longingly. He missed her so much.

"Hi David," Mariah said, sitting down across from him. David smiled his best smile, as he spoke.
"Hi Mariah," he said. "You look great. Thanks again for coming to talk to me."
"You're welcome," she said, smiling slightly.

The waitress came, and asked for their orders. Mariah asked for a burger and fries, and added a strawberry shake. David told the waitress to double it, and she left to get their food.
"Well I want to apologize again, for what I did you to that day," David said seriously.
He looked at Mariah squarely wanting her to believe what he said.
"I know David," Mariah said simply, as she took him in.

He looked really nice in the shirt, making her reminisce back to their beginnings and how good it used to be between them. Mariah thought of how sweet and sensitive David used to be.
How he used to always comfort her and tell her he loved her. Mariah sighed deeply and pushed the thoughts out of her mind.

David saw Aidan come in the door behind where he and Mariah were sitting. Aidan and Jaz sat in a booth by the door. David saw Aidan out of the corner of his eye spot him and Mariah. David reached over, and stroked her cheek as he spoke.
"Mariah," he began.
She pulled back from his touch.
"I love you baby. I want to be back with you," David went on. "Please tell me why you don't love me anymore."

Mariah began to talk, but David wasn't really listening. He was watching Elaine, as she slid in the booth beside Aidan, and began talking to him.
"Hi," Elaine said, as she sat down.

Aidan was a bit taken aback by her brashness. Jaz looked at her like she was crazy "Listen to me please," Elaine said quietly, turning her head, so they both could hear, but David couldn't see what she was saying.

"I need you to act natural Jaz," Elaine went on taking in the look she had on her face. She wasn't here to tell anyone about the two of them. Elaine had other business tonight. "Listen Aidan," she continued, as he looked at her.

"How did you know my name?" Aidan interrupted her.

"That's what I'm trying to tell you," Elaine started again. "Play along, and I promise you, this evening will be the best evening of your life."

Aidan and Jaz were confused. Something about her demeanor however, made them take Elaine seriously.

"OK, so what do you want us to do?" Jaz asked, relieved this wasn't some grand confrontation about her reluctance to commit to a relationship with Elaine.

"I need you to get up and wander off. But make sure Mariah doesn't see you," she went on.

"Then Aidan, I want you to pretend to be interested in being with me, and follow me out to this room we have set up," Elaine finished.

"David set this up didn't he?" Jaz hissed quietly.

"Yes," Elaine said plainly. "But he's the one who's in for the surprise tonight," she added hatefully.

"OK, I'm leaving. How long do I wait," Jaz asked.

"Five minutes. Then come to the room in the back, where they keep the pool table stuff," Elaine told her.

Jaz nodded and slipped out.

"Now Aidan, I need you to put on an award winning performance," she told him quietly.

Elaine supposed if she were straight, she would like him. Aidan wasn't a bad looking guy. He had really nice eyes. She almost laughed then. Jared, and the rest of those blockheads, still hadn't figured out she was gay yet. They all thought she was this super freak, who did any and everybody.

"I need you to kiss me," she told him.

Aidan wasn't sure until he saw David looking intently at them, and decided she must be telling the truth.

He leaned down, and kissed her lightly. Aidan saw David smile.
"OK now come on," Elaine told him, getting up to leave. Aidan dutifully got up, and followed.

David turned his attention back to Mariah.
"So I think its best if we just leave it like it is," she finished, waiting on him to respond.
"I guess I have to respect what you've said Mariah," David told her. "Will you come walk with me outside for just a minute?"
Mariah looked at David quizzically.
"I'm not feeling very stable right now, if you know what I mean," he said, sniffling slightly for effect.
"OK, let's go," she replied, as she got up to leave.

Jared saw David lead Mariah outside, and headed out himself. He didn't want to miss this! Once they were outside, David began walking toward the storage room. Mariah looked at him. He was very quiet. She knew she'd hurt him.
"David?" she said softly, looking at him.
He looked at her while she spoke.
"I'm sorry I hurt you," Mariah began. "I never meant to do that."

David tried to kiss her, and Mariah gently pushed him away. "Well, you can't blame a guy for trying," he said, sounding even more hurt.
"Hey, can we go into the storage room for a few?" David asked. "I really need to try and pull myself together."
After looking at him for a few moments, Mariah reluctantly agreed. He led her to the room, and stood behind her, letting her go in first. Mariah opened the door, and stepped in. David heard her gasp. He smiled, and stepped in behind her.

13

"Surprise asshole," Sherice said simply.
Elaine, Aidan, Jaz, Jared, and Nina were all there.
"What the --?" David sputtered.
"I don't understand," Mariah said, looking at David confused.
"I'm sure you don't Mariah, but David does," Aidan said coldly, looking right at him, taking Mariah's hand, and pulling her to him.
"David," she said softly. "What's going on?"
Elaine looked at David.
"Tell her," she said simply.

David didn't say anything. He was enraged. It showed all over his face.
"Guess I'll do the honors then," Elaine said. "David tried to set Aidan up. He wanted me to seduce him, and then you would walk in and catch us. Thus breaking you two up, and sending you, back into his waiting arms," she finished then looked at David.
"That about right?" Elaine asked him.
He still didn't say a word.
"Oh, but that's not the best part Mariah," Sherice piped up.
"Shut up bitch!" David growled at her.
"Fuck you," she said calmly. "Oh that's right. I already did that didn't I?" Sherice finished. "You see Mariah, David has been sleeping with me for the last six months, and I'm now two months pregnant, with his child," she said equally as calm.
"Shut up you lying tramp!" David yelled at her again.
"I don't hafta lie asshole! Here's the test!" Sherice yelled back, and shoved the paper in his face.

Mariah had definitely heard enough.
"Aidan," she said, almost in tears. "I want to go home."
"OK baby," Aidan said softly. "I'll take you home."

Sherice spoke again. "Mariah," she began, and Mariah looked at her. "I never meant to hurt you. David has told me a lot of lies too."

Mariah turned to David. "I hate you," she said simply, her jaw clenched. "I don't ever want to see you again. Ever!" she finished, as Aidan took her hand, and led her outside.

Jaz laughed, and followed.

"Serves you right, you dog!" she said as she left.

Elaine and Sherice walked out, with a final warning coming from Sherice.

"You better tell your parents they're gonna have a grandchild, and you're gonna have child support payments," she said venomously.

Nina told Jared to come on right now, or he was going to be without a girlfriend too. They left. David was alone and devastated. He'd lost Mariah forever, and Sherice was pregnant. His life as he knew it was over.

Aidan was holding her as she cried. Mariah was hurt and angry, all at the same time. He'd driven her car because she was too upset, and Aidan didn't trust Mariah to make it home. Jaz followed in their car.

They were sitting in Mariah's driveway now. *I can't let mommy see me like this,* she thought to herself.

Mariah knew Kayla would question her, and right now she couldn't talk about it.

"Are you going to be alright?" Aidan asked quietly, seeing that she had stopped crying.

Mariah looked at him for a long time before answering. "Yeah," she said softly.

Aidan knew she was hurt. Not so much because she was still in love with David, but because he had lied to her, and deceived her. Aidan reached out to touch her face. Mariah smiled at him. "Baby," he began, looking directly into her eyes. "I want you to know I would never hurt you like that. I would never cheat on you, or lie to you like that. Not ever," Aidan told her sincerely.

Mariah wanted to believe that. She wanted to have that assurance that not every guy was like David.
"How do I know that?" she asked him honestly.
Aidan sighed heavily, knowing the damage David's treachery had done. "Because I love you," he said simply. "And I only have eyes for you," Aidan finished, still looking intently at her.

Mariah smiled again. He'd admitted he loved her. That was a big step for a guy. She was impressed.
"I'm sorry," she said softly again.
Aidan smiled, and pulled Mariah close to him. He kissed her, told her he loved her again, getting out to walk her to the door.

Jaz was proud of her cousin as she watched them from her own vehicle. Aidan knew how to treat a woman, and she was glad he'd gotten together with Mariah. She'd never liked David, and tonight finally proved everything she'd ever said about him was true.

Jaz was just sorry Mariah had gotten hurt in the process. They'd made it to the door, and Mariah was telling Aidan goodnight.

"Thanks for being there for me, yet again," she said smiling sadly.
Aidan kissed her, and Mariah poured herself totally into the kiss. He was aroused when they parted, and she noticed. Mariah only smiled and said goodnight, as she closed the door.
Aidan walked back to the car and got in. Jaz teased him about a cold shower, and they both laughed as they headed home.

Mariah was upset about the events of the evening, but that wasn't what she was thinking about right now. She was thinking about Aidan, and his being aroused. Mariah had been very much turned on herself.

She began to wonder what it would be like to let him make love to her. She'd never really given it that much thought with David, but with Aidan it was different. She wanted it.
She couldn't help hoping she'd found the one in Aidan.
"We shall see," Mariah said aloud, as she headed to the shower, needing very much to cool off right now.

Kayla knocked gently on her door before she could get in.
"Come in," Mariah said pleasantly.
"Hi baby," her mother greeted her.
"Hi mommy, Mariah returned.
Kayla went on to tell her that David had called several times. Mariah simply frowned, which let Kayla know something was very wrong.
"Do you want to talk about it?" Kayla asked her.
"Not right now," Mariah replied. "Is that OK?"
"Of course," Kayla told her. "We'll talk whenever you get ready," she finished, as she was preparing to leave. Mariah stopped her, as she was walking out of the door.
"Mommy?" she asked.
"Yes?" Kayla responded.
"How did you know daddy was the one for you?" Mariah asked earnestly.
Kayla thought for a moment then told her daughter all the things about her father that made her fall in love with him. They both ended up crying, thinking about Black, but Mariah had a clearer understanding of what she felt now, with Aidan.
"Thank you mommy," Mariah said softly.

Kayla smiled, and kissed her daughter goodnight as she left her room. Mariah stood in the shower, allowing the water to wash away the unpleasantness of the evening.
"He's the one," she said softly, thinking of Aidan, and smiling.

David was still sitting in the storage room replaying the events of the evening back in his mind again. The night had gone horribly wrong.

"What am I going to do?" he asked aloud.

David thought of the hurt, and anger, he'd seen in Mariah's eyes. *What am I going to do with a baby,* he continued to think. *Damn! Why did it have to be with Sherice?!*

His cell rang as he finished his thought.

Please let it be Mariah, he silently prayed. It was Jared.

"Yeah?" David answered testily.

"Hey man," Jared began "I was just calling to check on you."

David sighed, he couldn't be mad at Jared. He'd made this mess all on his own.

"Guess I really blew it with her for good now huh?" he replied.

Jared sighed. He knew David was right. Mariah would never forgive him for this.

"Sorry man," was all Jared could think to say, "What you gonna do about Sherice?"

David hadn't even gotten that far yet.

"Do you think she'll go for an abortion?" he asked Jared.

Jared thought about it for a few minutes before he answered.

"I don't think so man," Jared replied. "She's really into you, and she's hurt because you still want Mariah," he went on. "So she'd probably have it, just to spite you."

David knew he was right. *How could I have screwed this up so royally?* He asked himself bitterly.

"Well man, I gotta go get my head right," David told Jared, as he prepared to hang up.

Jared told him to be careful, and give him a shout tomorrow. David needed a drink. He headed over to his friend Chase's house. They were always drinking and shooting the breeze.

They would let him drink, and not hassle him. Right now David needed to be somewhere where he could relax and forget. He got in his car and headed toward the house.

Aidan slipped out of the house after everyone was asleep, and headed back to the spot. He had some unfinished business. He arrived just as David was leaving. Aidan followed him to see where they'd end up.

David arrived at his destination, only to find there was no one at home. The street was in a small, residential neighborhood. The row houses lined the street.

They were all very well kept, with manicured front lawns, and numerous cars parked in the driveways, and on the street. It was also dimly lit, and Aidan decided it was perfect for what he had in mind. He parked his car four or five car lengths behind David's, and got out.

David was still knocking on the door of the small brick front home, hoping someone would answer. *Of course they wouldn't be here, the one night I really need them to be,* he thought to himself, disgusted.

David began walking back to his car. He didn't see Aidan standing in the shadows, waiting for him. As he reached for his door handle, Aidan stepped to him.

"That was a stupid ass stunt you pulled tonight," he told David, who whipped around, startled by the voice.

"What the hell do you want?" he returned to Aidan angrily.

"I'm here to tell yo' punk ass to stay the hell away from Mariah, once and for all," Aidan replied, standing directly in front of David.

David looked at him and saw that same cold, dead, look he'd had that Sunday at church. Still, he wasn't going to be intimidated.

"Man, fuck you!" he spat, and swung at him.

Aidan deftly ducked the punch, and hit David hard in the midsection. David fell to his knees, the wind knocked out of him. Aidan kicked him hard in the side, while he was on the ground. David couldn't catch his breath. Aidan continued his assault of kicks, until David was wheezing.

Aidan was careful not to hit or kick him in the face. He didn't want to leave any evidence he'd done anything to him. He got very close to David, who was still clutching his side, and trying to breathe.

"If you ever touch her again, I'll kill you next time," Aidan said calmly. "If you decide to punk out, and tell anyone I kicked your ass out here tonight, I'll come back and finish the job."

David couldn't talk. All he could do was shake his head. He just wanted this guy to leave him alone. He was sure he'd broken a couple of his ribs. Aidan kicked him once more for good measure, hard to his gut, and walked away, leaving him struggling to breathe.

Aidan smiled to himself on the way home. *Man that felt really good,* he thought calmly. He didn't understand where the depth of violence in him came from. Sometimes it scared him, but tonight it filled him with a sense of contentment.

He smiled again thinking of his kiss with Mariah earlier. *Yeah, things are moving right along,* Aidan thought of his plans to be her first and only lover, chuckling again as he arrived at the house.

David finally gathered himself enough to get into his car. He sat behind the wheel for a long time trying to pull it together. Finally, when he was able to focus, he started the car and headed home.

That fool is crazy! David thought to himself of Aidan. He had to admit he was slightly worried, but he just couldn't give up that easy. Next time though, he would be a lot more careful, David vowed as he drove.

14

Chris hoped Jackie would be in service today. He'd found out her name from her daughter Jasmine. She'd asked him to pray for her mother, who was sick at the time. She hadn't been to church in a couple weeks.

Chris thought Jackie was an extremely attractive woman, and he'd been drawn to her. He hoped he would get a chance to actually speak with her today, if she came to service.

Chris found himself yearning once again for a wife. It had been well over a month now since he and Kayla talked. They were both getting better at being comfortable with each other.

He knew that she and Jackie were friends. Their ability to get along made it easier for him to be around Jackie, when they were together. Chris went into his office to get his robe. He sure hoped she was in the congregation when he went out.

"Do you really think he's interested?" Jackie was asking Kayla, as they stood in ladies room at the church.
"Yes," she replied laughing. "You can't be that old that you've forgotten, can you?" she teased her friend.

Jackie thought about Pastor Lynch. He was a very attractive man and she'd found herself immediately attracted to him. She was intrigued when Jaz told her he'd inquired about her, on the couple of Sundays she wasn't there. She just chalked it up to being part of his job.

"How can you be so sure?" Jackie asked Kayla nervously.
"Haven't you noticed how he watches you the entire service?" Kayla asked her, laughing again. "He's definitely interested."
Jackie had to laugh herself. She was acting like she was seventeen again.
"So, how are you and Pastor Bradford coming along?" Jackie asked her friend, turning the tables.

Kayla smiled demurely. "We're fine," she said softly.
Jackie laughed at Kayla then.
"Don't like it so much when you're on the receiving end, huh?" she continued laughing.
The two women continued chuckling to themselves, as they left the restroom, headed for the sanctuary.

Thomas was sitting in his office thinking about Kayla. They'd been together more than a month now. Everything was good between them. She was becoming more and more open to him, and he was falling more and more in love with her.

He wanted to take her on a trip with him. He could arrange it so no one would know they were together. They'd done a good job so far of keeping their romance to themselves.

Only a few people knew, and they were all inside their inner circle of friends and family. Rachelle was still trying. She'd actually asked Thomas point blank the other morning why he wouldn't sleep with her.

Thomas was taken by surprise. He told Rachelle he thought she was a very attractive woman, but they weren't meant to be together.
"That doesn't mean we can't enjoy each other once or twice though," Rachelle replied simply.

He was still trying to gather himself. Thomas told her they really shouldn't be talking like this. It was inappropriate between the two of them.
"I want to know what you feel like," she'd told him again.
Thomas had to admit he was tempted. He hadn't been with anyone in over a year. Thomas dismissed the thought, as Kayla flashed in his mind. He loved her, and the only woman he wanted was her. Thomas gently told Rachelle they would never be together like that.

He also asked her if she thought it would be better, if she moved to another position in the church.
"No Pastor," she'd said quietly. "I promise never to bring it up again."

Thomas was satisfied with that, and left her alone. He got up to put his robe on. He felt good today. He hoped the service reflected the joy he felt in his own spirit this morning.

Jackie and Kayla sat next to each other. Mother sat on the other side of Kayla. Jaz and Aidan sat on the other side of Jackie. They all watched attentively, as the choir made their way into the stand.

They all spotted Mariah and smiled. She smiled back. Kayla turned her attention to the ministers, as they entered the pulpit. Thomas spotted Kayla and smiled. She smiled back.

Chris was elated to see Jackie was here today. He looked at her until she turned and locked eyes with him. Chris smiled at her, and Jackie blushed. He was amused, and knew she was interested.

I will definitely be making my way to talk to her today after service, he thought to himself, as he turned his attention back to the choir.

"Convinced now?" Kayla whispered to Jackie.

Jackie smiled, and shot Kayla a look. Kayla almost laughed out loud at that, but managed to control herself.

David was looking at Mariah singing. She'd ignored him since that night. She wouldn't return any of his calls. She hadn't spoken to him this morning when he saw her in the vestibule. His parents had questioned him at length about why they were apart. David just couldn't bring himself to tell them yet.

He saw that Aidan was still here. *I hate him so much,* David thought to himself, as he gave Aidan a look, thinking about the beating he'd given him.

He was going to have to deal with Sherice and that situation. She had flatly refused to have an abortion. *She is determined to ruin my life,* David thought, feeling sorry for himself.

Aidan was looking at Mariah, thinking about last night, when she was with him at home. They'd watched a couple movies together when they started playing around. He'd pinned her on the floor, and she was squealing at him to let her go. He'd told her it would cost her, and she laughingly asked how much.

He'd kissed her, and their passion had almost taken them completely over. He'd begun to touch her, and she'd responded. His hands were caressing her body, and Mariah was moaning softly at his touch.

He'd started to undress her. He'd removed her shirt, and was caressing her breasts through her bra. He took her shorts off and began caressing her. Mariah was still moaning softly as Aidan took off her bra. Her breasts were beautiful. He'd kissed them, and began to lick her nipples gently.

She'd reached up, and helped him out of his shirt. He'd looked into her eyes, and asked her if she were sure. She'd told him yes. He'd begun kissing her again. His hands began to caress her sensitive spot, and she gasped from his touch.

Then Jaz knocked and disturbed them. *This is not happening!* Aidan remembered thinking to himself. They'd dressed, and come out of the den to the kitchen, where his aunt had arrived home with groceries.
He had been so close. Aidan shook himself back to the present. This was definitely not something he should have been thinking about sitting in church.

Mariah had been watching Aidan. She knew from the look he had, he was thinking about last night. They'd almost made love. She still couldn't believe she was going to let him.

They had only been together over a month, but Mariah knew she loved him. Aidan made her feel wonderful. He made her feel safe and secure, that nothing bad could ever touch her. She loved the way he'd touched her last night. *Well there will be another time,* she thought to herself, as she returned her attention to the service.

Jaz knew what they were doing when she knocked. She'd heard them while standing outside the door. She hadn't wanted to stop them, but her mom came home too soon. She smiled to herself. She couldn't believe Mariah was going to let Aidan make love to her. She'd made David wait for over a year before she would even think about it, and he still didn't get the chance.

Jaz wanted to laugh out loud at that one. She really didn't like David. Of course no one but the two of them knew the real reason why. She hoped Aidan and Mariah would get the chance to finish what they'd started. Jaz wanted the pleasure of telling David personally. She smiled again, and returned her attention to the service.

Sandra Alston was watching Mariah intently as she sang. She sighed heavily to herself, thinking Mariah should have been her daughter, hers and Donovan's together.

She'd been in love with him for as long as she could remember. They'd graduated college together, and dated before the FBI hired him on. He'd left, and come back with Kayla and father to Mariah.

As much as Sandra wanted too, she could never bring herself to dislike Kayla, who was a wonderful person, and always genuinely kind to her. She'd been just as devastated when Donovan was killed, as Kayla. That was why she had to find out what had happened between Mariah and David.

She'd been elated a year and a half ago, when David told her he and Mariah were seeing each other. She would still have the opportunity to have Donovan as a part of her family.

Mariah was a beautiful girl, and Sandra knew she would make David a wonderful companion. *What has my stupid son done this time,* Sandra thought to herself tiredly.

David was just like his father, always doing things without thinking of the consequences. She was constantly getting him, and her son, out of various trouble and situations they got themselves into.

Sandra saw that Mariah was already seeing someone new. *No matter,* she thought to herself. She knew Mariah was a very polite and respectful girl. She would listen to her after church today.

Hopefully, Sandra could persuade Mariah to give David another chance. She didn't want to think of her not being a part of their family. She looked at her son then. He was looking at Mariah too.

He looks sad, Sandra thought to herself, taking another deep breath. *Well whatever it is, there's got to be a way to solve it,* she finished her thought, making up her mind to get the two back together.

Pastor Bradford had just given the benediction and everyone was making his or her way outside.

Sandra spotted Mariah near the choir stand, and began to make her way toward her.

"Hello Mariah," Sandra spoke, smiling at the girl.

Mariah smiled back and greeted her.

"Hi Mrs. Alston," she said pleasantly.

"May I speak with you privately for a few moments, please?" Sandra asked again.

Mariah had an idea what this was about, and she really didn't want to talk about it. She couldn't be rude to Mrs. Alston though, so she would oblige.

"Sure," Mariah replied. "Let's go into the choir room."

Sandra agreed, and the two of them left together.

David saw his mother and Mariah talking, then leave together. *I sure hope she can get her to change her mind,* he thought to himself. Then it dawned on him that Mariah might tell his mother about Sherice. David panicked for a brief moment, but then decided if she did; it was one less thing he would have to do.

Mariah and Sandra arrived at the room and were sitting down.

"Mariah," Sandra began gently. "I know that you and David have been going through some relationship issues," she went on. "But surely, you must know, seeing someone else won't solve them," she finished, looking at Mariah evenly.

Mariah knew from what she'd just said, David hadn't told her they broke up, just that they were fighting perhaps. "Mrs. Alston," Mariah replied, looking at her hands as she spoke. "David and I are over. We have been heading that way for a long time," she went on. "Neither of us wanted to admit it. Now that I have, he doesn't want to accept it," she finished, hoping his mother would just let it go.

Sandra took a deep breath. There was something Mariah wasn't telling her, and whatever it was, that was the real reason they were apart now.

"What made you come to that conclusion Mariah?" she asked softly, looking directly at her.

Mariah was becoming more and more uncomfortable with this conversation. She wanted out of this room right now. Sandra saw the girl becoming more distraught, and knew she had to make her tell.

"Mariah," she said softly, taking her hands into her own. "Please tell me what's going on. My son loves you, and unless I was terribly wrong, you loved him too," she finished.

Mariah was crying softly now. She didn't want to hurt David's mother. She was such a nice person, and she'd always treated her well.

"Please, Mrs. Alston," Mariah began, trying to speak through her tears. "I don't want to talk about this anymore."

Sandra felt terrible. Mariah was obviously in pain, but she needed to know. *How else could she fix it for them?* She thought to herself. Sandra hugged Mariah, and told her it was okay if she cried, but she had to tell her what was going on. Mariah took a deep breath, trying to staunch the flow.

"David wanted to have sex," she said quietly. Sandra was careful not to let her expression change. She knew there was more, and she needed to hear it all.
"Its OK honey, you can tell me," she said, still looking intently at Mariah.
"Well, when I wouldn't," Mariah went on. "David slept with someone else. He's been cheating on me for the last six months, and now has a child on the way with this girl," she finished softly, still looking at her hands.
My God! Sandra was thinking. *No wonder she broke up with him! A child?* She reached out and hugged Mariah tightly.
"I'm so sorry he did this to you Mariah," Sandra said, as she stroked her hair.
She pulled away, and looked at the girl. *There is no fixing this,* she thought to herself dejectedly.
"My son is a fool," she said simply, still looking at Mariah. "He's lost the most wonderful young woman he'll ever meet," she continued.
"I certainly hope you will continue to have a relationship with myself and his father though," Sandra finished hopefully.

Mariah was her last link to Donovan, and the thought of never being near her again, scared her. The girl brightened.
"Of course I'll be around to see you and Mr. Alston," Mariah said.
Sandra smiled, hugged her again, kissed her cheek and left her alone in the room.

15

Mariah sighed deeply. The encounter with Mrs. Alston had taken a lot out of her. She felt arms embracing her from behind. Mariah turned to find Aidan looking at her concerned.

"Hi," she smiled.

He smiled back, and asked her if she were okay. She told him she was, now that he was there.

"What did she want?" Aidan asked her softly.

Jaz told him who the woman was he'd seen talking to Mariah after service. He immediately began to make his way back here to her.

Aidan was about at his end with everyone trying to interfere in his relationship with Mariah. She was his now and he would destroy anyone who tried to change that.

"She wanted to know why David and I had broken up," Mariah told him.

"Why didn't he tell her?" Aidan asked, slightly annoyed.

She heard his tone and looked up at him.

"Because David wouldn't have told her the truth," she said plainly.

Mariah kissed him, and he softened.

"Can we go now?" Mariah asked him. Aidan smiled again.

"Of course," he told her, as he led her out to the car.

Sandra walked up to David, who was leaning on his car, watching for Mariah and Aidan.

"I want to see you at home, now," she said simply.

He could tell by her tone and the look she gave him, she knew.

"OK," David managed to mumble, as he looked down at the ground.

His mother was furious. *She'll still help me though,* he thought to himself, bringing some measure of comfort.

David got in his car headed to the storm he knew would be waiting at home.

Jaz was feeling pretty good. She'd watched David after service, loving the sadness she saw on his face. He'd hurt her badly, and she was glad he was suffering now. Her mom and Pastor Lynch seemed to be awfully chummy too, Jaz laughed to herself. She didn't mind. Her mom needed someone in her life. He was a good-looking man. Not like that last one she'd dated.

She often wanted to ask her mother were her eyes closed when she accepted a date with Julian. Maybe she and Pastor Lynch would hit it off and get married. That would be cool.

She had a pretty good idea of what David's mother wanted when she pulled Mariah to the side. She'd made sure she clued Aidan in on Sandra's angle. Jaz definitely did not want to see Mariah get back with David.

It'd been hard enough, watching them together the year plus they'd been dating. Jaz loved her best friend with all her heart, which was why she didn't tell Mariah the thing that happened between her and David.

Jaz knew it would hurt her deeply, and probably end their friendship. She'd known then David was a dog, and capable of anything. She silently thanked God again, for letting Aidan come and steal Mariah's heart away from David.

Now if they could only get the chance to actually make love, Jaz thought to herself, knowing that once it happened, Mariah would never ever think of being with David again.

As she continued sitting in the car waiting on her mother, Jaz thought about summer, a year ago.

"We really shouldn't David," Jaz told him as they continued to kiss, and touch each other.

"Please Jaz, You know you want to," he'd told her, as he continued to touch her.

Jaz had to admit she wanted it badly. She and David had been flirting here and there, but nothing serious. She knew he was with Mariah, and Jaz loved her friend. This particular day she'd unfortunately let her hormones get the best of her.

"Come on Jaz," David was pleading again, as he was lifting her skirt, and removing her panties.
"I can't do this David," she said, trying to push him away. David kissed her again, moved on top of her, and entered her.

The sex was okay. David wasn't the best she'd had. He'd managed to make her orgasm, but it wasn't something Jaz would be trying to come back for more of. They had regrettably gotten caught up, and not used a condom. Jaz found out she was pregnant a month later.
"So? What do you want me to say?" David asked her flatly. "You knew we were just screwing. I'm with Mariah," He finished, looking at Jaz distastefully.

She hadn't expected him to leave Mariah, or even want the baby for that matter. She did expect him to treat her like a human being though. His mother had been even worse.
"You will not be trapping my son into a marriage, or fatherhood, with this mess," she'd told Jaz haughtily.

They thought they were so much better than everyone, because her husband was a high profile attorney. Jaz had been devastated. All she wanted was help in getting an abortion, without her mother having to find out. These people had made her feel lower than dirt.
In the end, his mother took her to a private clinic, and Jaz had the procedure done.
"You better not ever tell Mariah about this!" David threatened her. "I'll tell her you were the one coming onto me," he continued. "What kind of best friend would that make you now, huh?"
Jaz was in tears. She'd just gone through one of the most traumatic experiences of her life, and this insensitive dog could only think about himself, still.
"I absolutely hate you, David Alston," Jaz told him evenly. "One day you will pay for how you're treating me today."
"Whatever, just get out of my car," he'd told her harshly. David peeled out of her driveway as soon as she closed the car door. She'd cried herself to sleep that night, and spent the next three weeks trying to get her sanity back.

Jackie's voice brought her back to the present.
"Did you hear me?" her mother was asking.

"Sorry ma," Jaz replied. "I didn't catch that."
Jackie told her again that she and Pastor Lynch were going to dinner, and he would drop her off at home.
"Oh okay. That's great," she said, smiling at her mother.
Her cell rang, as she watched her mother walk away.
"Hello?" she answered.
"Hey babe," Elaine said amiably.
Jaz smiled in spite of herself.
"Hey yourself," She replied. "What's up?"
"I wanted to see if you'd like to come over, and maybe spend some time," Elaine told her.
Jaz thought about it. It would give Aidan and Mariah the privacy they needed. "Well okay, but I can't stay long," Jaz replied.

Elaine smiled. Pleased she would get the chance to be with Jaz again.
"OK baby, that's fine," Elaine replied smoothly. "I'll pick you up from your house in about an hour, OK?"
Jaz told Elaine that was good, and she'd see her then.
This girl has got to come on and make up her mind. Elaine thought to herself, after she hung up.
She hated thinking of Jaz letting someone else touch her.
She sighed deeply, and went to shower. For tonight at least, Jaz was all hers.
Jaz wondered if Mariah would come home with Aidan.
With her mother gone, they would have the opportunity to finish what they'd started. Jaz wanted that to happen between them, very much.

She saw her mother and Pastor Lynch leaving, as Aidan got into the drivers side, and started the car.
"Where's Mariah?" she asked him.
"She wanted to go home and rest," Aidan replied. "She said she was feeling worn out after talking to David's mother," he finished evenly, careful not to let his annoyance show.

Aidan was tired of David and beginning to think he was going to have to forcefully remove him, permanently, from Mariah's life.

Jaz was disappointed, but she knew it would happen between them eventually. She could wait.

16

David arrived home about fifteen minutes after his mother. Sandra saw him pull into their driveway. *I am so damned angry with this boy right now,* she thought, as she sipped her wine.

His stupidity had cost them both. She hoped Mariah was being truthful, when she promised to visit still. *Why David?* Sandra thought again sadly. Maybe there was a still chance though.

She knew from Mariah's reaction, and the way she was crying, there had to be some emotion left for David. She would get to the bottom of this baby nonsense, and take care of this girl, just as she had that other one. Then she would make David crawl on his hands and knees if he had to, and beg Mariah to take him back.

Sandra heard him enter the house, and turned to go deal with him. David steeled himself, as he saw his mother coming into the den where he sat. Sandra sat across from her son and crossed her legs, looking at him intently the entire time.

"Who is she?" she asked simply, never taking her eyes from him.

David knew how this was going to go. He had done it before, and she'd gotten him out of it. He knew his mother was angry, but he also knew Sandra was fiercely protective of him, and his future.

A future she'd made up her mind, Mariah would be a part of.

"Sherice Collins," David replied.

His mother frowned deeply.

"Why would you take up with such a low class girl?" Sandra asked him.

"I don't know. She was easy I guess," he replied again.

Sandra could believe that. She knew the girl he was talking about. They lived in the low-income section of town. Her mother was pleasant enough she supposed, but

Sandra knew this was not the type of girl she wanted her son to marry, or have children with.
"Why would you be stupid enough to have sex, and not use protection?" she asked. "Do you realize how much you have hurt Mariah with this?"
David sighed heavily. Of course he knew. He saw it every time Mariah looked at him.
"Yes mother, I am very well aware of how much I've hurt Mariah," he continued. "It's all I think about. That and how I can make her forgive me," David finished quietly.

Sandra knew he was sorry. They always were. Her husband was the same way. She'd had to deal with him, and his numerous affairs, over the years. She'd basically grown accustomed to it now. She wasn't very fond of sex with him anyway, so it had been no great loss to her. Maybe if she'd married Donovan, her life would have been different. There was a man Sandra loved to have sex with, anytime and anywhere. She sighed heavily again, focusing on David now.
"What does she want to do?" she asked, already knowing the answer.
"She wants to have the baby," he said plainly.
Sandra figured as much. The girl was obviously a gold digger, and figured she had herself quite the meal ticket in David.
"Well, we'll see about that," Sandra said calmly.

David saw that look on her face. He knew it meant she was making plans. He almost felt sorry for Sherice.
"What are you going to do?" he asked, not sure he wanted to hear the answer.
Sandra simply smiled at her son, and told him not to worry about it. She'd let him know if she needed him. She dismissed David from the den, needing to make some calls.

"Hello Sherice," Sandra Alston said flatly, when the girl answered.
Sherice was shocked.

"Hello Mrs. Alston," she replied quietly.
"I understand you're pregnant, and claiming David is the father, is that correct?" the woman fired at her.
Sherice was scared, but she had to stand her ground. She had her child to consider.
"Yes I'm pregnant, and David is the father," Sherice said simply.
Sandra sighed heavily.
"I'm also assuming you want to have this child, yes?" she asked again.
Sherice told Sandra she had every intention of having the child, and she wanted David to take responsibility. "Oh, once the child is born, and the DNA proves that David is indeed the father, we'll be taking a lot more than just responsibility," Sandra returned ominously.

Sherice panicked. What the hell was his mother talking about? "I don't understand," the girl returned.
Sandra smiled to herself.
"If this child is proven to indeed be an Alston, we will take you to court, and fight for full custody," she told her emotionless.
Sherice was truly frightened. She knew they had money, and David's father was an attorney. She genuinely believed they could take her child from her.
"Why would you do that?" Sherice asked.

Sandra smiled again, thinking about the girl. She knew Sherice was terrified and Sandra was determined to make her suffer.
"That's simple," Sandra replied. "My grandchild is not going to be raised in low income housing, with low class surroundings, and a non existent future to look forward too because his mother is spending the child support on herself, her new boyfriend, and new babies she'll surely have," she finished.

Sherice was crying softly. Why did she have to be so cruel? They weren't bad people, and she would be a good mother.
"Please, Mrs. Alston," she said quietly.

Sandra heard the girl crying, and decided maybe she would be reasonable now.

"Well, you could always simply have the abortion, and be done with it all," she said.

Sherice sniffled miserably.

"I can't kill my child," she told Sandra simply. "It's not right."

Sandra sighed deeply. *She's one of those, is she?* she thought to herself.

"Well then, all I can tell you is if you insist on having this child, and naming David as the father, we will be forced to take legal action, to ensure the child's well-being," Sandra went on, hearing Sherice sobbing openly. "My attorney will be in touch with you in a few days," she finished, and hung up before the girl could respond.

There. That should scare her into having an abortion, and my son and Mariah can get back together, as they should be, she thought to herself, pouring a glass of wine to relax her own nerves. Sandra made a mental note to call her attorney later, and have him lean hard on the girl, and her family

Mariah was tired, drained, and glad to be home. The talk she'd had with Mrs. Alston had undone her. Mariah thought about that night again. It hurt so much still. She felt like such a fool, believing David all those months.

Actually beating herself up for not wanting to sleep with him. She knew David's father cheated on his mother. Half the town knew it. Mariah just thought David was different.

He'd been so loving and attentive, when they were dating. He was always polite and respectful, when he was with her. *Yeah, now I know why,* Mariah thought to herself, *he was busy having sex with Sherice.*

She wasn't upset with the girl. *Probably told her he was going to break up with me,* she thought again. Mariah decided she would take a shower and lay down. Her mother was out with Pastor Bradford again, so she didn't expect her back until later.

Mariah knew Pastor Bradford wanted to marry her mother. She hoped Kayla would say yes when he asked her. Mariah knew she was lonely. Her father had been dead for almost three and a half years now, and Kayla had never let another man touch her.

Mariah was getting undressed, when the phone rang. The number didn't appear on her ID.

"Hello?" she answered.

"Hi Mariah, Please don't hang up," David said quietly.

Mariah sighed heavily. *What did he want now?* she thought to herself, dreading what was coming next.

"What do you want David?" she asked tiredly.

David was so glad she hadn't hung up. He was hurting right now. He just needed to hear her voice.

"Please don't hate me, Mariah," he said again.

Mariah thought about what David said. She was angry yes, but she wasn't sure she hated him. Her mother often told her she had her fathers temper.

She knew that was true. Her mother seldom got angry, and if she did, she almost immediately forgave.

"I don't hate you David," Mariah replied.

"That's what you told me," he said softly.

Mariah knew she'd hurt him with that statement. She'd been so angry and hurt, finding out about his infidelity. She sighed deeply again.

"I know," she said gently. "I didn't mean that. I was just hurt."

David smiled. He had a glimmer of hope.

"I'm glad to hear that," he told her "I would never forgive myself, if I'd lost even your friendship," he finished hoping Mariah would at least agree to be his friend.

"David," she began again. "I'm not sure where you fit into my life right now," she went on. "But I can honestly say I don't hate you."

David thought about that for a moment, and decided it was better than nothing.

"OK Mariah," he said simply. "If you ever need to talk, please call me."
Mariah sighed again.
"I'll keep that in mind. I really have to go now, so goodnight," she finished.
"Good night Mariah," he returned. "Sweet dreams boo."

Mariah didn't realize the tears had fallen, until she saw the wet receiver. *Why am I still crying over him?* She thought to herself. *I have Aidan now. I'm over David, aren't I,* she continued thinking, as she headed for the shower.

David looked at the ceiling above his bed. She'd talked to him. Mariah had been civil, and she'd told him she didn't hate him. *You've got to still care for me somewhere inside you Mariah.* David thought to himself.
He would be patient this time. Not let his libido get him into trouble again. *If I can just get one more chance,* he thought again. *I'll never, ever, mess up again,* he promised himself as he closed his eyes and began to drift off to sleep.

Sandra put the receiver back into its cradle. She hadn't intentionally eavesdropped. She'd picked up the phone to call her attorney again, and heard them talking. She was glad Mariah talked to him.
Even David acted like he had an ounce of sense. *Once I get this baby situation taken care of, maybe, just maybe, I can get my daughter back,* Sandra mused to herself, once again picking up the phone.

Jaz was relaxing in her room, thinking about Elaine and the turmoil in their being together. Sighing lightly she recalled the first time they'd been intimate and how wonderful it'd been.
They entered the house, and Elaine asked if she wanted something to drink. Jaz told her yes, and Elaine left to get what she'd asked for. Jaz looked around the home while she waited. It was a very nice place. She loved the furniture. It was a contemporary corner grouping, with recliners on either end, in a bright, vibrant, cherry color.

There were colorful pillows tossed strategically on it, which made it really come alive and brighten the room. Someone has a serious crush on sunflowers, Jaz thought, chuckling to herself, at the various figurines she saw. Elaine returned with the drinks, and sat down beside her. She could tell Jaz was really nervous.

"We don't have to do anything you don't want to do Jaz," she said sensitively, looking intently at her. "I won't push."

"It's not that," Jaz started. "I just–,"she faltered.

"Just what, Jaz?" Elaine asked.

"I don't think I'm gay Elaine, I mean, I'm just curious," she replied, trying to gauge Elaine's reaction.

Elaine smiled, and kissed Jaz softly on the mouth.

"It's okay to be curious Jaz," she told her, still staying close to her face. "And if your curiosity is satisfied after tonight, so be it."

Jaz had to admit she'd enjoyed Elaine kissing her, and felt herself becoming aroused. Elaine saw her reaction, and kissed her again passionately, allowing her hands to caress Jaz's body. Jaz gasped from Elaine's touch, and moaned softly.

Elaine pulled away and took her hand, leading her to the bedroom. She walked in behind Elaine and took the room in. There were candles all around giving off both fragrant aroma, and seductive light. Elaine kissed Jaz again softly, and told her to relax. Elaine began kissing her neck and slowly making her way down her body. Jaz was moaning softl, and responding to her touch. She made her way down to Jaz's most intimate spot, and began to pleasure her.

Jaz was almost beside herself. She couldn't believe the way Elaine was making her feel. She was close. Jaz felt herself getting warmer and warmer, until she finally exploded, crying out loudly. Elaine smiled, as she let Jaz come down from the orgasm. Elaine began kissing her perfect lips again.

"Did you enjoy that baby?" Elaine asked her softly.

Jaz could only sigh, and shake her head yes. Elaine chuckled.

"So? Curiosity appeased now?" she asked.

Jaz smiled and told Elaine yes.

"Do you think you'll want to do this again?" Elaine asked, hoping that Jaz said yes.

"I honestly don't know Elaine," Jaz answered. "I mean, it was great, but I'm still attracted to guys too."

"That's okay Jaz. You don't have to make this grand decision to have one or the other," Elaine replied, careful not to let her face show her disappointment. "If you want to have both for awhile, that's okay with me." she finished, still hopeful.
Jaz smiled again.
"I think I might like that," she replied softly.

Of course they'd been together numerous times since then, and now Elaine was really pushing Jaz to commit. They'd argued about it as recently as yesterday and Jaz was truly at her end trying to decide if she really wanted to live a completely gay lifestyle or if the liaison had reached its end with her.

Sighing deeply knowing she wouldn't solve the problem tonight, Jaz pushed it out of her mind preparing to lay down, when her cell rang. Smiling slightly to herself seeing Chase's name on the caller ID she answered.
As they began to converse, Jaz found herself laughing and the thoughts of Elaine disappearing further and further from her mind's horizon.

17

They'd all gone out to dinner together. It had gone very well. Kayla found herself relaxed, and at ease, and she could sense both Thomas and Chris felt the same. Now she and Thomas were relaxing in his den, watching TV. She hoped Chris and Jackie would really connect. Kayla could tell the chemistry was there between them. She wanted them to be happy, like she was happy, now that Thomas was in her life.

He'd asked her about going out of town with him this week. She still wasn't sure. She knew Mariah would be okay. She was almost eighteen, which reminded Kayla she needed to plan a party for her daughter in the next month. She was scared. Going out of town with Thomas, more than likely meant sharing a room, and possibly a bed. Kayla didn't know if she could tell Thomas no, if he wanted her while they were there together alone.
It had been a very long time since she'd made love, and she thought about it often, especially when they were alone together like this, with him holding her in his arms.

Thomas looked at Kayla. *Wonder if she'll go with me,* he thought to himself. He wanted so much to take her on his trip. *Please say yes,* he thought again, as he stroked her hair.
"Have you given any more thought to what I asked you earlier?" Thomas asked.
Kayla looked him in the eye.
"Yes, I've actually been thinking about it all evening," she replied honestly.
Thomas wasn't sure what he would hear, but he wanted to know.
"Have you made a decision?" he asked again.
She sighed softly. Thomas was bracing himself for the no, he'd heard in her sigh.
"I'd love to go with you," Kayla said softly, still looking at him.

Thomas was ecstatic. He squeezed her tightly, and Kayla squealed at him that she couldn't breathe. He let her go, and immediately kissed her.
Kayla smiled at Thomas, with a mischievous twinkle in her eye. "You thought I was going to say no, didn't you?" she teased him.
He was so glad she hadn't. Thomas kissed her again, the desire beginning to rise in him. Their kiss grew passionate, and he found himself fully aroused. He pulled away from her.

"I need to go into the other room for a little while Kayla," Thomas told her honestly.
She looked at him and realized he was feeling the same things she was. Kayla wanted this man, and obviously he wanted her too.
"Can I come with you?" she asked softly, looking him in the eye.
Thomas was blown away. Was she saying what he hoped she was?
"Kayla," he began quietly. "You do realize why, I need to step out for a moment, right?" he finished, looking at her evenly.
She looked back at him.
"Is it for the same reason I want to go with you?" Kayla asked again, still looking intently at Thomas.

Thomas kissed Kayla, and took her hand leading her into his bedroom. After he laid her on his bed, he began to kiss her again.
"Are you sure?" Thomas asked once more, still softly kissing her neck.
"Yes," Kayla said simply.
Thomas began to undress her, taking the time to admire every inch of her. He undressed himself, as Kayla admired him. *Wow, all that was under that shirt?* She thought to herself, looking at his chiseled chest, and toned abs. He joined her in bed, and they began to explore each other. Thomas nibbled her breasts, and began to use his tongue to arouse her. He moved slowly down her body,

settling himself in her most sensitive area. He began tasting her, and Kayla moaned softly as she moved in rhythm with his tongue. She felt the heat in her body rising. She wanted to feel Thomas inside her. Kayla gently pulled him up toward her.

They began to kiss, as he slowly entered her. They began to move together, both their passion and longing, poured into this act. He couldn't believe how right this felt, and how good she felt to him.

Thomas felt himself getting close to his peak. He knew Kayla was too, as her pace increased. They both reached orgasm together. Kayla buried her face in his neck, as she cried out. Thomas let out a soft sigh, as he finished. They lay together afterwards, kissing and caressing each other.

"Kayla," Thomas said softly, looking down at her. "Being with you tonight was the most wonderful feeling I've had in a long time," he finished, as he kissed her again.

Kayla felt totally overwhelmed.

"Me too Thomas," she said softly.

Thomas knew then that Kayla had let go completely and was now ready to live life in the present, with him as her new mate. He began to kiss her again, and soon they were making love once more.

Kayla was sleeping peacefully, as he looked at her. Thomas knew they had to be married soon. He was still a pastor, and after tonight, there was no going back. He couldn't return to the days of not making love to her. He would ask her while they were on vacation together. He'd already known she was his wife. Now she knew it too. Thomas pulled her close to him, and was soon asleep himself.

Mariah looked at the clock. It was after midnight, and her mother wasn't home. Just then, she heard the car drive up. Mariah peeked out of her bedroom window. Thomas was opening the car door for Kayla to get out.

She saw them kiss, and say goodnight. She smiled, and returned to her own bed. Her mother knocked lightly on her door shortly after.

"Come in," Mariah called out.

"Hi there," Kayla greeted her. "What are you doing still up?"

Mariah decided she would have a little fun with her mother. "Waiting for you, young lady," she said, trying to look serious.

Kayla played along.

"Why?" she asked. "I'm here before my curfew," she said, trying hard not to laugh.

"I saw you kissing that young man outside," Mariah went on. "That is not proper behavior for you to be engaging in, all out in the open like that," she finished, this time bursting into laughter. Kayla joined her.

Her mother was looking at her seriously now. "Are you all right?" she asked softly.

She told Mariah she'd seen Sandra talking to her, and noticed how upset she was afterwards. Mariah told her what she and David's mother had talked about, and she was just overwhelmed by her day.

"I'm fine though mommy," she said. "I'm going to bed, now that you're home."

Kayla looked at her daughter, and saw herself. She didn't want Mariah wrestling with the same issues she'd faced at her age.

"Honey?" Kayla said softly, still looking at Mariah.

"Yes?" she replied.

Kayla wanted to choose her words carefully, before she spoke.

"I know that you and David had problems. I know he was unfaithful to you," she went on. "I just want you to be sure, the real reason you're with Aidan, is because you genuinely care for him. Not because you secretly want to get back at David, for hurting you."

Mariah understood what her mother was saying. She'd spent the better part of the night, thinking about that very thing.
"I promise I'll give it serious thought," Mariah replied, looking her mother in the eye.
Kayla smiled and hugged her daughter, giving her a goodnight kiss, and headed off to her own room.

Aidan had been thinking about his mother, and Mariah, all evening. He didn't call Mariah and disturb her, but he did call his mother. She hadn't answered, and he was worried. Where was she? She hadn't been home a lot lately when he called. Aidan already knew DeSean wouldn't be there, and thankfully, Wallace had never answered either.

He would try her again in a little while. Aidan knew it was after midnight, but he had to know she was all right. His thoughts turned to Mariah then. She was so beautiful, and he was crazy about her. He'd wished she had come home with them this afternoon. Aidan knew Aunt Jackie was going out, and they could have been together.

He wouldn't rush her though. He knew Mariah wanted him. She'd made that abundantly clear the other night. He needed to pick up some condoms. He wasn't going to mess up their future by getting her pregnant their very first time. Aidan saw his future with her. He heard his Aunt Jackie coming in the house. Jaz had returned a little while earlier.

Aidan made a mental note, to ask her about all the time she was spending with Elaine. He already knew Elaine was gay, he was wondering just what experimentation his cousin was up too.

Now, what her and that Pastor Lynch, been doing all this time? He thought, turning his attention once more to his aunt, chuckling to himself lightly.

Jackie was trying hard to be quiet. She'd bumped into the table, and cursed under her breath. *Geez,* she thought. *Why don't I just turn on a siren,* she laughed softly to herself.

She finally made it to her room, and turned on the light. She sat down and began to take her clothes off. Jackie reflected on the evening she'd spent with Chris.

They'd gone to the movies after dinner, then to the park, just sitting and talking. Jackie thought Chris was a wonderful man. They talked about both their failed marriages, and lack of current flames. She was glad to know he wasn't seeing anyone. He'd told her he was looking for a wife.

"So, do you think you might be interested in the position?" he'd asked her softly, looking her in the eye.

Jackie was so excited at the prospect of having this wonderful and gorgeous man in her life, she was afraid she couldn't speak.

"Yes, I think I may be interested at that," she'd replied, looking back at Chris.

He'd smiled then and kissed her. It had been almost nine months since she'd dated Julian. Jaz teased her about how unattractive he was. Jackie knew she was right. She was just trying to not be shallow. It didn't last. He was very possessive, and abusive. He'd hit her, and she'd tried to kill him. That effectively ended any more dates between them.

Now, here was this wonderful man in front of her, kissing her, and making her believe in love, all over again. He'd kissed her again, pulling her close to him this time. She'd responded by kissing him back, just as passionately.

"Wow," Chris said softly after they'd parted. "I can't wait till we get married, if this is what I have to look forward too."

Jackie blushed. He'd chided her, and told her it was okay.

"I'd like our relationship to be between us Jackie," Chris was saying, looking at her evenly.
"That won't be a problem at all," Jackie replied honestly. Outside of Kayla, she didn't really talk to anyone else at church.
"Good," he'd replied as he took her in his arms again.

Jackie thought about Jaz, and wondered if she would be all right with her being with Pastor Lynch. She didn't see why not. *At least he wasn't ugly like Julian,* Jackie thought to herself, laughing, as she headed to the shower.

Chris was happily whistling as he entered the house.
"I don't have to ask how your evening went, now do I?" Thomas teased, as he greeted his friend.
Chris smiled, sitting down, as he and Thomas began to talk about his evening with Jackie.
"She's wonderful," he said wistfully. "I think I've finally found the woman for me."
"Well, I'm glad to hear that," Thomas said. "I don't know how happy Gina will be though," he added mischievously.

Gina Peterson was his secretary Rachelle's friend, and she had set her sights on Chris. Chris gave his friend a look, and started to laugh.
"Please don't bring her up!" Chris said, still laughing. She had been pursuing him since the first day she met him. She'd basically done everything except show up at his front door in a fur coat, with nothing underneath.

Thomas decided to have some fun with his friend. "Oh, don't tell me you never thought about it," he teased. Chris laughed. "I ain't gonna lie," he admitted, still chuckling himself "I thought about it once or twice. But I knew that would have been suicide, for real."

They both laughed again, thinking of the two women, and the drama they'd endured with them. Thomas began talking to Chris about his trip, and telling him what needed to be done, while he was gone.

"Did she say yes?" he asked Thomas, referring to Kayla. Thomas smiled, and Chris knew she had.
"I'm going to ask her to marry me, while we're there," Thomas told him.
Chris smiled again. "Good luck man," he told him sincerely. "You two deserve to be happy, together."

Thomas was a little worried. "Do you think she'll say yes?" he asked Chris, looking at him evenly.
Chris thought about it, and decided she would.
"Yeah, I think she will," he told Thomas, bringing a huge grin to his face.
"Well I'm going to bed," Thomas told Chris, leaving him in the den with his thoughts.

He was thinking about Jackie again. Chris wanted to make love to her. *Better go hit that cold shower,* he thought to himself, finding that he was fully aroused, from just thinking about her.

"I think he's gay Rachelle" Gina told her friend. Rachelle sighed deeply.
"I just don't know what to say, girl," she replied.
They'd been talking at length about Thomas and Chris and their inability to seduce either of them.
"I mean they haven't talked to any woman in the church," Rachelle said.
"Maybe they're dating someone outside the church," Gina said.
Rachelle sighed again.
"I don't know. I mean, Thomas never says anything about his personal life, and you know I can't ask," she told her.
Gina told her she understood.
"I've done everything, except show up naked on his front stoop, and this man has not paid me an ounce of attention," Gina lamented.
"We've got to come up with a sure fire way to see if they're gay, or straight, girl," Rachelle told her.
"What?" Gina asked.

Rachelle told her she wasn't sure yet, but she was definitely thinking on it.

"OK, but on to other things," Gina told her, as they began to talk about the various clients they commonly knew from the shop, and the various happenings that were going on.

"So she was messing with him and Alfred?" Rachelle asked, as they were talking about one of the women in the church, who also frequented the shop.

"Girl yeah, with her nasty self," Gina replied. "And now, she don't know which one she's pregnant from," she finished. Rachelle sucked her teeth.

"I always knew she was a ho!" she told Gina, who readily agreed with her. "But you know, Alfred messing with Tasha too," Rachelle told her.

"Girl for real?" Gina asked, amazed.

Rachelle confirmed they were indeed involved.

"Girl it is so much drama going on up in that church, it ain't even funny," Rachelle told her.

"Well, I wish I could get my own drama going, with a certain Assistant Pastor I know," Gina replied laughing. Rachelle joined her.

"Girl, me and you, both," she replied. "Do you see the bodies they both got on them, and I know the jewels have got to match," Rachelle quipped, and Gina concurred.

"If I could just wrap my legs around that waist, and feel all that power, I would be in heaven," Gina said, and they both laughed.

"Well let me get dinner on the table, my bighead nephew, K.C., and his friend Cedric, will be here soon," she told Gina.

"Girl you do realize, Cedric got himself an older woman crush on you, don't you?" Gina teased.

Rachelle told her she knew, but that wasn't what she wanted. Gina laughed, and told her she understood completely. They said their goodbyes, promising to call each other tomorrow, and hung up.

Aidan dialed the number again. "I better get an answer this time," he said half aloud to himself. Liv answered on the third ring.

"Hello?" she greeted the caller.

Aidan breathed a sigh of relief.

"Where have you been mama?" he asked her, his voice full of concern.

Liv felt so guilty. She'd been out with Big D again, and she'd missed his call.

"I'm sorry baby," she began. "I was out with a friend," she said simply.

Aidan thought it was odd she'd never mentioned a friend before.

"Are you seeing someone mama?" he asked guardedly.

Liv was quiet for along time. She knew she could trust Aidan. He wouldn't tell Wallace, or DeSean. She just wasn't sure what he would think.

"Yes, I am," she said softly.

Aidan thought about that for a moment. Maybe this guy would be good to her, and help her to leave Wallace, and his abuse.

"Tell me about him," Aidan replied gently.

Liv was relieved that he wasn't angry. She began to tell him all about her new friend.

Aidan smiled, as he recalled his conversation with his mother. She was so happy. He was glad that D had come into her life. He'd warned her to be careful though. Aidan knew what Wallace would do to Liv, if he ever found out, and then Aidan would definitely have to kill him.

He hoped Liv would leave now. Maybe he'd get a chance to meet this guy when he went home for Christmas break. Aidan remembered then, that Mariah's birthday was next month. *I've got to get her something special, he* thought to himself, as he closed his eyes to go to sleep.

18

DeSean walked into the house at 8:00 a.m., just as his father was leaving for work.
"Where you been all night?" Wallace asked him roughly.
DeSean didn't feel like fighting with his dad.
He always wanted to hit or bully him, like he did his mother all the time.
"I stayed over at Cameron's," he answered simply.
His father grunted, but didn't make an issue of it.
"What you gonna do about school?" Wallace asked again.

He knew DeSean hated school, and he was flunking out anyway. *Might as well just get his GED or something,* Wallace was thinking to himself.
"I ain't going back," DeSean said simply.
He didn't need school now. He had his money from the game they were hustling, and they'd started selling drugs too.
"Will you talk to mama for me?" he asked his father.
"Yeah, I'll handle her," his father said. "You need to at least get your GED though."
"I know. I'll get it," DeSean lied.
He had no intention of doing anything, other than making money now.
Wallace knew he was lying, but what could he do? The boy was almost grown. He'd be seventeen in a few months. DeSean and Aidan were only 11 months apart.

He'd gotten Liv pregnant again, right after she had Aidan. Wallace wasn't going to be supporting some other man's child, without one of his own.
"I gotta go to work," he said again, still looking at his son.
"We'll talk tonight, when I get home," he finished, the meaning very clear.
Wallace wanted DeSean home tonight.
"Yeah, okay, Dad," DeSean replied.
He would be here tonight, but he wouldn't stay. He had business to take care of. DeSean headed off to his room to change his clothes.

Liv heard DeSean in his room, and got up to go talk to him. "Hi stranger," she said.
DeSean didn't detect any anger in her voice, so he decided to reply.
"Hey mama," he replied.
"You OK? You eat?" Liv asked him concerned.
He took a deep breath and sighed. She was only concerned about him, and he was so mean to her most times.
"Yeah mama," DeSean replied. "I'm OK, and I had something at Cameron's."
She saw he was changing clothes.
"You leaving again?" she asked him calmly.

Liv really didn't like arguing with her son. She was scared for him. She'd heard rumors about the things he, and Cameron, were up to now. She didn't want to bury him.
"Yeah, I'm going to hang out with Cameron again," DeSean said plainly.
He hoped she didn't start in on one of her world famous lectures about how he was throwing his life away. He just wanted to live his life, on his own terms, without being hassled about it.
"OK," she replied. "Will you be home for dinner tonight?" Liv asked him gently.
DeSean looked at her, and saw the love and concern in her eyes for him. She was still his mother. He walked over and hugged her.
"Yeah mama," he told her. "I'll be here."

After she released him from the embrace, DeSean walked over to the door to leave. He stopped and turned back to Liv. "Can we have meatloaf tonight?" he asked.
Liv smiled. It was his favorite dish.
"Yes baby," she told him softly.
He smiled back, as he headed out the door.

Liv sat down at the kitchen table. She thought about her youngest son, and how different he'd been when he was younger. *Wallace has poisoned his mind,* Liv

thought tiredly. He was always convincing the child that she favored Aidan, over him.
It just wasn't true. She loved both her children. Liv sighed heavily again, knowing she couldn't change him now. She would just continue to hope and pray DeSean made it to adulthood.

Liv got up to get dressed. She was spending the day with Big D. They were going to breakfast, and then to the hotel. She laughed to herself, thinking about their sex life. Big D was one of the best lovers she'd ever had. Liv hadn't felt like this in years. Not since her daily sessions with Dezi.

Thinking of Dezi, made her think of Aidan. He had a birthday coming up in the next few months. He would be eighteen, and she'd promised herself she would tell him about his father.

Oh God, Liv continued to think to herself. *How do you tell a child, his father was a criminal, and a killer,* she sighed again, and pushed it out of her mind. She still had a few months. Liv instead thought of Big D, and their plans. That brought a smile to her face as she headed for the shower.

"What we doing today?" DeSean asked Cameron. They were trying to establish territories, and get dealers for the drugs they were moving.
"We gonna meet up with them Broughton boys," Cameron replied smiling.
The Broughton Boys were a dangerous gang that controlled the housing project they lived in, with the same name. They were perfect for what Cameron and DeSean had in mind. They could supply the product, and effectively eliminate any competition. They could also be useful in the expansion of their sales territory. He and DeSean had a big vision of what they wanted their hustle to grow into. They wanted to be living high, and enjoying the benefits of their labor.

DeSean saw Shay when she came back into the house. He looked over at her. Big D was old enough to be her grandfather, almost. *She's fine as hell,* he thought to himself, looking her over once more.

Shay was slender, but she had nice breasts and legs. Her butt was perfectly proportioned to the rest of her. Her eyes were almond shaped, and she had a cute almost button nose, with full lips. She kept her hair bleached a platinum blonde, in some unique style or other, but always looking good.

She needs to figure out she can do better, DeSean thought, as he got up to go into the kitchen where Shay was, leaving Cameron engrossed in his phone conversation with one of their girls.

Big D arrived at the restaurant to find Liv waiting for him. He smiled, and she waved at him.

"Hey baby," he greeted her, as he leaned over to kiss her. Liv supposed she shouldn't let him do that, since they were in public, but they were on the other side of town, and no one looked familiar in here.

"Hey yourself," she replied, smiling at him.

They ordered breakfast and talked, while waiting for their orders. The restaurant was packed with early morning commuters trying to grab a quick bite and go. The waitress was busy, but polite. The place had been around for a while, judging by the aged tile floors, and cracked, chipped, plastic chairs. It was clean though, and the prices good, which kept people coming back. The waitress returned with their food, and they proceeded to enjoy it.

"So?" Big D asked, looking hungrily at her, after they'd eaten. "You ready to explode again?"

Liv laughed lightly.

"I'm definitely ready for that," she replied, still smiling. They paid their check, and headed to the hotel to spend the day together.

"Hey," he said simply, looking at her again.
"Hey Sean," Shay said quietly.
She never called him DeSean, always Sean.
"How you feeling?" DeSean asked her again.
She looked at him quizzically. *No one else seems to give a damn how I am,* Shay thought to herself, still looking at him.
"I'm OK," she said simply.
"Why you lyin'?" he asked, stepping very close to her.

Shay was getting turned on, with him standing this close to her. She shouldn't be feeling this way. "I'm not lyin'," she replied.
"Yes you are," DeSean chided her. "You trying to be with that joker, knowing he too old for you," he went on, still standing close, and speaking softly in her ear. "You let him hurt you, and for what? He don't really care about you," he finished, and kissed her gently on the neck.

Shay knew what DeSean was telling her was the truth. She just didn't want to hear it.
"Please stop Sean," she said softly.
He pulled her to him, and began caressing her breasts. Shay was really getting turned on now. She had to make him stop.
"No, Sean. Stop it," she said quietly, as he slid his hand up her dress and thighs, and between her legs.

Cameron and DeSean left the house shortly after his encounter with Shay in the kitchen. DeSean was glad his friend was so engrossed in his conversation, knowing there would have been hell to pay had he caught the two of them together.

They met up with the Broughton Boys, and talked about their plans for partnership.
"So what are we getting out of the deal?" Carlos Browning asked. He was the leader of the gang. He was intelligent, and articulate. Not an imposing figure physically, standing only about 5'7", slight build, and sleepy expression. He was however, extremely vicious, and deadly.

"You get your products to a larger, and more elite, clientele base," Cameron told him, explaining that the girls had local celebrity johns, as well as working class johns. Carlos nodded thoughtfully, as they talked.

"So where is Big D?" he asked.

He was the one who'd originally set up the deal. Carlos wasn't too sure about the two sitting in front of him right now.

"He's handling some other business," Cameron replied a little testily. "Look, we here to do the job. Is there a problem?

Carlos regarded him for a moment before answering.

"No," he replied. "It was simply a question," Carlos finished, looking back at the two.

"Tell Big D everything is square, and we'll be ready for the first portion tonight," He told them.

"He can send one of ya'll to get it, and distribute it, like he want it," Carlos continued. "All I care about is getting my money, which is fifty-five percent, agreed?" he finished.

Cameron told him that was fine, and yeah, the percentage was straight.

"I'm looking forward to very lucrative partnership gentlemen" Carlos finished, effectively ending the conversation.

Cameron and DeSean told him they were too, as they left.

"I'm going to end up killing that one," Carlos commented to his boys, about Cameron.

He already didn't like him, and he had a smart mouth.

"He has one time to fuck up, and it's his ass," Carlos finished coldly, still looking in the direction the two left in.

19

"**A**re you sure she doesn't suspect anything?" Kayla asked Aidan, who was her co-conspirator in the deed they were planning.
He laughed and told her no.
"OK, good," she replied. "Have her here by 8:00," she told him.

Aidan laughed again. He loved Mariah's mother. Kayla was one of the warmest people he'd ever met. *I'm going to like having her for a mother-in-law,* Aidan thought to himself chuckling at his long range plans for him and Mariah.
"I promise she'll be there," Aidan replied.

They hung up, as each went back to their assigned task. Aidan had asked Mariah if they could spend her birthday together, and she'd agreed, saying her mother told her she wasn't giving her a party this year.
He had to go to the mall, and pick up her gift.
She'd teased him about being older than he was.
"We're only six months apart," he'd told her, as she ribbed him.

Thinking about Mariah made Aidan smile. He went back to the den, where she was waiting for him.
"So?" Mariah asked him.
Aidan was confused. What was she talking about? She gave him a look.
"The sodas you were going to the kitchen to get?" Mariah reminded him.
Aidan laughed. He'd completely forgotten the excuse he gave her for leaving.
"Oh yeah," he said, laughing again. "Be right back," he told her, as he headed back to the kitchen.

Mariah teased him about being slow, when he came back. They began to wrestle, and Aidan once again, pinned Mariah to the floor.
"Give up?" he asked, smiling at her.
She was still giggling.

"No!" Mariah squealed, as Aidan began to tickle her.
He stopped, and looked at her. She was so beautiful, and she was his.
"Happy birthday, baby," Aidan told Mariah, still looking at her.
"Thanks," she replied, still smiling.

He leaned down, and kissed her passionately. Their heat began to grow, and he began touching her.
"Come up to my room with me," Aidan said softly, looking her in the eye.
Mariah wanted him, and they'd already come close, a couple of times.
Today was a perfect day she supposed, it was her birthday.
"All right," she replied, getting up to leave with him.
Aidan glanced at the clock. They had plenty of time. He was ready to cement their relationship once and for all.

Aidan led Mariah to his bed, and kissed her again, as he sat her on it.
"I want you so much," he told her, still caressing her.
Mariah smiled again.
"I want you, too," she replied.
They began to kiss once more, and Aidan undressed her.
"You are so beautiful," he told her, as he began exploring her body with his tongue.

Mariah was moaning softly now, and Aidan was fully aroused. He kissed his way to her center and began tasting her. Mariah's breathing became ragged and uneven, and Aidan knew she was almost there.
She cried out softly as he buried his tongue deeper inside her and he felt her body tremble, alerting him she'd reached her peak.
Now to permanently erase David from her mind forever, Aidan thought as he reached over, onto the nightstand, and got the condom.

Mariah helped him put in on, and guided him to her entrance. Aidan kissed her again passionately, as he slowly, and carefully, entered her. He didn't move immediately once he was inside her.

Aidan, taking his time, began to kiss and caress Mariah almost to her peak once again, before he thrust into her. They were moving together, and Mariah was expressing her pleasure. Aidan held her tightly enjoying the feel of her as he consumed her.

"Aidan," Mariah breathed in ecstasy, as she reached orgasm again.

Aidan came then, pulling her body even closer to his own. Her body was still trembling from her orgasm, as he held her.

"I didn't hurt you, did I?" Aidan asked her gently, once they'd composed themselves.

Mariah looked at him, and smiled.

"No. You were wonderful," she told him.

Being with her had been everything he hoped it would be and more. Mariah would never be touched by any other man, and Aidan would kill any fool crazy enough to try and come between them.

Next time, I think I want to feel her, Aidan thought to himself of making love to Mariah. He shook the thoughts and looked at the clock again. It was after six. They'd better get a move on.

"Come on baby," Aidan said, getting up. "I want to take you someplace," he finished, looking at her, smiling.

Mariah looked at him evenly, and spoke.

"Someplace other than the planet you just took me too?" she said, smiling now.

That comment made Aidan feel ten feet tall. He smiled back, and kissed her again. "Come on," he said, pulling her up this time. "You're gonna get us in trouble," Aidan laughed, as Mariah headed to the bathroom.

Jaz was sitting in the den, still smiling, and enjoying the revelation that Mariah and Aidan had been together having heard them as she stood outside of Aidan's closed bedroom door.

She knew just when she was going to tell David too. Jaz knew he would show up at Mariah's party, even though he wasn't invited. David still wasn't taking no for an answer when it came to Mariah.

Jaz actually chuckled out loud at the enjoyment she would get seeing the hurt on his face, when he found out Mariah had given herself to someone else. She had to be careful not to show any emotion when they came into the den. Jaz knew Mariah would tell her later, and she would act surprised.

"Where ya'll going?" she asked nonchalantly, when Aidan came in to get his keys.

"To the mall," he told her, knowing Jaz already knew the plan for the evening.

"Happy birthday girl!" Jaz said cheerfully, to Mariah. Mariah laughed and told her thanks.

"What is my big head cousin getting you?" she asked, looking at Aidan.

Mariah laughed again, and told her she had no idea.

"Come on, let's go," Aidan said, sticking his tongue out at Jaz.

"Bye you two, and behave yourselves!" Jaz laughed. She watched them get into the car, and leave. *I can't wait to see you tonight, Mr. David Alston,* Jaz thought to herself, laughing loudly, and polishing off her popcorn.

David was looking at the calendar. Today was Mariah's eighteenth birthday. He'd had his own, a month earlier. He planned to take her gift to her later tonight. *Maybe she'll talk to me again,* David thought to himself.

She'd been cordial to him, and even held a conversation here and there, in the months since they'd broken up, but nothing even close to them getting back together. David still loved Mariah so much.

His mother was really doing a number on Sherice. She had her attorney leaning hard on her. They weren't in

the position his family was, and David knew they could easily prove her unfit.
Sherice was fighting tooth and nail to keep this baby. They had to do something soon, or she would be too far along, even for the private clinic his mother knew of.
"We can always take her out of the country," she'd told David, when he expressed the time limitations they had.

His phone rang, and jolted him out of his thoughts. The number was blocked. *Maybe it's Mariah,* David thought hopefully, as he answered.
"Hello?" he answered.
"Make your mama stop, David," Sherice said.
He could tell she was crying. David had no sympathy for her.
"I told you you'd made a mistake, didn't I?" he told her coldly.
Sherice cried harder.
"It's not fair David!" she yelled at him. "This is my baby!"

David smiled then, knowing she was close to breaking, and this nightmare was close to being over for him.
"Well, unfortunately, my semen gave you that baby, and I want no part of you," David said again, as coldly as he could.
Sherice continued to sob.
"Give it up Sherice," he told her plainly. "You can't win this one," David finished harshly.

Sherice managed to compose herself, and speak.
"Why are you trying to hurt me like this David?" she asked him quietly.
He almost laughed out loud at that question.
"I honestly loved you," Sherice went on "All those nights we were together, I fell in love with you, and the wonderful person I thought you were," she finished sounding defeated.

David didn't care about her declarations of love. He wanted Mariah. She was all he'd ever wanted, and Sherice had effectively ruined that for him.

"I have never loved you, Sherice," he told her again coldly. "I've never been in love with you," David continued. "I was only screwing you, because I couldn't make love to the woman I wanted," he finished dryly.
Sherice began crying again.
"You'll get yours David," she said quietly, and hung up before he could reply.
David thought to himself, *I've heard that before from the other bitch.* He wasn't impressed either time. He got up, and headed to the jewelers, to pick up the gift he'd picked out for Mariah.

"You've got to calm down," Dr. Blanding was telling her. Sherice had been admitted because she'd started spotting.
"Do you want me to give you something to help you rest?" Dr. Blanding asked.
Sherice said she did.
"OK, let me do another ultrasound first and check on the baby, and then I'll tell the nurse to bring you a sedative," Dr Blanding told Sherice, as she left to go find the ultrasound tech.

Sherice looked at Elaine. She'd been sitting quietly in the chair the whole time, and heard the conversation with her and David. Sherice knew Elaine was angry, but she didn't say anything. She'd brought her to the hospital, and stayed with her since she got here.

Elaine was watching Sherice intently. *What the hell does she see in that jackass?* She thought to herself. Sherice was her best friend in the world, and Elaine was completely in love with her, still. They'd kissed a couple of times, but Sherice had always stopped herself. Except for the one time she'd allowed Elaine to pleasure her.

They'd been drinking, and she supposed Sherice was a little drunk. Elaine wasn't, she held her liquor very well. Sherice knew she was gay. It hadn't changed their friendship, and Elaine was glad of that.

This particular night, she made her feelings for Sherice known. *"I've never thought about it," Sherice told her. "Well let me just show you," she'd replied, kissing Sherice softly on her neck. Sherice sighed softly, and allowed Elaine to continue touching and kissing her.*

Elaine gently lay her down and continued to arouse her. She'd sucked her breasts, and even tasted her. Sherice was moaning in pleasure and enjoying every moment of it. Elaine was too. She was so aroused while she made love to Sherice.

Elaine felt her orgasm, and she kissed Sherice softly again. "Did you like it?" Elaine asked her friend.
Sherice admitted she did. "But I miss the hardness," she'd answered honestly.
Elaine told her she could fix that next time.
"We can't," Sherice had replied.

She'd pushed Elaine away, and went to the bathroom. They'd never talked about it again. Elaine still loved her, but she knew Sherice wanted no part of that again. She sighed gently, as the doctor returned with the ultrasound machine.
Dr. Blanding squeezed the gel onto Sherice's stomach, and smoothed it with the ultrasound wand.
"Let's see here," she said, as she began to look at the image.
The machine was turned so Sherice couldn't see, but Elaine could.

She saw the concern register on Dr. Blandings face, and followed her gaze. Elaine saw the screen, and the image of the baby. There was no heart beating, as there had been earlier.
"What's wrong?" Sherice asked seeing the doctor's face.
Dr. Blanding sighed deeply, and looked at the young woman.
"I'm sorry Sherice," she began. "The baby has died."

Sherice screamed in horror, and began to cry. Elaine got up and went to her, taking her in her arms, and holding her. Dr. Blanding sighed gently.

"I'll send the nurse in, to prep you for the procedure," she told her.
Sherice just continued to cry.
"This isn't fair," she told Elaine miserably.
"I know," Elaine replied, and continued to hold her friend.

20

Kayla was busy making sure everything was in place. Thomas was laughing, and chasing her around the house, as she moved from room to room.
"Slow down, baby," he told her, finally catching up with her in the kitchen. "Everything looks wonderful," he told her again. "The caterers are doing a fine job, and Aidan promised to have her here on time."
"Now come and sit down," he said, smiling at her.

Kayla just wanted everything to be perfect. Mariah was her only child, and she loved her so much. She couldn't believe her daughter was eighteen years old. Kayla remembered having her, like it was yesterday.

Thomas was watching her closely. He knew this was an emotional day for Kayla. Her daughter was all grown up now, and would be moving on with her own life.
"Have you made any plans for our wedding?" Thomas asked, trying to take her mind off her thoughts.
Kayla smiled at Thomas, and caressed his face.
"Yes, as a matter of fact, I have," she told him.

Kayla wanted something small and intimate, but neither Mother, nor Mariah, was hearing that. She'd been afraid of mother's reaction when she told her that she and Thomas were getting married.
Kayla had no reason to be. Mother was genuinely pleased. Mariah had squealed her delight when Kayla told her, and immediately began to help her plan.

She knew Thomas had talked to Mariah about what she would call him, once they were married. Mariah honestly told him she couldn't see herself calling anyone else daddy, but her father, so they'd settled on dad. Kayla was happy they got along so well, it made everything so much easier for her.

She was going to give Mariah a very special gift tonight for her birthday, once they were alone. Kayla heard the bell ring, bringing her back to the present. She got up to open the door, as the first of the guests began to arrive.

Sandra knocked lightly on David's door.
"Come in," he called out.
David was coming out of the bathroom, putting on his shirt.
"Where are you going?" she asked him, seeing he was getting dressed.
"To take Mariah her birthday present," he replied, looking up at her.

Sandra was looking very intense.
"What is it?" David asked her cautiously.
"It seems we won't have to worry about Sherice anymore," Sandra told him, waiting for his reaction.
"Why?" David asked, still guarded.
He'd just talked to Shercie an hour ago. His mother took a deep breath, and exhaled.
"Evidently the stress of the situation caused her to miscarry," Sandra went on. "I had our own doctor go to the hospital. He just called me, and verified the report," she continued. "So once again, you've been spared from yourself," she finished, looking at him hard.

"Now," Sandra began again. "I want you to do whatever you have to do, to get Mariah back into your life," she finished evenly.
"I'll try mother," David told her softly. "Do you want to see what I got her?"
Sandra softened. She knew her son loved Mariah, and he was trying. He'd been faithfully pursing her since they broke up. She made a mental note, to do a little investigating of her own, concerning the boy Mariah was seeing now. Maybe she could help them along to their reconciliation.
"Yes, David," she replied. "Let me see it."

He brought her the box, and Sandra opened it. It was the most magnificent heart pendant she'd ever seen. It

was twenty-four carat gold, with brilliant diamonds, completely encompassing it.
"David, this is absolutely beautiful," she told him, smiling up at him. "Mariah will absolutely love it," Sandra finished; sure that she would indeed love it.
"I hope so mother," he replied, looking wistfully out of the window.

"Go to her David, and make her remember why she fell in love with you in the first place," his mother said softly, looking him in the eye.
David hugged her, and told her thanks for once again being there for him.

He grabbed his keys, and picked up Mariah's gift, heading out the door to see her. *Please let her forgive him,* Sandra thought to herself, as she headed downstairs to have a glass of wine, and make some new phone calls.

"Hello Sandra," Alexander boomed into the phone. "I hear the crisis is over!" he said again.
She chuckled lightly.
"Yes thankfully," she replied. "Maybe my son can get his life back together now," Sandra finished.
Alexander chuckled again.
"I need you to work on something else for me," she told him.

He was intrigued. Sandra always had the most interesting assignments for him.
"What can I help you with?" Alexander asked her.
"There is a boy I want you to investigate. I need to know everything you can find out about him, his history, criminal activity, his parents, the works," Sandra told him.
"Ok, so what's his name?" Alexander asked.
"Aidan Preston," she replied.
Alexander wrote down the name.
"Do you at least know where he's from? That's always a good starting point," He asked again.

Sandra thought about it for a moment. She'd only learned his name from someone she'd overheard talking about him.
"No, but I do know that Jackie Pierce is his aunt," she replied.
Alexander told her that might help a little, but he couldn't do much without speaking to the woman, and that would send up flags.
"Does he go to school here?" he asked trying a different angle.
"Yes, he goes to the same high school as David," She replied.
He smiled.
"That will work," Alexander told her.
He knew it would be much easier to get his information from the school. He already had a contact in place he would call.
"How quickly do you want it?" He asked her.

Sandra thought for a moment and decided she needed it soon. She couldn't allow Aidan and Mariah to become too much closer, or David would never stand a chance at winning her back.
"Yesterday," she replied.
The attorney laughed loudly.
"Oh the usual," he replied, telling her he would get right on it. "I'll call you as soon as I have anything that would interest you," he told her.

Sandra thanked him again for his help, and his professionalism, as they hung up. *Well, hopefully he will find what I need to destroy this pathetic relationship, and secure my son's future.* She thought to herself, heading upstairs to her bedroom, alone again.

Everyone was in place, waiting for their arrival. Aidan called from the mall, saying they were on their way. As they saw the headlights, Kayla told everyone to be quiet, and get ready. Aidan helped Mariah out of the car.

"It is so not like mommy to be so forgetful," she was saying.
Kayla called and asked Mariah to stop by the house, and check the stove. She was too far away, and almost positive she'd left it on.
"We all have our days," Aidan told her as she opened the door, and walked into the darkened house.
"Surprise!" everyone screamed at once, turning on the lights.

Mariah was shocked. They'd managed to pull this off without her suspecting a thing. She looked at Aidan, and he was smiling. *He was in on this too!* Mariah thought to herself, as she laughed. Everyone was telling her happy birthday, and hugging her.

The house was alive with multi color balloons, streamers, and flowers, as well as a huge banner proclaiming her a happy eighteenth. The music was starting, and people were making their way into the other room to dance. Mariah finally made her way through the well wishers, to her mother, and Thomas.

"You guys are terrible!" Mariah told them both, hugging them as she laughed. "I should have known you were up to something, when you told me no party."
Kayla hugged her again, and told Mariah how much she loved her, and how proud she was of her.

"I have something special for you later," Kayla told her. "When we're alone."
Mariah told her OK, she was looking forward to it.
"Come on birthday girl!" Thomas laughed, grabbing Mariah's hand. "Let's dance!" he finished, heading to the living room.

Everyone was dancing, and having a wonderful time. Kayla was enjoying watching Mariah, when Thomas came back and grabbed her, pulling her out onto the dance floor with Jackie and Chris.

Mariah was catching her breath when Jaz came over to talk to her.

"We got you didn't we?!" Jaz laughed, as they hugged each other.
"Yes!" Mariah laughed. "You guys are awful."
She leaned close to Jaz's ear.
"I have something to tell you," she said, smiling slyly. Jaz pretended to be perplexed.
"Come on," Mariah said taking her hand so they could go talk.

They ended up on the rear deck of the house. Jaz was looking at Mariah expectantly, waiting for her to speak.
"I'm off the island," she said quietly, looking intently at Jaz.
Jaz feigned shock, and whispered. "You and Aidan had sex?"
Mariah shook her head yes. Jaz squealed, and hugged her telling her she was happy for her.
"So?" Jaz asked, looking sly herself. "How was it?" she finished, giggling.
"Definitely all that," Mariah said softly, with a faraway look in her eye.
"Well I'm really happy for you two," she told her best friend.
"Did he give you your present yet?" Jaz asked, then added, "I mean your other present."
Mariah laughed and told her no.

"He says he wants to give it to me later, alone," she told her friend.
"I think you'll like it," Jaz said.
Mariah smiled. "I'm sure I will," she laughed, and they went back inside to the party.
Aidan saw them come in smiling, and knew what they'd been outside talking about. He smiled and made his way to Mariah, ready to give her his gift now.

David arrived to find the party in full swing. He was a little hurt that Kayla hadn't invited him, but he had

to remember he and Mariah weren't officially together anymore.
David checked his outfit once more. He was wearing her favorite color again, and the shirt was form fitting, the way she liked it. He picked up the gift bag, and headed for the front door. David knew Kayla would let him in. She would never be rude, and close the door in his face.

Jaz saw him drive up and get out, making sure she answered the door when he rang the bell.
"What do you want David?" Jaz asked, looking him up and down distastefully.
Look at him, tryna be sexy, like Mariah is really gonna take him back, she thought to herself, and almost chuckled aloud.
"Look Jaz," David started, trying hard to keep his cool. "I'm not here to see you. Where is Mariah?"
Jaz stepped out, and closed the door.
"She's with her boyfriend, on the deck in back," she said casually, watching his reaction.

David was trying really hard not to be mad, and he knew Jaz was enjoying watching him. *This bitch is really going to work my last nerve in a minute,* he thought, as he continued to try and hold his temper.
"Well I'd like to leave her gift with her mom then," David told Jaz, again, trying to step around her.
"Mrs. Black is having a good time. Why would I let you ruin it, by coming inside and upsetting her?" she asked, blocking his path again.

He'd had just about enough of this girl for tonight. "Look Jaz," he said, his anger evident. "Get the hell out of my way," he told her evenly.
Jaz looked at David hard. *Let me go ahead and burst this fool's bubble,* she thought, as she geared up to tell him.
"Guess what Mariah just told me?" Jaz asked him, still holding his gaze.
He rolled his eyes.
"What the hell do I care what she just told you?" David asked, trying not to lose his temper.
Jaz smiled as she answered.

"Oh trust me. You wanna hear this," she said, looking at David hard again.

Obviously she had something on her mind, so he would try to get her to tell it, and leave him alone.

"OK Jaz," David told her, as he exhaled deeply. "You're dying to tell me, so spill it!" he said, as he crossed his arms to listen.

She looked him over, then back in the eye.

"Mariah told me she wasn't a virgin anymore," Jaz said flatly.

He tried to cover, but she saw it. David was stunned.

"Why don't you stop lying and playing games Jaz," David spat at her venomously.

Please let her be lying! He thought panicking, but trying to maintain his composure.

Jaz chuckled lightly. "I don't have to lie to you, David," she said again, without emotion. "Follow me to the rear deck, and I'll let you see for yourself," Jaz finished, challenging him.

David thought about it. He had to know if she were telling the truth. He couldn't believe Mariah would sleep with Aidan so soon. He followed, as Jaz led him to the deck, and to a spot where they could see and hear, what was going on.

Aidan and Mariah were sitting on the deck. "Are you having a good birthday baby?" Aidan asked, as he kissed her.

David didn't want to see that, but he stayed put.

"Yeah, of course," Mariah told him, smiling back.

David was looking at how beautiful she still looked. He loved Mariah so much. *Please don't let her have slept with him.* He prayed silently, as he continued to watch them.

"I have your gift," Aidan told her, looking at her slyly.

"You mean my other gift?" Mariah said mischievously.

He laughed. "This afternoon was without a doubt all that," Aidan told her softly, as he looked into her eyes.

David was crushed. He knew then, that Jaz had told him the truth. Jaz was watching David intently, seeing that he was deeply hurt. She didn't feel bad for him. He deserved it, after all the pain he'd caused everyone else. David didn't want to hear anymore, but he couldn't bring himself to move.

"Baby," Aidan said, taking Mariah's hands. "I want to give you this," he told her, producing a ring box. She gasped when he opened it to reveal the half-carat solitaire, set in twenty-four carat white gold ring inside. "I know we both have a lot of school ahead of us," Aidan began. "But I want you to know, I want to spend the rest of my life with you by my side."

Mariah was crying softly.

"So baby," he began again. "Will you promise to be with me?" he finished, waiting for her response.

Mariah was so overwhelmed she couldn't speak. All she could do was cry, and shake her head yes. Aidan smiled and hugged her. He put the ring on her finger and kissed her. Kayla and Thomas both emerged from the party, finding them on the deck.

"What's wrong baby?" Kayla asked, seeing her daughter crying.

Mariah smiled at her mother, and showed her the ring. Kayla smiled and hugged her daughter, then turned and hugged Aidan.

Thomas congratulated them both, and told them he was available for the ceremony. They both laughed, and said it would be a couple of years away. They all returned to the party, leaving Jaz and David alone in the darkness. He turned to Jaz, and handed her the bag.

"Please give this to Mariah, and tell her happy birthday for me," he said quietly.

Jaz saw David in the soft light, trying hard to control his emotions. This time she did feel bad. She'd wanted to get back at him, but the pain and hurt she saw in David's eyes, she wouldn't have wished on her worst enemy. Jaz watched him walk slowly to his car, and drive away.

I guess what they say is true, she thought to herself, *revenge is never as fulfilling as you think it's going to be,* Jaz sighed heavily, and headed for the party. She would put his gift in Mariah's room, on her bed. She'd find it later when she went to sleep.

Jaz peeked inside, and saw there was a card, so Mariah would know who it was from Jaz thought to herself as she went back to the party. She dialed Elaine as she walked back inside. Jaz was feeling low and really wanted to hear her voice. She got her voicemail.

How odd, Jaz thought to herself and dismissed it, as she made it back inside.

21

David's mind was reeling. *Mariah had sex with Aidan, and she's going to marry him,* he kept thinking over and over. He still couldn't believe it, and he'd heard it all for himself.

It's over, I have no chance now, David thought miserably to himself for a while, before new inspiration took hold. *OK, so she'd slept with him. He could forgive that, and they weren't married yet,* he thought again.

David made up his mind he had to pull out all the stops. He knew his mother had connections that could help. He would find out everything he needed to know about Aidan, and beat him at his own game. Mariah was supposed to be with him, and he wasn't going to just roll over and play dead.

David arrived at home, and went immediately to fix himself a drink.

"After what I just heard, I need this," he said aloud as he gulped down the whiskey straight.

"What exactly did you just hear?" Sandra asked softly, walking into the den where he was.

David looked at his mother. He needed her help, and he needed it now.

"Mariah is engaged to Aidan," he told her flatly.

Sandra needed a drink herself now. Her mind was reeling.

"What kind of nonsense are you spouting?" she asked him, still not believing what he'd told her.

"I saw and heard them for myself," David told her again. He went on to tell her how he ended up witnessing the event.

"They've slept together," David told her, the pain in his voice obvious.

Sandra couldn't be upset with Mariah. David had hurt her deeply. This boy had obviously used that to seduce her.

"You can't be upset with her about that David," she told him softly.

David sighed deeply, and looked at his mother again.
"I know that," he began. "I completely forgive her for that," he went on. "I just want Mariah back that's all, and I need your help," he finished looking at her evenly.
"What do you want me to do?" Sandra asked him.
David began to tell his mother what he needed from her.
"When do you want me to invite her over?" she asked him.
"Tomorrow," David told her.

He would make sure his car wasn't there, and his mother was to tell Mariah he was out. He would take care of the rest from there. Sandra told him she would call. David hugged her, and headed off to his room. She thought about him after he left, and hoped his plan would work.

David was thinking ahead to tomorrow. Mariah will have gotten his gift by then. He would surprise them by coming home early, and finding her there. His mother would of course excuse herself, and he would talk to her. David had to make her see reason. He had to make Mariah admit there was still a part of her that loved him. David said a silent prayer then closed his eyes, waiting for sleep to take him.

The evening had been wonderful. Mariah was reflecting on everything that'd happened. She and Aidan would be married, and she would spend the rest of her life being loved and happy.

She saw the gift bag on her bed. *This must be what mommy had for me,* Mariah thought to herself, as she pulled the box out of the bag. She opened the box to reveal the most beautiful diamond heart pendant she'd ever seen. *This is amazing,* she thought, smiling to herself.

Mariah looked for the card, and found it still inside the bag. She opened it and began to read. *No matter how long we're apart, or how far you go, you will always have my heart. Love always, David.* Mariah was speechless. *How did this get here? Did he bring it,* she wondered. Mariah looked at the pendant again, and felt tears come to her eyes. This was the David she remembered. The way he used to be before he started taking her and their relationship for granted. Mariah sighed heavily.

She would call David tomorrow, and at least say thank you for his gift. He needed to move on. Mariah put the box back into the bag, and placed it on her nightstand. She didn't want to think about him, or them, anymore.

There was a soft knock on her door.

"Come in," Mariah called out pleasantly.

Kayla entered her room and smiled at her.

"How was everything baby?" she asked her daughter softly. "Did you enjoy your party?"

Mariah smiled and hugged her mother tightly.

"Yes," she replied still smiling.

Kayla looked at her.

"I wanted to tell you how much I appreciate you," she began. "And how much I love you for accepting Thomas in my life now," she went on. "Now that I'm marrying him, there is something I have to let go of, and because I never want to be far from it, I'm giving it to you."

Mariah was perplexed. Kayla took her hand, and gently placed the wedding rings that Black had given to her, when they were married. Mariah began to cry.

"Mommy," she said, through her tears. "Thank you so much for trusting me with these."

Mariah knew how much these rings meant to Kayla. She knew it wasn't her mother letting go of her father, just Kayla moving on with her life.

"I love you so much, Mariah," Kayla told her. "You were the most wonderful gift your father ever gave me," she finished, hugging her daughter tightly.

Mariah was still crying. The depth of emotion she felt at this moment was indescribable. Kayla knew she was overwhelmed. She kissed Mariah softly on the cheek, and told her goodnight.

Mariah got up after her mother left, and placed the rings on the pink ribbon she had attached to the frame containing the wedding picture of her mother and father. She cherished this gift more than any other she'd received tonight.

"I love you daddy," Mariah whispered softly, touching the photo.

She turned to go shower and get ready for bed. Her phone rang as she passed it. *Who is this? It's after midnight,* Mariah thought to herself.

"Hello," she answered, still trying to compose herself.

"Hello Mariah," Sandra said softly.

Mariah smiled as she replied. "Hello Mrs. Alston."

Sandra was so happy to hear her voice.

"Happy birthday sweetie," she told her pleasantly.

Mariah was glad to hear from her. She felt guilty, since she'd promised to visit, but hadn't.

"Thank you so much, Mrs. Alston," she replied again.

Sandra chose her words carefully to complete the mission she was on.

"I was wondering if maybe you and I could have our own little celebration tomorrow, since we haven't had a visit in a while," she said softly.

Mariah didn't have a problem with that. She only had one question.

"David won't be there will he?" she asked quietly.

Sandra knew she would ask.

"No sweetie. I'll make sure of it," she told the girl.

"Well alright then. What time?" Mariah replied again.

Sandra asked her to come around 1:00. They would have lunch and talk.

"That'll be great. I'll see you then," she replied, and they said goodnight.

Mariah was reflecting on the conversation, and the planned visit. *Please don't let him be there,* she thought to herself. She couldn't explain it, but Mariah just knew she couldn't handle seeing David right now. She looked at her hand, and the engagement ring again, smiled to herself, and headed off to the shower.

Talking to Mariah always made Sandra's mind go back to Donovan. Tonight was no exception. She'd absolutely loved him.

"Donovan, why are you going to California?" Sandra asked him the last time they talked.

They were dating then, and she thought they would get married.

"It's a wonderful opportunity honey," he'd answered her.

"I don't want to leave," she'd told him stubbornly.

He'd sighed deeply, and asked her to please reconsider.

"I love you Sandra, please come with me," he'd begged.

Sandra told Donovan no again and again, until he'd finally given up, and left without her.

"Stupid me," she said aloud, thinking of it now. Sandra wished with everything in her, she could have that chance back. She would run to the plane to leave with him. She'd endured watching Donovan and Kayla together for years, watching them in love with each other, and raising Mariah.

Sandra watched what a wonderful father he was. She'd been elated when Kayla asked her to watch Mariah for her one day. She and the child had a marvelous time. Mariah was such a good child, not demanding and spoiled like David. They'd played together, and Sandra felt completely fulfilled, having Donovan's child in her arms.

She was almost positive Kayla knew how she felt about Donovan, but she'd never mentioned it, or acted any differently toward her. Sandra felt guilt for secretly harboring the jealousy she felt toward Kayla all these years. She drained her wine glass, and headed up to bed. Her husband was working late, again.

The new day dawned with the sun shining brightly as Sandra looked out of the huge pane window and admired the brilliance of God's landscape. Sandra was instructing the cook on what she wanted for lunch. They were having lasagna. It was Mariah's favorite.

This has to work, she thought again. Sandra couldn't see herself never having Mariah near again. She genuinely loved the girl. Sandra only hoped her son had truly learned his lesson, and wouldn't put Mariah through the hell his own father had made her endure.

"Hello Sandra," Maurice boomed, as he walked into the room.

Maurice Alston was her husband, David's father. He was a prominent defense attorney, who was well respected in the judicial circuit. He was considering a bid for judge next year.

A good-looking man, Maurice stood a solid six feet, with a lean, toned, frame. He had beautiful dimples, much like Mariah's, and big brown eyes. His hair was sprinkled with gray, making him look more distinguished.

"Hello Maurice," Sandra replied, rather distracted.

"Is the queen stopping by?" he asked her jokingly, seeing all the activity at the house.

She smiled slightly.

"No, Mariah is coming by for a visit," Sandra said evenly, watching his reaction.

Maurice looked up from his mail, and smiled himself.

"Good," he said softly.

Sandra knew what he was thinking. Maurice loved Mariah as much as she did, for his own reasons of course, but they had the same end in mind. They'd discussed at length, what a wonderful choice for David she was.

"Is David going to be here?" Maurice queried again.

"No, not initially," Sandra replied.

Maurice knew what that meant. She and David had devised a plan. He hoped it worked. He missed having Mariah around. She was an absolutely wonderful girl.

"Well good luck with everything," Maurice told her, planting a peck on her cheek, and heading out the door.

Sandra sighed watching him leave. *I used to love him so much,* she thought to herself, as she went back into the kitchen, to check the progress of lunch.

David parked the mustang in the garage and closed it. Mariah wouldn't suspect he was there. David couldn't wait to see her. He wondered how she liked his gift. He would ask her when they talked.

David looked himself over in the mirror once more after he returned upstairs to his room. He had on an outfit similar to the one he'd worn on their first date. He wanted Mariah to remember, to think back to the time when they were happy.

I have been such an ass, he thought to himself again. He'd had the perfect woman, with the perfect relationship, and he took it all for granted. *Never again,* David continued thinking, as he looked out the window to watch for her approach.

Mariah was pulling into the Alston's circular drive, looking for David's car. She didn't see it. *She promised he wouldn't be here,* Mariah chided herself. She hoped she looked okay. It was only supposed to be her and Mrs. Alston. She got out of the car, and headed for the door.

David saw Mariah get out, and she took his breath away. She was wearing a cute blue wrap dress that accentuated her perfect figure. Her hair was down today. He took a deep breath, and quickly headed down the back staircase and out to the garage to wait.

"Hello Mariah!" Sandra exclaimed, as she hugged her and ushered her inside the house.

Mariah laughed and returned her greeting as they made their way to the den.

"Tell me all about your birthday!" Sandra said, smiling still. She was so happy to have her sitting here again in her home. Mariah began to tell Sandra all about the party, and

the surprise of it all. Sandra glanced at her hand, and noticed Mariah wasn't wearing the ring today.
"Well I hope you're hungry," Sandra said, rising.
Mariah followed, and they headed to the dining room.
"We're having lasagna," Sandra said, looking at her quizzically. "You do like lasagna, right?"

Mariah laughed, and told Mrs. Alston to stop teasing. They both laughed, and sat down to enjoy lunch. After they ate, the cook brought in a small cake, with a single candle on it. Mariah was very moved, and hugged Mrs. Alston tightly, telling her thank you. Sandra kissed Mariah on the cheek, and told her she was welcome.
"Come on, let's go back into the den, and visit some more," Sandra suggested, as they rose.

They'd been talking for the last thirty minutes, about Mariah and college, when David appeared.
"Hi Mother I'm –," he stopped mid-sentence, after seeing Mariah.
"Hi," he said softly, looking at her.
Sandra had to play her part now.
"David, what are you doing home?" she said crossly. "I asked you to not come back until after my meeting," she finished, looking at him evenly.
"I'm sorry. You didn't tell me it was Mariah you were meeting," David said again, still looking at her.
"And this is exactly why!" Sandra told him. "You're upsetting Mariah, and I don't want that," she finished, shooting him a look.

Mariah didn't want her to be upset, and it honestly wasn't his fault.
"It's OK, Mrs. Alston," she said quietly.
Sandra looked at her.
"Are you sure?" Sandra asked again.
"Yes. It's okay," Mariah replied again.
"Mother, I'd like to speak to Mariah alone, if that's okay with her," David said to Sandra.
She looked at Mariah. "You don't have to say yes, if you don't want to," she told her.

Mariah looked at her, and smiled again. "It's OK," she said softly.
"Very well then," Sandra said, rising to leave.

They were alone now, as David sat down next to her. "Happy belated birthday," he said softly.
Mariah smiled, and told him thanks.
"I got your gift," she replied again. "Thanks again."
David looked at her. This was awkward, but at least they were talking.
"Did you like it?" he asked, still looking at Mariah intently.
She smiled again at the memory of it.
"Yes, it was perfect," Mariah said again, very softly.
"Like we used to be, before I messed up?" he asked.
She sighed, and David knew he'd struck a nerve.
"Yeah, I suppose so," she said sadly.

David knew this would be his only chance to let Mariah hear his heart, and he had to take it.
"Mariah," he began. "I know I hurt you," he went on. "I took you and our relationship for granted," he continued. "I'm sorry," David finished, going on to tell her other things he felt about her.
"As for me messin' around on you," he started anew. "There's no excuse for that," he went on. "I just want you to know, there won't be a baby to constantly remind you of that," he finished, looking at her again.

Mariah looked at him, her mind reeling in so many different directions, her emotions churning. She was feeling things she shouldn't about David. Things she thought were long dead and buried.
"Why?" Mariah asked, not looking at David now, referring to the baby.
David was glad she was still sitting here. He'd thought she might leave when he got there.
"She had a miscarriage," he said evenly.
Mariah shook her head, and sighed heavily.
"I'm sorry for that," she said softly.

David loved that about Mariah. She was concerned for Sherice, even though she'd been his partner in crime.
"Can we be friends Mariah?" David asked her quietly.
Mariah took a deep breath.
"David, they're some things I need to tell you," she said quietly, looking him in the eye.
He already knew what she was going to tell him. He would spare her, and himself, that again.
"I already know about you and Aidan," David said simply, looking away.

She'd seen the hurt, and pain in his eyes.
"You were there last night, weren't you?" Mariah asked again, still looking at him.
David shook his head yes.
"What did you hear and see?" she inquired.
David looked at Mariah steadily, and smiled a sad smile.
"Everything," he told her.
She took another breath, and looked away.
"It's OK Mariah," David said gently, making her look at him. "I understand. I really do."
Mariah was still confused. She didn't know what to say to David now, or how to feel about him. This was the David she remembered. This was the David she fell in love with.

He saw Mariah struggling with her emotions, and as low down as it seemed, he would take advantage of it. David leaned over, and kissed her softly. Mariah gasped lightly, but didn't push him away.

David saw the tears glistening, and knew she was thinking about their beginning. He kissed her again gently, the tears falling this time. *Well it's now or never,* David thought to himself, taking Mariah in his arms, and kissing her passionately.

She allowed him to kiss her, feeling her body responding to him. David had begun caressing her, and stroking her gently. His hand was traveling up her dress, toward her center.

"David, no," Mariah said, pushing him away.
He stopped, and looked at her.

"I don't think you really want me to stop, Mariah," David told her, as he tried to kiss her again.
"David, stop," Mariah replied pushing him away once more.

David was frustrated with the mixed signals she was giving him. "Mariah, why are we playing this game?" he threw at her angrily. "I can tell you want me, so why are we going through this," he added breathing hard and looking directly into her eyes.
Mariah sighed deeply and moved away from David.

"This is why we can't be friends David," she began as David tried to control his temper. "You always try to bring it back to us being together and I've already told you, we are over," Mariah told him never taking her eyes from him.

David sighed deeply before speaking. "Mariah, tell me you didn't want me five minutes ago?" he challenged.
"I won't deny that David," Mariah replied trying to stay calm herself now. "But it's not going to happen, I'm with Aidan and that's how it is," she finished.

David exploded. "I don't wanna hear that shit," he told her angrily as he got up in her face. "I watched you and him last night with all that romance and future shit," David spat.
Mariah rose to leave as David snatched her back to the couch and held her there.
"I love you Mariah," David hissed still holding her. "Yeah I messed up, but I'm trying to make it right, stop trippin' and let's work this out," he finished as Mariah continued to watch him closely.

Finally David let go of her and Mariah rose once again.
"I have to go David," Mariah told him coldly ending the discussion, as she gathered herself. "How 'bout you don't call me anymore," she told David as his mouth dropped.
"We can't be friends," she continued.
"You don't really want that, and I can't give you what you really want," she told him sighing lightly again. "Move on

David, it's the best thing you can do right now," she finished.
"What about us Mariah?" David pleaded. "Please, baby, don't do this."
"There is no us anymore David, that's what I've been trying to get you to understand," she told him quietly. "Please tell your mother I said goodbye," she finished, heading for the door.

David stopped her long enough to try once more. "OK Mariah, I get it," he told her. "Give me a little time, and I promise I can be just your friend."
Mariah looked at David long and hard for a few moments before speaking again.
"Prove it," she said calmly and left the house headed to her car.

22

The last few months had been some of the best she'd had in a long time Liv was thinking to herself. Aidan was coming home for a week during his Christmas break. She had to go grocery shopping, she reminded herself to put on her to do list today.

Wallace had hit her last night. Liv looked at her face and saw she didn't have a bruise or black eye, thankfully. She knew Aidan would have the same reaction Big D had, when he'd seen it the last beating. *"That muthafucker needs to stop putting his hands on you," he'd growled, looking at her face.*

Liv told him she was used to it, and didn't want to talk about it anymore. Big D kissed her then, and made love to her. He always knew just what to say and do, to make her feel better. *"Why don't we get a place together?" he'd asked her.*

Liv finally made up her mind, and told him two days ago, that she would. She was going to wait until she told Aidan during his break, and then leave, after he was safely back at Jackie's.

Liv was happy her sister had married again. Pastor Lynch was a fine man. She'd met him, when she went to their wedding, last month. She'd met Aidan's fiancée Mariah. She was a beautiful girl.

Her mother looked familiar to Liv, but she couldn't place her at the time. She'd just gotten married three weeks before Jackie, to the other Pastor of the church. Liv was going to celebrate Aidan's birthday while he was home. He would be eighteen, and she was also going to tell him the truth about his father.

She didn't look forward to it, but he had a right to know. Liv hadn't seen DeSean in the last week. He came and went pretty much as he pleased these days. Wallace had beaten her the one time she forbade him and he'd told his father. Since then, she'd said nothing.

Liv wasn't telling DeSean of her plans. He was too close to his father. The key turning in the lock brought her out of her thoughts. Wallace entered the house. Liv could see he was in a foul mood. She would just go out to the store, and leave him alone. Maybe she could avoid any conflict.

Wallace looked at Liv hatefully. He had not had a good day. He'd gotten fired from his job. Marie told him she was pregnant with his baby, and gave him an ultimatum. DeSean had gotten locked up for dealing, which Liv probably didn't know, because he'd called Wallace at work, and not at home.

Liv didn't say a word, as he glared at her. She didn't want him to have a reason to hit her again.

"Where the fuck you going?" Wallace asked her acidly.

Liv looked down at the floor, and answered as evenly as she could.

"To the grocery store," she replied.

Wallace looked at her again. He had too much going on right now. He needed a beer. He walked over to the fridge, and opened it.

"Where's my beer?" he asked ominously.

Liv knew DeSean had to have taken the last one. She didn't drink beer.

"I don't know honey," she tried to sound loving. "But I'll get you more while I'm out," Liv finished, picking up her change purse.

Wallace slapped her hard, making her nose bleed.

"Bitch, you know I like my beer in the fridge when I get home!" he screamed at her.

Liv scrambled backwards crab-like against a wall. He began walking toward her.

"Please Wallace!" she began to scream, as he reached for her. "Oh God! Please! No!" Liv continued to plead, as he beat her mercilessly.

He'd finally spent himself, and looked at her. She wasn't moving. Wallace wasn't sure she was even breathing. He'd gone too far, and he knew it. He'd been so angry. "Liv?" he called, trying to rouse her now.

He bent down, and began to shake her. He shook her harder, and called her name loudly. Liv still didn't move. Wallace picked up the phone, and dialed 911, gave them the information, and left the front door wide open, as he walked away from the house. The ambulance arrived ten minutes later. They found Liv, crumpled against the living room, wall barely breathing.

"We have an African American female, badly beaten," the EMT was telling the hospital, as they prepared to take her to the emergency room. "Breath sounds are shallow and uneven," he continued. "Massive head trauma," he finished, looking at the other EMT. They exchanged knowing looks.

They'd seen this kind of domestic violence before, and the results were usually the same. They ended up hearing about a funeral. They got Liv loaded onto the stretcher, and put her into the ambulance. They left, heading for the hospital, sirens wailing.

A crowd had gathered outside the apartment, when the ambulance and the police arrived. Big D had been on his way to meet her. They were walking to the store together. He'd seen the commotion, and wandered over to investigate.

His heart sunk when he saw them take Liv, and put her in the ambulance. He was heading to the hospital now. Big D prayed she would be all right, but he had a bad feeling.

He knew DeSean was her son. He'd found out by accident one night, when Liv was complaining about him, and how he was getting involved in the wrong things. She described him, and called Cameron by name, then Big D knew exactly who she talking about. He would go down to the county lockup and tell him about her later.

She'd also given him her sister's number, just in case, Liv told him. *Guess she always knew huh?* Big D thought to himself, tiredly. He would call her after he got to the hospital and found out what shape Liv was in.

The ambulance arrived carrying Liv, and the EMTs wheeled her into the ER. Doctors cleaned her up, and checked her vitals. She was still clinging to life, but it didn't look good at all.

They took her up to do a scan, and saw she was bleeding in her brain. There was nothing they could do to stop that. They just had to hope the swelling would go down, and it would stop on its own.

They briefly thought about opening her skull, to allow her brain to expand, but decided to wait and see. The ER doctor went into the waiting room, to see if anyone was with the woman.

"Is there anyone here with Olivia Guthrie?" he asked.

Big D walked over to him, and told him he was.

"Are you a relative?" the doctor asked him.

"No," Big D replied. "I'm a good friend."

The doctor looked him over, and saw he seemed to be genuinely concerned. He didn't think this was the person who'd done this to her.

"Well," he began, talking to Big D. "If you know how to reach any of her relatives, you need to call them," he went on. "She's bleeding in her brain, and we honestly don't expect her to make it," he finished gently, looking at Big D evenly.

Big D thanked the doctor for his candor, and left to go make his calls. He was still in shock. He'd finally found a woman he truly wanted to be with, that he truly could say he loved, and she was dying.

He thought about Wallace, knowing he was responsible for this. *I'ma kill that muthafucker if she dies,* Big D thought coldly to himself. He pulled himself together. He still had to call her sister, and let her and the other son know.

Shay was visiting DeSean. She had been near his mom's house when the ambulance came. She'd seen it, and walked down the street. They were gone when Shay got there, but one of the neighbors told her what

happened. She felt bad having to tell him about it, with him being locked up and everything.
They'd been together now for the last couple months, ever since they'd been together that morning in the kitchen. She'd thought about what he said, and decided to leave Big D alone.
Big D hadn't been mad when Shay told him she was getting out of the game. He told her it was all good, and he was glad she'd found someone to make her happy. Shay never told him it was DeSean. They still did business, and she didn't want to mess anything up.

DeSean was seated in front of her now, smiling. Shay picked up the phone, and he picked up the other.
"Hey baby," he said sweetly, still smiling at her.
She smiled back and told him hello.
"Sean," Shay said softly, and her look changed.
Oh shit, DeSean thought to himself, *she's gonna break up with me cause I'm in here now.*
"Baby, your mama is in the hospital," she told him quietly.

He was shocked. He was glad she wasn't leaving him, but this was just as bad.
"What happened?" he asked, already having the sinking feeling he knew.
"The neighbor said, her and your daddy got into it, and he beat her up pretty bad," She told him, looking him in the eye.
DeSean was hurt. He knew his dad slapped his mom around, but he never actually thought Wallace would hurt Liv.
"How bad is she?" he asked Shay.
"I honestly don't know baby," she told him.
DeSean asked her if she would go by the hospital and check.
"You know I will," Shay told him. "I'll come back, and let you know tonight," she finished, getting up to leave.

Visiting hours were over for now. He blew her a kiss and she smiled. DeSean watched her leave. Shay was the best decision he'd made. He was glad he'd approached her that day, and talked her into leaving Big D alone. She was pregnant. She'd told him right before they locked him up.

DeSean figured it would happen. They never used birth control when they made love. Shay thought he'd be mad, but he wasn't. DeSean was going to show everyone he did know how to be a man, and raise his child the right way. He'd wanted to tell his mother when he got out of here.

They were releasing him in a few days. They couldn't find any evidence, and were dropping the charges. The extra days were for a minor ticket he hadn't paid. *Things are gonna be different when I get outta here,* DeSean thought to himself, both about his life, and his mothers.

Big D dialed the number Liv had given him. A man answered, and he guessed it was her sister's husband.
"Hello, May I speak to Jackie Lynch please," Big D said, once the man greeted him.
"Certainly," Chris replied. "May I tell her whose calling?"
"Um, tell her it's a friend of Liv's," Big D told him.

Chris thought it was odd the man didn't want to give his name, but called his wife to the phone anyway.
"Who is it honey?" she asked him.
Chris just shrugged, and told her what he'd said.
"Hello?" Jackie answered.
She had a bad feeling about this. Why hadn't Liv called her herself.
"Hi, Mrs. Lynch," he spoke. "This is D. I'm a friend of Liv's, and she gave me your number."
"Hi D," Jackie said. "Is something wrong?" she asked, not wanting to hear the answer.

Big D took a deep breath.
"Yes, I'm afraid there is," he told her. "Liv has been hurt real bad and she's in the hospital," he continued "The doctors don't think she's gonna make it, and they wanted her family to come as quickly as possible."

Jackie screamed, and Chris ran to the phone. He took the receiver from her. She was hysterical. He was trying to comfort her, and talk at the same time.

Big D repeated what he'd told Jackie. Chris told him they were walking out the door right now. He held Jackie, and calmed her down.

"I can't tell Aidan," she whispered, still shocked. "What am I going to say to that child?"

Chris told Jackie he would tell Aidan. He needed her to go upstairs, and get a bag together for them. They needed to get to Virginia Beach, as soon as possible. Jackie looked at Chris and hugged him, silently thanking God again, for sending her this wonderful man.

She left to pack, and Chris left to go outside and find Aidan. Chris found him outside on the grass with Mariah.

"Hey Uncle Chris," Aidan greeted him, when he walked up to them.

"Hey Aidan," he said.

Mariah didn't like the look Pastor Lynch had. Something was wrong.

"Aidan," Chris began seriously. "Your mother is in the hospital," he told him, still looking at him evenly.

"She's been hurt badly, and is not expected to survive," he went on, ignoring the look on Aidan's face. "We're getting ready to leave within the hour to get to her. Please get a bag packed, so we can go."

Aidan was livid. He didn't have to ask. He knew exactly what had happened to his mother, and he knew exactly who had done it to her. *I'm going to kill Wallace if anything happens to her,* Aidan thought bitterly to himself, as he got up to go inside.

"Do you want me to come?" Mariah asked him.

Aidan looked at her. He didn't want her to see his mother like that. He didn't want Mariah to know what he was capable of, when he saw his stepfather.

"No baby," he told her gently, hugging her close to him. "I'll be alright. Aunt Jackie and Uncle Chris will be there," Aidan finished, kissing her softly.

Mariah looked at him, and asked if he were sure. He told her he was. Aidan kissed Mariah again, passionately, and told her he loved her. He left her in the yard, as he headed to the house.

Mariah was heartbroken for him. She knew how much Aidan loved his Mother. She'd met her when Jackie and Chris got married. Liv was such a sweet lady. Why would anyone want to hurt her? Mariah sighed.

23

Big D was still at the hospital when they arrived. He recognized Jackie and Chris from the wedding pictures Liv had shown him.
"Hey, I'm D," he said to Jackie.
She gave him a small smile, and returned his greeting, introducing him to Chris.
"The doctor will be back in a little while," he told her.

Just then Aidan walked in. He'd been parking the car, and had just made his way to the ICU waiting area. Big D looked at the boy, and had a flashback.
"Damn, he looks just like Devastator, gray eyes and all," he said softly, under his breath.
"Excuse me?" Chris said, looking at him.
"Oh, nothing, just thinking out loud," Big D covered.
Chris walked ahead to catch up with Jackie, who'd gone to the nurse's station.

Aidan saw the man looking intently at him, and walked over to him.
"You're D?" Aidan asked, as he looked him over.
"Yeah," Big D said simply.
Aidan smiled. "My mom told me a lot about you," he said.
If he had dimples they'd almost be twins, Big D thought, once again picturing his lost friend.
"Your mama is one sweet woman," Big D said honestly. He'd fallen hard for Liv, and wanted more than anything to make her happy, and give her a good life. It obviously wasn't meant to be.
"You made her very happy these last few months. I'm grateful for that," Aidan continued, still looking at Big D intently. "I only wish she'd left with you a long time ago," he finished sadly, looking around at the ICU waiting room.

Big D felt the same way. He'd pleaded with Liv to leave last month. He'd gotten the place for them, and he had money enough to take care of them. Liv kept putting him off. *If only she'd come with me then,* he thought to himself, dismayed at the current situation.

Jackie and Chris returned to the waiting room, with the doctor in tow. He gave them all an update on Liv's condition, saying they didn't expect her to make it through the night.
"Who's Aidan?" the doctor inquired.
"I am," the young man said quietly.
"She's been asking for you, as she goes in and out," he replied. "If you like, you can come sit with her for a little while. She may wake up for a moment or two," he finished, looking at Aidan sympathetically.

Aidan followed him to his mother's room. The doctor warned him of her appearance before letting him in. He still wasn't prepared for what he saw. His mother was almost unrecognizable Wallace had beaten her so badly. He sat down by her bed, and held her hand. Liv immediately stirred.
"Aidan?" she said, almost inaudibly.
He bent close to her ear, so she could hear him.
"Yes mama, it's me," Aidan said softly.
Liv was struggling to breathe, as she tried to speak.
"Don't talk mama," he told her.

She squeezed his hand tightly, and started speaking. "There's a box in my closet," Liv said haltingly, stopping to breath between each word. "For you only," she went on "Your father's in there," she continued. "He never knew about you. Be a good boy, and a good husband to Mariah."

Liv had a coughing fit, and Aidan didn't think she would survive it. Liv managed to catch her breath again, and look at him with her one open eye.
"I love you, and DeSean," she said softly, a single tear escaping and rolling down the side of her face.
"We love you too, mama," Aidan replied softly, trying to hold back the tears himself.

Liv relaxed, and the monitor alarm sounded. The doctor and nurses came in quickly, checking her vitals. Aidan was ushered out of the room, as they worked to save her.

They were all in the waiting room, when the doctor came out and informed them that in spite of all they'd done, she'd died. Chris held Jackie as she cried, and tried to accept what she'd just been told.

Big D was sitting in a chair trying not to cry himself, anger and rage building up in him, every minute more that he sat thinking about Liv never coming to him again. He looked over at Aidan, and his blood almost froze. The boy had the coldest look he'd ever seen, at least in the last eighteen years, since he'd looked into Devastators face.

That's got to be his son! Big D thought to himself, recalling a conversation he'd had with Liv.

"You're son's are as different as night and day," he'd said to her.

She'd laughed, and told him they had two different fathers. Aidan's father died before he was born was all Liv would say about him. Now sitting here looking at him, Big D knew. Dezi Gianni had fathered the young man sitting in that chair. He wondered if the boy knew who his father really was. Big D wanted to talk to Aidan, and tell him about his dad, but that would have to wait. Right now, they had to unfortunately talk about burying his mother.

Shay had just made it to the ICU, and was standing around the corner, when she heard the doctor come out and call Liv's family together. She'd heard him say she was dead. *How am I going to tell Sean his mother is dead?* Shay thought to herself, the sadness of it sinking it.

She saw his brother, recognizing him from Sean's description of him. She guessed that was the aunt and uncle he'd told her about. They didn't have any other family they were close too. They had distant relatives here and there, but none as close as the ones they'd gone to visit.

Shay saw Big D, and finally realized Liv was the woman he'd been seeing all this time. She felt bad for him too. Shay knew from DeSean, he'd loved this woman and wanted to move-in with her. Shay quietly left the hospital, heading back to the jail where she would have to tell DeSean the horrible news.

"I'm going to take Jackie back to the hotel to rest for awhile," Chris told Aidan.
"Then you and I will go about making arrangements for your mother," he finished still looking at him evenly.
Aidan simply nodded, and told Chris he was going to the house.
"OK, give me directions, and I'll come on over once I get your Aunt settled," Chris told him again.
Aidan wrote the directions, and gave them to Chris, who then left with Jackie. Big D walked up to Aidan.
"Will you let me know if you need help with anything, and when the service will be?" he asked.
Aidan told him he would, and asked for his number, which Big D promptly supplied.
"Thanks again," he told him softly.
Big D looked at Aidan quizzically.
"For making these last few months of her life, wonderful for her again," he told him.
Big D shook his head that he understood, gave him a small smile, and headed for the elevator. *He had some business to take care of. He needed to find that no account husband of hers, and settle the debt he owed him,* Big D thought to himself, as he boarded the elevator.

Aidan sighed deeply. *This has got to be the worst day of my life,* He thought to himself, as he also headed out of the hospital, back to the home they'd lived in.

Shay was back in the visiting area waiting for DeSean. She still didn't know how she was going to tell him about his mother. She thought about the child she herself carried.

Shay was glad DeSean hadn't been mad. She really wanted this baby, and she really loved DeSean. He'd been so good to her, and treated her like she was his queen. He'd never hit her, like his father did his mother. He'd talked about it, and even threatened her, but in the end he always walked away, or just left her alone. Shay shuddered, thinking of the pain his mother must have endured before her death.

She was so deep in thought DeSean had to tap the glass, to get her attention. Shay jumped, and then looked at him. He was looking at her intently, waiting on her to pick up her phone. She picked up the receiver, and DeSean began to question her.

"Did you go by the hospital?" he asked.

She shook her head yes.

"So? How is she?" he asked again.

She had to tell him, but she surely didn't want to. Shay took a really deep breath. DeSean steeled himself for what he was about to hear.

"Your mama passed away, a few minutes before I got there," Shay said softly, looking right at him.

She saw the shock and the hurt in his face immediately.

"Are you sure?" DeSean asked quietly, looking ready to cry.

"Yes," Shay replied softly. "Your brother, and Aunt and Uncle were there too."

DeSean was glad for that at least. Liv hadn't died without anyone being there that cared about her.

"What about my dad," he asked, already knowing the answer.

"No, I didn't see him," she replied.

DeSean figured as much. He was the one that had killed her. *I'm going to find him and pay him back for this when I get out of here,* DeSean thought to himself angrily.

"I need you to go by the house, and tell my brother, where I am," he told her.

Shay nodded that she would and got up to leave as visiting hours were once again over.

"I'm sorry baby," she told DeSean before she left.
He gave Shay a small smile, and told her he loved her and their baby. She smiled, and told him they loved him too. Then she was gone.

DeSean returned to his cell. He was completely devastated by his mother's death, even more so, that his father had killed her. *I never believed he would hurt her like this,* DeSean thought to himself. He was thankful that he'd gotten a hold on his own anger, and learned from his father's example, not to put his hands on women anymore.
He would never hurt Shay the way Wallace had hurt his mother. DeSean thought of his mother, and how badly he'd sometimes treated her. The guilt and hurt set in, and he began to cry.

Aidan arrived at the house and entered. He cringed in horror at the blood on the wall, and the various medical paraphernalia lying around. *Damn!* he thought to himself, *this place looks like a war zone.*

Aidan walked straight into the bedroom, and looked in her closet. He found the box she'd told him about. He needed to know now more than ever, about his father. If he was still alive, Aidan wanted to meet him. He wanted to try and have a relationship with him, to know if he had other brothers and sisters. Aidan wanted to know why he acted the way he did sometimes. Why he felt the way he did sometimes.

Aidan placed the box on the bed in his old room. He hadn't felt comfortable anywhere else. He opened the box, and found the information he'd waited all his life for.

Aidan found some of his baby things, his hospital birth certificate with his footprints on them, a lock of hair from his first haircut. He smiled at the things his mother kept. Then he found the scrapbook. It was tied with a blue ribbon, and had his name on it.

Aidan untied the ribbon and opened the book. There were pictures of him as a baby, pictures of his mother while she was pregnant. These made him smile again. Then he turned the page, and found the articles.

Aidan looked at the man in the photo under the caption. This was his father. The articles talked about a crime cartel and the demise of its creator. His father was a criminal, a deadly and vicious killer, according to the articles Aidan was reading.

He looked at the dates on the articles. They were all written months before he was born. *That's why she said he never knew. He was already dead,* Aidan thought to himself. He continued to look through the book, finding more photographs of the man who'd fathered him, realizing his mother had given him his fathers name too, his middle name being the same as his father's last name. Aidan turned another page, and almost dropped the book.

There was a picture of his father with a woman. The woman looked almost exactly like Mariah. Aidan read the caption and found out the woman in this picture was Kayla DeWitt. Now she was Kayla Bradford, Mariah's mother. He read the article and found out she'd been dating his father. Aidan also saw mention of the FBI agent that killed him in the shootout, Mariah's father Donovan Black.

Aidan guessed that was how he and her mother had met. He was reeling from the information he'd just learned. Aidan wished he could talk to Kayla about his father. He needed to know so much more than these articles were telling him. He heard a knock at the door, interrupting his thoughts. Aidan went to see who it was.

He saw the girl standing there, but didn't recognize her. "Hi, can I help you?" Aidan asked her amiably enough.

Shay smiled, and told him who she was. She then told him where DeSean was, and that he'd sent her.

"Does he know about mama?" he asked, looking at her evenly.

Shay shook her head yes.

"When will he get out?" Aidan inquired again.

Shay told him, DeSean would be released in two days. Aidan thanked her for coming, and letting him know. He also thanked her for telling DeSean. She smiled, and told him he was welcome, and then once again left him alone with his thoughts.

Chris arrived shortly after that. He too was shocked by the brutality of the scene when he arrived. He immediately cleaned the wall, and floors, as best he could, then he and Aidan began to make arrangements for his mother.

Big D was waiting outside Marie's apartment. He'd seen Wallace before, and followed him here one day. Liv didn't know it, but he'd made it a point to see her old man. *Always wanna know what the competition looks like,* he'd thought to himself that day, as he followed her home. Now Big D was waiting for Wallace to appear. *I know that low-life scum is up in there,* he fumed to himself.

Big D had his switchblade with him, and he was planning on carving Wallace up good with it. He'd killed the love of his life and Big D wanted payback. He thought about her oldest son again. *I've got to talk to that boy.*

He needs to know who he really is, he finished thinking, as he saw Wallace ease around the corner, heading to Marie's front door. *I knew that dog would show up sooner or later,* Big D thought to himself again. He saw Wallace let himself in. Big D knew Marie wasn't there, he'd seen her leave earlier headed to work.

Big D stepped off the curb, and headed to the door. He didn't care if anyone saw him or not. His mind was on one thing. Arriving he put his ear to the door, and listened. He heard Wallace talking, and assumed he was on the phone.

Big D couldn't hear what was being said, but he sounded agitated. *Probably trying to find out how to get outta town right quick,* Big D thought again. He knew Wallace wouldn't open the door if he knocked.

He would be too scared and paranoid to do that, so Big D had to figure another way to get in. He looked around and saw the units had big bedroom windows. He knew Wallace was in the living room, because he could hear him loudly.

Big D went around to the back of the apartment. Fortunately for him, she'd left the window open. He climbed onto the air conditioning unit, and hoisted himself up. Big D easily slid himself in the window.

He heard Wallace still talking. "I need to get outta here now man!" he was saying angrily, to the other party on the phone. "The folks are gonna be looking for me!" he went on. "I didn't mean to kill her man. It just happened!!" he was explaining still. "Look, are you gonna help me or not?!" he finally finished, listening to the response from the other person.

Big D walked up behind him, flipping the switchblade out, and locking the blade. Wallace was so engrossed he never heard it click. He never heard Big D walk up behind him.

Big D looked down at him from behind, grabbed his hair, and pulled his head back, exposing his throat. Big D slit it in one fluid motion. Blood gushed from the exposed jugular, as Big D held him allowing the flow to continue.

Wallace was trying to get up, but couldn't because of the angle Big D held him. Wallace was helpless. Big D was looking into his eyes as he died.

"This is for all the pain you've ever given Liv, and for taking her away from all of us that loved her," he told him coldly, as Wallace gasped his last few breaths of air.

After he was sure he was dead, Big D released his head and let Wallace slump over onto the couch. He cleaned his knife and left him there, going back out the way he'd come in, wiping the sill, and anything else he'd touched while he was there.

He thought of her as he walked home.
"It's all good now baby," Big D said aloud, hoping Liv could hear.
He thought about Aidan again, and made a mental note to go see him tomorrow.
"A man ought to know where he came from," Big D said aloud again, as he walked into his own apartment, and closed the door.

24

These had been the longest three days of his life. Aidan and Chris made all the arrangements for Liv, and now they were here at the service. Aidan looked around at all the people who'd come out.

Some he recognized, some he didn't. DeSean had gotten out and come home yesterday. They'd talked, and he'd found his younger brother very much a changed man.

Aidan found out about him and Cameron, and how he'd ended up in jail. He'd been spared the worst of it, because Cameron had been carrying all the dope, and they'd arrested them blocks apart. Cameron was facing a lot of time, and there was no deal being offered.

Aidan was thankful his younger brother wasn't going to spend the majority of his adult life, in prison. DeSean had gone immediately down to register for his GED classes after he was released. Aidan knew his mother would be proud of DeSean, and told him so.

It was a miserable day. It was misting lightly, and the wind was blowing hard, making the mist sting, adding to the unseasonable cold for this time of year. They were standing at the graveside, and Aidan was saying goodbye. He'd heard they found Wallace dead at some woman's apartment. The police thought she'd killed him, and were still investigating it.

Aidan didn't care who'd killed him, he was just glad he was dead. His only sorrow was not being able to watch Wallace take his last breath himself. He'd taken their mother from them, and Aidan had nothing but hate for him.

"Say youngblood," Big D said, as he stood beside Aidan looking at her grave.

"Hey D," the young man replied.

Big D looked at him evenly, and then spoke.

"Did you ever ask your mama about your daddy?" he asked.

Aidan looked at him quizzically. *What an odd question,* he thought.
"No. I never got the chance," he told him.
Big D nodded, but didn't say anything else.
"Do you know something about him?" Aidan asked him.
"I'm not sure we'd be talking about the same person, since your mother never told you anything," Big D said matter-of-factly.
Aidan looked at him again, and then spoke.
"If you're talking about Dezi Gianni, then we'd be talking about the same person," he said slowly, watching Big D's reaction.
Big D smiled slightly.
"Yeah, we'd be talking about the same person," he replied.
Aidan was elated. Here was someone who actually knew his father and could tell him more than biased newspaper articles.
"When do you wanna talk?" Aidan asked him.
"Whenever you're ready to know, youngblood," Big D returned.
They agreed to meet later that night. Big D gave him his address, and told him to stop by. Aidan returned to the waiting car, and went back to the hotel. They were flying out in the morning.

He'd talked to Mariah before the service. *I miss her so much. I can't wait to get back to her,* Aidan thought to himself, on the ride back to the hotel. He also couldn't wait to talk to Big D tonight, and find out what he needed to know about his father.

Big D was smoking a joint and thinking about today. It was almost more than he could stand, watching them bury his Liv. His only satisfaction came from knowing Wallace was dead too.

He was waiting for Aidan to come by. Big D knew he would have a lot of questions, and he hoped he could answer them all for him. Big D knew how Liv felt about

Aidan knowing who his father was, since they'd talked about it at length.
He just hadn't known then that Dezi Gianni was the father she was talking about. Big D figured this was the least he could do. The knock at the door brought him out of his thoughts. He opened the door, and motioned Aidan inside.

Big D offered him some smoke, but he declined.
"You want something to drink?" he asked him now.
"Coke if you got it," Aidan replied.
Big D got him the drink out of the fridge, and headed back to the living room.
"So?" Big D asked. "What do you know about Dezi?"

Aidan sighed, and told him nothing much past what he read in the articles, his mama saved for him. Big D nodded, and began to tell him about back in the day, and about The Clique. They talked for the next three hours, Aidan asking questions, and Big D trying his best to answer them.
"Was he as cold blooded as they say in these articles?" Aidan asked again, intrigued with his father's ruthless reputation.
"Only when he had to be," Big D answered. "Devastator was a businessman. He did what he had to do, to secure his business."

Aidan asked about the nickname, and Big D explained. Aidan shook his head and smiled slightly. His father was definitely a force to be reckoned with from what Big D told him. Now he understood just a little better why he was, the way he was.

He took the newspaper article out of his pocket, and showed it to him.
"What can you tell me about her?" Aidan asked, referring to the picture of Kayla.
Big D looked at the picture of the woman and smiled.
"Yeah, I remember her," he said. "She was the love of his life," he told the boy, looking at him evenly. "Devastator loved this woman to death, literally," he went on.

"That's how they finally got him. He'd come here to get her, and the baby, so they could be together," Big D finished, still thinking wistfully about it.
"What baby?" Aidan asked guardedly.
"They'd had a child together," Big D replied. "I never got a chance to see the baby, but he'd told me all about it as he was coming back here," he finished.
Aidan was getting ill. He thought about Mariah. She was the only child Mrs. Bradford had.

He thought about those dimples she had, that he loved so much. His father had the same ones. *Fuck no,* he thought to himself, *have I been screwing my sister?!* He was getting sicker by the moment. He'd heard enough for now.

Aidan looked at his watch, and told Big D he had to go. "Thanks for everything man," he told him as he left. Big D hugged the boy, and told him to be cool.
"Remember who you are man," Big D told Aidan, as he closed the door behind him.

Big D turned the letter over in his hands after the young man left. He'd gotten it today. He smiled again thinking of the contents, as he headed to his bedroom to lie down.

Mariah was anxiously awaiting Aidan's returned. She wanted to make sure he was OK. Jaz had flown down for the service, but he'd told her not to come. Mariah asked him why, and Aidan told her he just didn't want her too. She'd been a little hurt, but she understood he wanted to say goodbye to his mother on his own.

Jaz called her from the airport a little while ago, and she was expecting Aidan to call soon. He'd been very distant when she talked to him earlier before their flight. Mariah chalked it up to grief, and let it pass.

Aidan was staring out of the window, wondering how he was going to face Mariah. He needed to get to her mother, and fast. He knew Mariah would want to see him, want to kiss, and make love.

He just couldn't touch her, not until he knew for sure about her parentage. Aidan tried not to think of them together. He got ill every time he did. It was a repulsive thought to think he'd been bedding his own sister all these months, and asked her to marry him.

Please, he began to pray silently, *let Mrs. Bradford tell me it's all a mistake.* Aidan finished making a mental note to call her as soon as he got home.

"Hey, we're here," Jaz said, bringing him back.

They were pulling into the driveway. Aidan had been so preoccupied he hadn't noticed. They all got out of the car, and headed inside.

"I'm going to lie down for a while," Jackie said tiredly. Chris told her he would join her, and they left together. Jaz told Aidan she was going up to her room too.

After they left, and he was alone, Aidan dialed Kayla's number. She and Mariah had separate lines, and right now he was thankful for that. He needed to see her before he talked to Mariah.

"Hello?" she answered.

Aidan took a deep breath, and proceeded. "Hi Mrs. Bradford," he replied.

"Oh, hello Aidan," Kayla told him.

Aidan could hear the smile in her voice.

"Mrs. Bradford I really need to see you, and talk to you," he said evenly.

Kayla thought it was strange that he would call, and she couldn't imagine what he needed to see her about, but she agreed.

"All right Aidan," she said pleasantly. "When you would like to come over?"

He thought about it, and decided they needed to meet somewhere else. He didn't want to chance running into Mariah, not yet.

"Can we meet somewhere besides your house?" Aidan asked her.

Now she was really perplexed.

"Well, yes I suppose," Kayla replied again. "Where would you like to go?"
Aidan thought for a moment.
"How about Gamby Park?" he asked.
He knew it was where they were building their new home. It was quiet, and they could have plenty of privacy to talk.
"That'll be fine Aidan," she told him. "When?"
He needed to see her right now. He hoped she was free.
"Umm, how about in an hour?" Aidan asked, holding his breath.

Kayla was completely confused now. He sounded anxious, like there was something weighing heavily on him. She thought about her day. She had time, so she would go see what had him so distraught.
"That's fine Aidan," Kayla replied. "I'll meet you there."

He breathed a sigh of relief, and told her thanks, as they hung up. He turned to take his bag upstairs, when the bell rang. Aidan went to the door and opened it, finding Mariah standing there smiling.

25

"Hi baby," she said sweetly, coming in and throwing her arms around his neck.
Mariah tried to kiss him, and he pulled away.
"What's wrong?" she asked, hurt that he'd rejected her.

Aidan didn't want to hurt Mariah. He just had to know the deal before they did anything else he might live to regret. "Nothings wrong Mariah," he told her.
She knew that was a lie, because he'd called her by name. Aidan seldom did that.
"Are you sure?" Mariah asked him softly, looking him in the eye.
Aidan had to look away. "I just need to take care of some things right now, and be by myself, OK?" he told her, looking back at her evenly.

Mariah didn't understand. Why was he being so distant and cold to her?
"Have I done something wrong Aidan?" she asked quietly, almost in tears.
He didn't want to make her cry, but he couldn't be with her yet. Not until he knew for sure. He took a deep breath.

"Baby," Aidan began, forcing himself to call her that. "Its nothing you've done. I swear. I just need some space right now, OK?" he lied, hoping she believed him.
Mariah still wasn't convinced. There was definitely something going on with him.
"OK," she said simply, as she turned to leave.

Aidan watched her leave, and go down the highway. *I'm so sorry Mariah,* he thought to himself, as he headed out to meet Kayla. *Please let her tell me what I want to hear,* he pleaded silently, as he drove.

Mariah was hurt. *What did I do,* she asked herself. Even though Aidan told her it wasn't her fault, it had to be. They were fine before he left. Why would he be acting so differently now? *What happened while he was home,* she wondered.

His old girlfriend, Mariah thought becoming even more hurt and jealous. Maybe Aidan and his girlfriend had reconnected and he wanted to end their relationship now. The thought crushed her as she drove aimlessly for a while, finally finding herself at the cemetery. She parked, got out, and headed for her fathers grave. She needed to talk to him.

Mariah was surprised to find Mrs. Alston there. Sandra didn't see her, so Mariah didn't interrupt. Mariah stood and watched her, while she sat there at his grave. "Donovan, I miss you so much." Sandra was saying. "Mariah is such a beautiful young woman now. You would be so proud of her," she went on.
"I only wish she and David had stayed together," she sighed heavily. "Now, not only have I lost the man I've always loved, but now I've lost any link to him I've ever had." She was crying softly now.

Mariah was stunned. Had her father and Mrs. Alston had an affair? *No,* she thought to herself, *her father would never do that to her mother.* Mrs. Alston was speaking again, as Mariah turned her attention to her. "If only we'd stayed together after college," she said softly, drying her tears. "I love you," Sandra said simply, as she turned to leave.

Mariah stepped behind the large tree she was standing next to, and Sandra passed by her unseen. She stood there, taking in what she'd witnessed. Now Mariah understood why Mrs. Alston was always so loving and protective of her. She'd wanted Mariah to be her child, from her father.

She finally walked over to her fathers resting place herself now, sitting down where Sandra had been moments earlier, and began to talk to him. Mariah never heard David walk up.
He knelt down beside her, as she lay on the stone crying. David picked her up, and pulled her to him.
"Shhh," he told Mariah, trying to soothe her. "It's OK."

Mariah was taken aback at his presence at first, but she hugged him back tightly now, needing desperately to be held. David held her until she'd spent herself. He wiped her tears, and gave her tissue to blow her nose.

"What are you doing here?" Mariah asked him quietly, after she composed herself.

David looked at her, taking in how beautiful she still was to him.

"I come out here a lot," he answered simply, not telling her he'd followed her after seeing her driving through town.

Mariah looked at him quizzically.

"Why?" she asked.

David smiled, as he sighed.

"Its peaceful, and I talk to your dad sometimes," he lied.

Mariah didn't know that. She was glad he'd come today. She needed a friend right now.

"What's the matter?" David asked, as he walked back to her car with her.

"Nothing really," she replied.

David looked at her, and knew she was lying. Mariah was a terrible liar. It always showed all over her face.

"I thought we were friends," he said quietly, looking at her intently.

"We are," Mariah replied.

"Then tell me the truth," David said.

She took a deep breath, and looked him in the eye.

"It's personal," Mariah replied, and looked away.

David knew then, something was going on with her and Aidan and he was elated.

"You mean it's about you, and your fiancé?" he told her smoothly, showing no emotion.

Mariah looked at David closely. They'd been getting along pretty well and he hadn't said or done anything close to suggesting they get back together. Even now, he wasn't acting jealous, or being mean spirited. He seemed to be genuinely concerned about her.

"Yes," she said softly.

David had to play this right. He still loved her, and he would take any opportunity offered to be with her. Hopefully he could ease her into a break up with Aidan and then the two of them could get back on track, the way they were supposed to be.
"You wanna discuss it over some ice cream?" he said smiling.
Mariah laughed, and it brightened his day.
"OK," she told him, turning to her car to follow him.
He stopped her, and told her he'd drive, and then bring her back to get her car after they were done.
"That's fine," Mariah replied, smiling at him again.
David's heart was jumping for joy. He was going to let Mariah talk as long as she needed, glad for the chance to spend some time with her.

Kayla arrived at the house site to find Aidan waiting for her. He looked nervous and upset. *I wonder what's so urgent,* she was thinking, as she exited her car.
"Hi, Mrs. Bradford," Aidan greeted her. "Thank you so much for meeting me, on such short notice."
"Is everything all right Aidan?" Kayla asked him, concerned.
"I'm hoping it will be after we talk," he said simply.
They walked into a semi-finished section of the house, and sat on the stairs.
"What is this about Aidan?" Kayla asked uncertainly.
Aidan wasn't sure how to get started.

He needed the information this woman could give him, but he didn't know how to ask her for it.
"Mrs. Bradford," he began tentatively.
Kayla gave Aidan her full attention. She could sense he had something serious on his mind.
"I need your help with something that's very important not only to me, but to my future with Mariah," he said, looking at her now.

Kayla continued to watch Aidan intently, waiting for him to speak again.

"I found out while I was burying my mother, how I got my middle name, and why," he told her.
Kayla was perplexed. *What did that have to do with her and Mariah?*
"Go on," she told him gently.
Aidan took a deep breath, and looked her in the eye.
"My middle name is Gianni," he told her.

Kayla gasped, putting her hand over her mouth, to stifle the cry she felt rising up. Aidan saw her and knew she remembered. Kayla had to take a few deep breaths and collect herself, before she could speak again.
"What do you want to know Aidan?" she said quietly, letting her mind travel back almost twenty years, to her time with Dezi.
Aidan didn't waste any time getting to his point.
"I need to know if Mariah is my sister?" he blurted.

Kayla looked at him, and understood finally his urgency. She took a deep breath, but didn't speak. Aidan was practically beside himself. Her taking this long to answer him couldn't be a good thing.

Kayla knew the young man was anxious, but she was thinking. *He's Dezi's son,* she was thinking to herself somewhat elated at the thought. *What if he's like his father? Would he hurt Mariah?* Kayla was still thinking the fear creeping in now.

Would he make Mariah's life a nightmare, like hers had been? She didn't want her only child to go through that. She knew Mariah loved Aidan, and he seemed to adore her. She'd never seen him act like the darker side of Dezi. Kayla was confused. She didn't know what to do.

Aidan continued to look at her and see the torment she was going through. *Fuck, it must be true,* he assumed, jumping up. Kayla saw him, and turned to him.
"It's OK Mrs. Bradford," Aidan said, backing away from her. "I know the answer."
Kayla got up to follow after him.
"Aidan please wait!" she called after him.
He stopped long enough for her to catch up.

"Aidan, I'm sorry it took me so long to answer you," Kayla told him. "This is a part of my life I've fought hard to put behind me," she went on. "But simply put, to answer your question, No. Mariah is not your sister," she went on. "Donovan Black is her natural father."

Aidan breathed a deep sigh of relief. He loved Mariah, and he didn't want to believe he'd done something so twisted.

"Mrs. Bradford?" he questioned.

Kayla looked at him expectantly.

"Tell me why this part of your life upsets you so much," he implored, "I never knew my father, and I'd love to learn as much about him as I can," Aidan finished and hoped she would answer him.

Kayla took a deep breath, and sat down.

"About twenty years ago I met a handsome, exciting, and dangerous man. He was charming and intelligent, and treated me like a queen," she said softly, looking into space as she talked, the love she still felt for Dezi coming to the surface. "We had a wonderful romance in the beginning," she continued.

"I knew he did some things that were illegal, but he always kept me shielded from that part of his life. I didn't find out about the true extent of his activities, until I met Mariah's father," Kayla continued looking at Aidan now, tears forming in her eyes.

"He and I fell in love while he was investigating Dezi," she finished taking another deep breath.

"He was arrested as he was trying to abduct me, and take me out of the country," she told him. "Black was the one who arrested Dezi, and afterwards he and I began dating seriously," she went on. "Dezi made a deal with the prosecution almost four months later, and got out."

"I was terrified of him at this point, and I thought he would come after me to hurt me. I'd also just found out I was pregnant," she was crying softly now. "I left, not telling anyone where I was," Kayla stopped to wipe her tears.

Aidan's heart was breaking watching her suffer through this story, but he was also grateful she was sharing it with him.

"Black found me when Mariah was two days old," she went on looking at him again. "He came to the hospital, and fell in love with her on sight," she smiled, and Aidan smiled back.

Kayla sighed. "I had to break his heart, and tell him she wasn't his."

Aidan sighed gently, feeling her pain

"He asked me for a paternity test, and I asked him why. I thought she was Dezi's child," Kayla started again. "They had the same dimples. He was insistent though, so we had the test done," she continued.

"Dezi found me too eventually," Kayla continued her story. "He'd come to my house, and was waiting for me when I got home. He held Mariah for the first time, and he too fell in love with her immediately," she went on. "He'd come to take us away. Someplace out of the country, because he knew the FBI was on his trail. Black had come too, and they'd surrounded the house," Kayla took another deep breath, before continuing.

Aidan was listening intently. This was something he'd been waiting all his life to find out.

"We managed to get Mariah out safely," she started. "I'd just gotten on the ladder to get out myself, when Dezi came into the bedroom, and lunged at Black. They fought, as his partner pulled me off the ladder," she went on.

"I don't know exactly what happened, or what was said, since Black never talked about it after that day. But it ended with Dezi being killed, and him being shot in the shoulder," Kayla continued, even though she looked as if she couldn't take saying another word.

"I went to Dezi's funeral. I needed closure, and of course, I still thought he was Mariah's father," Kayla said. "When I returned, Black pulled me aside, and gave me three envelopes."

"I opened the first, and it contained a picture of a woman with a baby," she continued breathing deeply. "The second had an adoption certificate, for him," Kayla said, looking at Aidan closely.

Mariah's father was adopted? I wonder if she knows that, he thought, as he continued to listen.

"The third was the paternity test result. I didn't want to see that. I already knew what it said, so I started to fold it, when Black finally told me to actually look at it," Kayla took Aidan's hands into her own.

"Like I told you before, Donovan Black is Mariah's father," she said softly. "She is not your sister. She got those dimples from Black's natural mother," Kayla told him, finally spent.

Aidan's mind was spinning from everything he'd just learned. Things were much clearer for him. He understood his father's possessiveness with Kayla, and his own with Mariah. Seemed he and his father had very similar tastes in women.

He was sorry his father had been killed; he would have loved to have seen the great man in action. He wanted to experience the power Dezi obviously wielded.

"I love your daughter with all my heart, Mrs. Bradford," he told her honestly, still looking at her.

Kayla smiled, and told him she believed him.

"I have to go now Aidan," she told him, rising to leave.

He thanked her again for telling him the truth, as he watched her head for her car, and leave.

Aidan needed to call Mariah and see her. He knew he'd hurt her earlier, and he needed to make it up to her. He could now, without guilt or fear, because he finally knew the truth.

Talking to Aidan brought it all flooding back for Kayla. All the days of stress and agony, wondering who'd fathered her child. She'd been excited at first then scared. She'd thought about how she'd been with both Dezi, and Black, within a weeks time period.

Kayla remembered Dezi and his temper. She thought about the scene she'd had with him at the abortion clinic. He would have killed her, if he knew Mariah wasn't his. She shivered at the thought.

Kayla remembered how loving and kind Black had been, and how much she'd enjoyed making love with him. She thought about Dezi, and how out of control he'd gotten at the end. He'd scared her to death. He'd drugged her, and tried to kidnap her.

She didn't want Mariah to go through what she went through. *He's not Dezi though,* she thought to herself, as she really thought about their love affair in earnest.

Kayla continued to reminisce, remembering what an attractive man Dezi was. Tall, with those beautiful teeth, and pool deep dimples, he was absolutely breathtaking. Kayla thought of the first time they'd made love together, how he'd had her favorite dinner, and the rose petals, and the perfect drawn bath.

She thought of how he'd touched her, and caressed her, and gave her pleasure upon pleasure. Kayla found herself aroused again at the thought. *He really was wonderful at one time,* she thought sighing deeply.

She also remembered then, the death and destruction that came from being with him. It still pained her to think about Taea after all these years. Jackie reminded her so much of her. Kayla chuckled at the thought.

Both of his friends were dead too. Then Dezi himself had been killed. That was a very dark, and painful, part of her life and she was scared to death now, knowing Aidan was Dezi's son. Kayla just hoped and prayed with everything in her, that Mariah wouldn't pay for her sin, and mistakes of the past.

26

David was having a wonderful time with Mariah. They were enjoying their ice cream, and she was laughing at the story he'd just told her.
"Feeling better now?" he asked her.
Mariah smiled, and told him, yes she was.
"You want to go to my house for a little while?" David asked, hoping she'd say yes. "We can check out some DVD's, or just chill and talk some more," he added, still waiting on her answer.

Mariah thought about calling Aidan, but decided against it. She didn't want to be rejected again. If he was going to break-up with her, then he'd have to do it when he made the call, not her.
"Sure we can go for a little while," Mariah replied. "Are we going to disturb your mother?"
David knew his mother was at her weekly bridge game, besides which, Sandra would never consider Mariah a disturbance.
"She's not there," he told her simply.
David was thrilled Mariah was coming. They got into the car, and headed for the house.

Arriving shortly afterward, they entered the house sitting down to talk.
"Where have you decided to go to school?" he asked her as they watched a movie in the den.
"Probably Duke, I guess," Mariah said wistfully. David knew she was thinking about her father. He'd graduated from there, before going to the Academy, and on to the FBI. Mariah wanted to do that too, it was her dream. His dream was to be there by her side when she did.
"Good choice," David told her, as he poked her in the side.
Mariah laughed, and told him to quit it. Her phone rang just as David was about to tickle her. Mariah laughed and moved away.
"Hello?" she answered.

Aidan smiled.
"Hey," he said back.

Mariah smiled. She was glad to hear from him now that he sounded like himself again. David saw her, and knew it was Aidan. He watched her intently as she talked.
"I'm sorry about earlier baby," Aidan said simply.
Mariah smiled again.
"I was wondering if we could spend some time?" he asked her.

She definitely wanted that. "Sure, I'll be there in about an hour okay?" Mariah replied.
Aidan told her he'd be waiting.
"Baby?" he queried.
"Yes, Aidan," Mariah replied.
"I love you," he told her softly, and disconnected before she could reply.
Mariah turned to David.
"Will you please take me back to the cemetery, to pick up my car?" she asked.

David was crushed. He thought this was the end of her and Aidan, and he'd worked hard gaining her trust all this time. He wanted her to stay here with him.
"Sure, just give me a few, OK?" he told her.
He couldn't show his true feelings. That would make Mariah not talk to him again, and he really needed to keep her trust he thought as he formulated a plan.
Mariah was excited about seeing Aidan. *I guess he was still a little upset about his mother,* she thought to herself of his earlier mood. She didn't care why. Mariah just wanted to be with him, and make love to him.

David came back into the room with his drink, and began looking around.
"Do you know where I put the keys?" he asked, as he pretended to look for them.
David was trying to stall and buy some time. He knew they were alone in the house, and he just couldn't let her leave right now. Mariah began helping him retrace his steps.

"Well dag David, they can't be that far," she told him chuckling, as they continued to look.

David walked behind Mariah as she was checking the sofa cushions, and pushed her gently onto them. He lay on top of her, effectively holding her there. Mariah was alarmed.

"David what are you doing?!" she asked, beginning to become afraid.

"Mariah, didn't our being together for almost two years mean anything to you?" David asked, looking at her hard.

Mariah was terrified. His eyes were blazing, and she could tell from his tone, he was angry now.

"David please, that's over," she told him gently.

He kissed her hard, and began talking to her again.

"You love me! So why don't you stop trying to pretend you don't!" David told her, even angrier now.

He was tired of this. He loved Mariah, and he was meant to be with her. Not that damned Aidan. David was going to take back what was his, and he was taking it back now.

"David please, you're hurting me," Mariah told him, near tears now.

"I'm sorry about that, but I'm not letting you leave here, without you telling me the truth Mariah," he told her again. "I want you, and I want to be with you," David went on. "I'm the man you're supposed to marry, the man you're supposed to have children with," he continued to rail, as he began undressing her.Mariah knew what he was planning. She couldn't let that happen. She began to try and reason with him again.

"David please, I don't want it to be like this!" she yelled at him.

He looked at her quizzically for a moment, trying to decide if he should believe her.

"I want to be with you David, but not like this," Mariah said again, trying to calm down.

She just needed him to get off her.

David kissed Mariah again, gently, and she kissed him back. He began to relax. He continued to kiss her, as she seemingly responded to his touch. David finally moved off her, so he could undress himself.

Mariah saw her chance and took it. She pushed him as hard as she could, and ran for the door. David caught her, and grabbed her shirt, trying to pull her back into the room.

Mariah fought with him, and he slapped her hard across the face. She didn't give up. She continued to fight until the material gave and tore in his hand, allowing her to bolt out of the door. She ran away from the house, hearing him scream her name. David grabbed his keys from the hiding place he'd placed them, as he raced off to catch her.

Mariah was terrified. She heard David start the car, and come out of the driveway. She hid in the nearby woods adjacent to their house. David zoomed by her, and she let out the breath she'd been holding. Mariah touched the pocket on her pants, thankfully finding her cell. She dialed the only person she could call right now.

Sandra was sitting in the den, drinking her wine, and anxiously thinking about what she'd heard earlier. David was obviously trying to attack Mariah. She'd gotten downstairs too late to stop him.

"Please let her be alright," she prayed aloud about Mariah. She was going to kill David when he returned. *How dare he do that to her!* Sandra thought to herself. She knew he was still in love with Mariah, but he'd been dead wrong. What if she called the police? Sandra couldn't let his future be ruined like that.

She would be forced to lie and say that Mariah had consented, then changed her mind afterward. Sandra didn't want to do that. She still loved Donovan so much, and that would be such an insult to his memory if she did it. David was her son though, and she couldn't let him be destroyed, even if he was stupid and brought it on himself.

Sandra heard the car return, and rose to meet him at the door.

"Where is Mariah?" she asked him angrily.

David looked at his mother, shocked and surprised. He hadn't known she was at home.
"When did you get home?" he asked.
"I've been here all night," she told him, the meaning very evident.

David hung his head shamefully.
"What the hell were you thinking?!" Sandra yelled at him.
"I lost my head," he replied. "I never meant to hurt her."
Sandra took another deep breath.
"Where is Mariah?" she asked again, slowly and deliberately.
David told her he couldn't find her.

"She must have made it to the road," he told Sandra. "I've been up and down the highway at least four times, and I didn't see her anywhere."
Sandra told David he had to find her, and they had to make sure she was all right.
"This is a nightmare David," Sandra told him again.

David wondered if Mariah still had her cell. He picked up the phone and dialed. He handed it to his mother, in case she answered. The phone connected, but no one spoke.
"Hello? Mariah?" Sandra said anxiously into the receiver.
"No Mrs. Alston, this isn't Mariah," the female voice said angrily.
Sandra exhaled deeply. She didn't recognize the voice, but she could tell from the tone they knew about the incident.
"May I speak with Mariah please?" she asked, trying to remain calm.
"She's not in any shape to talk to you right now," the voice replied again. "I'll tell her you called," they said preparing to hang up.
"Please, young lady, I just want to know she's alright," Sandra said quietly.
Jaz smiled, she loved the idea of Mrs. Alston begging. *Haughty bitch,* she thought to herself.
"Hold on, I'll see if she'll talk to you," Jaz told her.

Mariah asked her who it was, and she told her.

"Hi Mrs. Alston," Mariah said softly.
Sandra breathed a sigh of relief.
"Mariah, honey, are you all right?" she asked, her voice full of concern.
Mariah knew Sandra was genuinely concerned, so she wouldn't punish her anymore than Mariah knew she had to have already been.
"I'm okay Mrs. Alston," she replied. "I'm not going to report this or anything."

Sandra smiled gently. "Thank you honey, but I am really worried about you," she replied "Are you sure you're okay?" she asked. "David didn't force –," Sandra faltered, not able to bring herself to finish the question.
Mariah heard her voice break, and knew she was in pain.
"No, Mrs. Alston, he didn't hurt me like that," she replied.
Sandra told her she was glad.
"I love you Mariah, please believe that," she told her honestly, crying softly.
Sandra knew Mariah would never come to visit again, and that she'd lost her final link to Donovan.
"I know Mrs. Alston," she said softly. "I need to go now, OK?"
Sandra told her goodnight, and not to hesitate to call her if she needed anything. Mariah thanked her and disconnected.

Maurice arrived home shortly after the phone conversation and Sandra told him what'd transpired. "He did what?!" Maurice bellowed.
David heard his father yelling, and knew he was in for some serious punishment. He might actually follow through on that threat to send him to military school for the rest of his final year.

Maurice was furious with David, but he tried to be reasonable. "Maybe this is partially our fault," he said tiredly, sitting down across from his wife.
Sandra looked at him like he was insane.

"How the hell could any of this be our fault?" she asked, looking at him hard.
Maurice took a deep breath.

"We've been pushing him to be with Mariah, since we discovered he had a crush on her in ninth grade," he told his wife. "Then when she broke up with him, we made him feel like it would never be right again until he got back with her," he went on, as Sandra continued to look at him. "Hell, I can genuinely understand where he's coming from," Maurice finished wistfully.
"What are you talking about Maurice? How can you identify with where he's coming from?" Sandra asked, genuinely perplexed.
"Come on Sandra," he began. "You honestly think I didn't know you've been in love with Donovan Black all this time?"

She was dumbfounded. She couldn't speak.
"I loved you, so it didn't matter. I was actually glad when he came back with Kayla and Mariah, but it didn't seem to dampen your obsession," Maurice went on.
"I've had affairs with other women, just to get out from under the shadow of the man you really wanted to marry," he finished softly, looking directly at her.

Sandra was so ashamed. She'd treated Maurice so badly all these years, trying to chase a dream that would never happen. Especially now, with Donovan being dead, yet here she was still trying to hold on.
"I'm sorry Maurice. I never realized how much I hurt you," Sandra told him honestly.
"Was Donovan the only reason you wanted David to be with Mariah?" he asked her.

Sandra had to think about it for a moment, before she answered.
"That was a big part of it, I won't lie," she began. "But Mariah is a wonderful girl in her own right. She was absolutely perfect for David, and he loves her unconditionally, even now," she went on. "All I want is for my son to be happy."

Maurice shook his head in agreement. He felt the same thing of Mariah. He always gave Donovan and Kayla credit for raising a fine young woman.

"But we have to let David live his own life," Maurice told her.

"Tonight could have been a disaster, of major proportions," he went on. "Thankfully, Mariah wasn't hurt and now we should back off, and allow David to choose his own companion."

Sandra nodded her head in agreement. Still, she hoped in the back of her mind that they would end up together. She felt Maurice's eyes on her, and she looked up. He was taking her in, feeling that familiar longing to be with her.

"Do you think we could go upstairs, and create some magic of our own?" he asked her huskily.

Sandra actually wanted him right now. Maybe she was finally seeing the diamond she'd been treating like coal all these years.

"Yes, I'd like that very much," she replied, as she took his hand, and they began to ascend the stairs together.

27

David was anxious. He couldn't believe how he'd behaved earlier. He was also worried about her telling Aidan. He'd had one run in with the guy he didn't need another. His mother told him Mariah said she wouldn't report it. So maybe she wouldn't tell Aidan either.

His cell rang and he answered. "Hello?" he said into the mouthpiece.

"You are one shady bastard David," Jaz spat at him. David recognized her voice.

"What do you want Jaz?" he asked her impatiently.

"I want my cousin to beat the hell out of you," she said flatly.

He didn't like where the conversation was going.

"I'm going to tell him what you did to Mariah tonight," she hissed into the phone.

So, Jaz had been the one to pick Mariah up, David thought to himself. *If she didn't call him, then she must not be planning to tell him,* he reasoned.

"Look Jaz, I wouldn't do that if I were you," he replied darkly.

Jaz was even angrier.

"Why the hell should I be scared of you?" she spat back.

David knew he had a little leverage, and he used it.

"Well, Mariah still doesn't know you screwed me, and were pregnant with my baby, now does she?" he said coldly.

Jaz immediately felt the fight leave her. She was livid that David was going to once again, get away with something.

"Whatever David!" she told him, trying to still sound brave.

David knew he had her, and he moved in for the kill.

"You'd better keep your mouth shut, unless you want to lose the best friend you've ever had," he told her and hung up before she could reply.

Jaz hated him. She wanted Mariah to tell Aidan what he'd done to her, but she'd refused. She said she wanted to forget it, and move on. *There's got to be a way I can clue him in, without actually telling him,* Jaz thought to herself. She couldn't let Mariah find out about what she'd done with David. She would come up with something. Jaz wasn't going to sit back, and see that dirty dog get away again. She returned to the car where Mariah was waiting. "You ready to go now?" Jaz asked Mariah.

She told her she was. Jaz started the car and drove them to the cemetery to get the other vehicle. Mariah called Aidan, and told him she was running behind. He'd told her it was fine, and he'd see her when she got there. Once they disconnected, Jaz began to question her. "How are you going to be normal with Aidan, after what just happened?" she asked.

Mariah told her it wasn't the same. She loved Aidan, and she didn't mind him touching her. She wouldn't allow David to win, by coming between her, and the man she loved.

"Why won't you tell him Mariah?" Jaz asked again.

Mariah sighed heavily.

"You already know the ending to that story as well I do," she replied, giving Jaz a look.

Jaz chuckled softly. She did know. Aidan would beat David to a pulp.

"How long have you and Elaine been seeing each other?" Mariah asked, effectively changing the subject. Jaz was surprised. She thought she'd been doing a good job of hiding their connection.

"What do you mean?" she asked evasively.

Mariah gave her another look.

"I'm not stupid Jaz," she replied. "I see how she looks at you, and I see how you are around her," she finished.

Jaz sighed deeply.

"Are you upset?" she asked her best friend.

Mariah smiled at her.

"Why should I be?" she replied. "If you care for her, and she cares for you, isn't that all that matters?" Mariah finished, still chuckling softly.

Jaz loved her for that all by itself. She should have known Mariah wouldn't abandon her.

"Well all I know is you and my big head cousin need to be quiet when ya'll getting freaky," Jaz chuckled trying to lighten the mood. "Making all that noise, and waking everyone up."

Mariah looked at her and blushed.

"Do you really hear us Jaz?" she asked, mortified at the thought.

Jaz laughed heartily. "Sometimes, but its okay Mariah," she continued to laugh. "Damn girl, lighten up!"

Mariah was still embarrassed. She made a mental note to try and control herself from now on. Jaz saw her discomfort, and laughed again.

"Stop," she told her. "If its good girl, it's just good!" she laughed again, and this time Mariah laughed with her.

Aidan was glad to see her. He apologized to her again for his behavior earlier. Mariah laughed, and told him it was okay. His aunt and uncle were gone for a couple days. They wanted to unwind from the unfortunate events of the past few weeks.

They had the house to themselves.

"You want a snack or something to drink?" Aidan asked, as he kissed her neck.

Mariah giggled, and told him yes.

"Coke okay?" he asked.

"Yes, that's fine," she replied, still laughing.

She'd pushed the incident with David out of her mind for now. Mariah was where she wanted to be, and with the man she wanted to be with. Aidan returned with their drinks, and they began to talk.

"Are you alright?" she asked him gently, looking into his eyes.

Aidan smiled, and told her he was fine now.

"I wanted to come to your mother's service," Mariah told him.

He sighed gently.

"I know baby, but you know I didn't want you there for that," Aidan told her, as he caressed her face.

He noticed a slight discoloration. He started to ask her about it, but Mariah started talking again, interrupting his thought.

"I know, but I really felt like you needed me," she told him, beginning to touch him back.

Aidan felt that familiar longing to be with her, and began kissing her. She'd missed him, and she wanted him badly. Mariah felt her body begin to respond to his touch. Aidan was slowly undressing her, taking the time to gently kiss, and caress, each part of her.

He got to her shirt, and removed it. He took off her bra, and saw several scratches near her breast.

"Mariah?" Aidan questioned.

"Hmm?" she answered softly, her mind still on him touching her.

"How did you get these scratches?" he asked, concerned.

Mariah opened her eyes. She hadn't thought there were any marks on her. She looked at Aidan, and he was waiting expectantly for an answer. Mariah didn't want to lie to Aidan, but she couldn't tell him David had done this to her.

"I, um, must have done it the other day, helping mommy in the yard," she lied, hoping he believed her.

Aidan looked at Mariah closely. She was lying to him, and he wanted to know why.

"Mariah," he began gently. "You are a terrible liar. Now tell me what really happened," he said softly, and kissed her for good measure.

Mariah didn't want to do this. She already knew Aidan's next move if she told it.

"Please Aidan, its no big deal. Can we talk about it later? I just want to be with you," she pleaded.

Aidan took a deep breath. Why was she being so evasive?

"Mariah," he said simply, giving her a look.
She felt the tears come. Mariah was scared. Not for herself, but for David. She knew Aidan already didn't like him. He pulled her to a sitting position. Mariah tried to reach for her shirt, but Aidan wouldn't let her put it back on.
"Be still," he told her, as he carefully examined every inch of her, removing her jeans and panties as well.

Aidan found bruising on her inner thigh, and hip. He spoke slowly and deliberately this time. "I want you to tell me what happened to you, Mariah," he began. "And I want you to tell me the truth."
Mariah knew he was angry. She should have gone home, and seen him tomorrow. Now it was too late, and she was cornered. Aidan wouldn't let her get dressed. She was still naked, and he was looking at the bruising and scratches, his frown getting deeper and deeper.

Aidan took the time to examine her face again, where he'd originally seen the discoloration. It was deeply bruised near her neck, beneath her cheek. Mariah was crying softly. Aidan covered her with the sheet, but still wouldn't allow her to dress.
"Tell me," he said again, trying to control the coldness that was coming over him.

Mariah took a deep breath, and began telling him about her day. She told him how she was really hurt earlier, and had gone to visit her father's grave. She told him about David finding her there, and them spending time, and then going back to his house.
"Is that where you were when I called?" Aidan asked, looking at Mariah evenly.
"Yes," she replied quietly. "I asked him to take me back to my car as soon as I hung up with you."
Mariah told him about David losing his keys, and them looking for them.
"He pushed me on the couch, and held me there," Mariah said, beginning to tremble slightly.

Aidan felt himself growing colder with anger, as she continued.
"He began saying things to me, and trying to undress me," she went on. "I got the scratches and bruises as I was fighting him." Mariah looked up at Aidan fearfully.
He caressed her face, and smiled gently.
"Go on baby," he told her.

Aidan was seething inside, but he couldn't let her see that.
"He grabbed my shirt, and it ripped. I ran out of his house and into the woods," she told him. "Then I called Jaz, and she came and got me," Mariah finished, still looking at him and trying to gauge his reaction.
Aidan couldn't let her see how deeply angry he was. He was going to kill David, literally.
"Aidan," Mariah began, and he turned his attention to her again. "Please, I know you're mad, but don't do anything to David, OK?" she pleaded. "I mean, its over, and I just want to forget it, and move on."

Aidan didn't like lying to Mariah, but he would this time. "OK baby," he replied. "If that's what you really and truly want, then I'll do what you ask," he finished, and then kissed her again.
Mariah smiled, and told him thanks. They began to kiss again, making love to each other twice, before spending themselves. Aidan watched her as she slept.
I'm sorry Mariah, he thought to himself, stroking her hair gently.

I'm going to have to break this one promise. I have a serious date with David Alston, he thought venomously, the Gianni blood beginning to boil inside him. Aidan closed his eyes, thinking of the bodily harm he was going to inflict on the young man.

Early the next morning Aidan kissed Mariah goodbye, and watched her drive down the highway, before turning to find Jaz. He knocked on her bedroom door.
"Yeah?" she answered.

"I need to talk to you," he told her, waiting for her to open the door.
Jaz told him to come on in, and he entered the room.
"Tell me about last night," Aidan said simply, sitting on the end of bed.

She looked at him, and saw the anger in his eyes. *Does he know?* Jaz was wondering. She'd promised Mariah not to tell, and she didn't want to break her promise.
"What do you mean?" Jaz returned, trying to feel her cousin out.
Aidan sighed deeply.
"I mean about you picking Mariah up, after David tried to rape her," he said, slowly and deliberately.
Jaz had never heard Aidan sound so cold. It actually chilled her.
"What do you want to know?" she asked quietly.
"Did he succeed?" he asked first.
Jaz emphatically told him no.
"Mariah fought him, and got outta there," Jaz told him.
"How was she when you found her?" Aidan asked again.

Jaz told him that she was cold and frightened, with only her bra, and jeans on.
"She was crying," Jaz went on. "But other than that, she was fine," she finished, still trying to gauge Aidan's reaction.
He thought about all that Jaz had just told him, and took another deep breath. He didn't say anything for a while.
"Are you going to hurt him bad?" Jaz asked quietly.

Aidan turned to her, and he didn't need him to utter a word. His look told Jaz everything she needed to know. She gathered herself from the initial shock of his reaction, and spoke again.
"Well, let me know if you need my help," she replied.

Aidan smiled gently, and told her thanks. He hugged her tightly, and prepared to leave.
"By the way," he began, turning to Jaz again. "Are you and Elaine serious, or is this just an experiment for you?" Aidan finished, waiting for her answer.

She was stunned. *Damn, does everyone know?* Jaz thought to herself, of her family.
"It's not an experiment," she replied softly. "It's complicated," she added.
Aidan continued to stare at her, making her uncomfortable.
"So are you going to disown me or something?" Jaz asked, hurt by his silence.
Aidan chuckled lightly.
"Why would I do that, big head girl?" he asked, as he continued to chuckle.
"Well, you haven't said anything" Jaz replied.

Aidan sighed, and leaned against the doorframe, taking in the unique room. There were posters ranging from rap stars, to country stars, to sixties icons. Jaz had love beads hanging over the closet entrance.

A multicolor, bean-bag chair, adorned the corner and her Minnie mouse comforter still covered her bed.
"I just want you to be happy Jaz," he told her honestly. "I don't want to see you hurt by anyone, male or female."
Jaz smiled, and told him thanks.
"I don't ever want to lose you, or Mariah," she told him, her voice wavering.
What else is behind that comment? Aidan thought to himself.
"Jaz?" he queried.
She looked up at him.
"Is there something you need to tell me?" Aidan questioned.
Jaz thought about it. She wanted so much to share what'd happened with her and David. She needed to unburden herself, and let it go.
"Not right now," Jaz replied, backing down once again.

Aidan studied her a few moments longer, before letting it go and leaving. Jaz fell back onto her bed once he'd closed the door, and began to cry. Aidan heard her sobbing through the door.

He wanted to go back and force her to tell him what was so wrong, but he decided against it. Whatever was going on, Jaz was going to have to make the decision on her own to tell him about it. Aidan sighed again, and left. He had plans to make.

David felt like there was sand in his eyes when he opened them. He'd barely slept last night, after his father finished chewing him out. *What the hell was I thinking?* He asked himself, replaying the scene with Mariah, again and again, in his mind.

I've messed up completely, he thought to himself. Mariah would hate him now, and never speak to him again. He was also still worried that she might change her mind, and tell Aidan. David didn't want another confrontation with the guy.

He thought about carrying one of the guns his father owned. He wasn't going to give this guy a chance to mess him up again, like he had last time. David picked up his cell. He had to make sure at least one loose end was still tied up.

"Hello?" Jaz answered.

He'd blocked his number so she wouldn't know it was him.

"Did you keep your mouth closed bitch?" David growled into the phone.

Jaz sighed deeply. She hated him, and here he was, calling and threatening her again. "I didn't tell him, if that's what you want to know," she replied dryly.

David grunted. "Good," he replied hatefully. "And if you want to keep him and Mariah in your life, you better keep it that way."

Jaz sighed deeply again. "Did you want something else asshole?" she queried.

David chuckled lightly.

"No, that will do for now," he told her.

"OK," Jaz replied and disconnected.

David smiled to himself headed into the bathroom. He was glad he didn't have to worry about that much. *Let's just hope Mariah doesn't have an attack of conscience, and tell him,* he thought to himself tiredly.

David still wanted to see her again. He loved her so much. Why did he have to hurt her like that last night? Thank God he hadn't actually raped her. He could never forgive himself, if he'd done that to her.

His shower had been invigorating. Now David was dressed, and ready to go. He had to go to the school and make sure his records were being sent to the schools he'd applied to for college.

Duke was first on his list. He knew it was where Mariah would be going. He still hoped they could get past this storm, and be friends. He couldn't bring himself to give up on her yet.

David stopped by his fathers study, and took out the snub nose .38 he kept in the drawer. He dropped it into his book bag. He would keep it in the car. *Just in case.* He thought to himself.

David yelled a goodbye to his mother, as he grabbed an apple from the fruit bowl, heading to his car. He started the fire red mustang and peeled out of the driveway. He was so consumed with his own thoughts he didn't notice Aidan following him.

David met up with Chase after arriving at school, who invited him to the end of the year bash they were throwing tonight. He cheerfully accepted glad to have something to do that would keep his mind off of his loss.

Just as he rounded the corner with Chase, still discussing the party, David saw Mariah. She was coming out of the guidance office with Mr. Willingham, the counselor.

They were smiling, and talking to each other as they walked down the hallway. She hadn't seen him, and he was grateful. David sighed wistfully, as he watched Mariah walk away.

He made up his mind to get completely obliterated at the party tonight. Maybe if he got drunk enough, it would ease the pain he was feeling right now, watching the woman he loved, walk out of his life.

28

"So, are you coming tonight or what?" Chase asked again.
He'd been talking to her for the last ten minutes, and Jaz hadn't said a word back. She'd been fine before that. He didn't understand what gave.
Jaz had to reel her mind back in. Her head was still spinning from what she'd just seen. Chase was giving her a ride home, and as usual trying to hit on her.
They'd been enjoying their conversation, and bantering back and forth, when Jaz saw the car. They were passing Sherice's house, on Chase's way to buy some weed.

Just as they got near enough for her to actually see the house, she saw Elaine and Sherice standing in the doorway kissing.
Chase was so engrossed in conversation he never noticed the sight. Jaz was absolutely crushed. *I knew she was lying about that bitch,* she thought to herself spitefully.
Her mind immediately traveled back to the last argument she and Elaine had. *"Have you slept with someone else?" Elaine asked out of the blue.*
Jaz was surprised. She didn't know why Elaine had asked her that.
"No!" she replied emphatically. "Why would you ask me that?"
Elaine sighed, and shrugged. Jaz was a little angry.
"Don't you trust me?" Jaz asked.
Elaine looked at her levelly for a few moments.
"I really don't have the right to trust, or not trust you, now do I?" she returned.
Jaz knew where Elaine was going with this.
"Why do we have to fight about this again?" Jaz asked.
Elaine cared deeply for Jaz. She wanted her to commit. "Because, I can't stand the thought of someone else kissing you, or making love to you." Elaine told her, becoming angry herself.
Jaz had a few questions of her own she wanted answered.
"Really?" she returned agitated. "Well, what about Sherice?" she asked, looking at Elaine hard.
"What about her?" Elaine returned.

They were both angry now.
"She's my best friend. So what?" she asked again.
"So have you slept with her?" Jaz accused. "You two are awfully damned close all the time."
"What do you care if I slept with her?" Elaine yelled back. "You only wanted your curiosity appeased, remember?"
Jaz was furious. "Don't you dare try and turn this around. I asked you a fucking question, and I want a damn answer!" she yelled again.

Elaine looked at her, but didn't answer.

"You did!" Jaz screamed, tears streaming down her cheeks. "What happened Elaine? Did she push you away, so you decided you would come after me?" she continued, sobbing and screaming. "So you figured I was better than nothing? If she wanted you back, you'd go to her, wouldn't you?!" Jaz accused.
"I won't be second to your damned best friend, who you're completely in love with!" she finished, still sobbing deeply.
Elaine came over and tried to comfort her.
"Don't touch me!" Jaz said harshly.
Elaine knew Jaz was hurt, but she hadn't meant to hurt her.
"Baby, I'm sorry," she said softly. "I never meant to hurt you, and you're not second to anyone," she continued. "Please believe me. I care so much for you. Please give us a chance," Elaine finished, still holding her tightly.
Jaz was sniffling quietly.
"But you are in love with her aren't you?" she asked again, the pain in her voice evident.
Elaine sighed deeply.
"It's complicated Jaz." She replied.
"Explain it to me." she told Elaine, looking at her evenly. Elaine took a deep breath, and told Jaz she had a lot of feelings for Sherice, but she knew they would never amount to anything.

"What I felt for you Jaz, was not a result of Sherice turning me down," Elaine told her, looking at her closely. "I am genuinely attracted to you, because of you."

Jaz still didn't say anything for a while.
"Are we going to be okay?" Elaine asked her finally.
Jaz sighed deeply.

"I don't know. I have to think, and sort out some things," she replied tiredly

"Girl are you ignoring me?" Chase asked again, chuckling lightly and breaking Jaz's thought.

Jaz forced a smile.

"No boy," she replied, forcing the laughter. "I'm trying to decide whether I'm coming tonight?"

Chase laughed harder and told her okay. She had to get home. Jaz needed to think. Why would Elaine lie to her? She thought she'd been there for her, that she'd done everything she'd asked of her. *What more could she want from me?* Jaz asked herself miserably, Elaine's request that she commit to a relationship coming to mind. She sighed deeply.

"Yes, Chase," she replied, as he pulled into her driveway. "I'll be at the party tonight," she giggled.

He smiled widely.

"That's good to hear Jazzy-J," he laughed.

He looked at her for a while not speaking.

"What is it boy?" Jaz laughed, seeing him staring at her.

"I, um," Chase began, stuttering a little to get it out. "I'm really feeling you Jaz," he told her earnestly.

Oh God, not now, she thought to herself. Jaz had enough to deal with. Still she wouldn't hurt his feelings. Chase was really a nice guy, a little out of control sometimes, but a nice guy.

"Well that's sweet," Jaz replied, smiling and looking into his eyes.

Chase smiled and leaned over, kissing her gently on the cheek.

"See you tonight Jazzy-J," he said softly.

Jaz smiled and let herself out, waving at him as she went inside. Aidan saw her come home with Chase.

"Why you riding with that stoner?" he asked jokingly.

Jaz smiled slightly, and told him Chase was really nice.

"I know that," Aidan replied, looking at her closely. "I'm just kidding."

"What's wrong?" he asked, cornering her in the kitchen.

Jaz really didn't want to get into this right now. She tried to move around him, but Aidan blocked her path.
"I asked you a question," he told her evenly.
She looked up at him tears in her eyes.
"Please Aidan," Jaz told him quietly. "I don't want to talk about it right now," she finished, the tears spilling down her face.
Aidan remembered her crying earlier, and decided this time he would push.
"No," he replied, hugging Jaz tightly. "You're going to tell me this time why you're so unhappy."

His hug broke the dam, and Jaz began to sob deeply, clinging to him for support. Aidan's heart was breaking seeing his cousin in so much pain. After she'd quieted down, and cleaned her face he probed again.
"Tell me what's going on Jaz," he said softly.
She sighed deeply, and looked at him.
"OK," she replied. "But let's go upstairs to my room," she told him, heading up the stairs.

Aidan followed, and took and seat on her bed again, once they entered the room. She looked up to find him watching her expectantly. Jaz took a deep breath, and told him everything. She told him about last summer, and the thing that had happened with her and David.
She told him about her and Elaine, and how she'd seen her with Sherice this morning. She told him about her conflicted emotions in her attraction to Chase.

Jaz talked for the better part of the afternoon with Aidan listening intently. Once she was finished, she looked at Aidan to gauge his reaction to everything she'd told him.
Aidan was reeling. He hated David Alston even more now, and was more determined than ever that his plans for him, not fail. Not only had he hurt the woman he loved, he'd hurt his favorite cousin, whom he loved like his sister.

"So why don't you confront Elaine about what you saw," he told her. "I mean it's only fair. Since she's sneaking around, you should let her know you saw her," Aidan told her again.

Jaz thought about it and decided she liked the idea.

"Don't even worry about David," Aidan told Jaz softly. "I'm going to take care of all of that."

Jaz was happy she'd told him about it. She felt lighter, freer that she had in a long time. Aidan hadn't judged her or called her names. He'd understood, and even told her he would defend her. Jaz loved her cousin so much, and she hoped he would indeed give David Alston just what he had coming.

After Aidan left her room and she was alone, Jaz picked up her cell and dialed Elaine.

"Hey Jaz," Elaine answered.

Jaz sighed heavily.

"I need to see you," she said plainly.

Elaine was slightly alarmed by the tone of her voice.

"What's wrong?" she asked.

Jaz sighed again.

"I think you already know that," she replied evenly, trying to contain the growing anger she felt.

Elaine's mind was spinning. *What the hell is going on?* she thought to herself. There was no way Jaz could know about this morning. *Not unless Sherice had called her,* Elaine thought to herself, and then dismissed it. She knew Sherice would never do that.

"OK, when do you want to talk?" Elaine asked guardedly.

"I'm on my way there now," Jaz replied.

Elaine sighed, and told her okay she'd been waiting. Jaz disconnected without saying goodbye and went downstairs, yelling over her shoulder to Aidan she would be right back.

Elaine hadn't liked Jaz's tone one bit, and the only thing that kept flashing in her mind eye was the Jaz did indeed know about what happened between her and Sherice earlier this morning.

She'd gone over to Sherice's house after her best friend called and chided her for not spending any time with her, since hooking up with Jaz. Elaine was still smiling as she rang the doorbell. Jaz had sent her a text message, wishing her a good day, and telling her she missed her.

Sherice opened the door, and Elaine nearly dropped the carton of juice she was carrying. *Shit!* Elaine thought, taking her friend in from head to toe. The paisley blue sundress Sherice was wearing was spaghetti strap, with a deep v-neck, made of curve hugging lycra.

She had on her push-up bra; making her already pert breasts sit even higher, inviting closer inspection. It was dangerously short, barely covering her perfect behind, and the thong panties she was obviously wearing, let the imagination run wild when you looked at her.

Elaine felt herself becoming immediately aroused. This was going to be a long morning, she thought, as she followed Sherice inside, and to her room.

"So what you wanna do?" Sherice asked innocently.

Elaine had to take a deep breath before she answered.

"Let's catch up a little," she told Sherice, trying hard not to look at her.

She is so damned fine, and that dress is killing me, Elaine thought, as she tried not to react. Sherice chuckled lightly, and began telling her the latest gossip. They were soon both laughing, and completely relaxed with each other.

"So, then, she caught them in the athletic room girl!" Sherice was saying, as she and Elaine both laughed.

"I got my tattoo," she told Elaine.

Elaine was intrigued. She knew Sherice wanted one, and had said she was going to get one, but Elaine thought she was just bluffing.

"Really?" she replied curiously.

Sherice smiled again.

"Yep. You wanna see it?" she asked.

Elaine shrugged, and told her sure. Sherice came over to Elaine as she sat on the side of her bed, removed the bra, and pulled the strap of the dress down exposing her breast.

The tattoo was a cherry with juice flowing, drawn on the side of her breast, going down between the two.
"Do you like it?" Sherice asked softly, as Elaine stared at the tattoo, her breast, and her hard nipple.
"Very much," she replied softly.
Sherice smiled knowingly, and moved closer to her.
"You can touch it if you want," she said gently.

Elaine sighed softly. She wanted to touch Sherice with every fiber of her being, but knew she shouldn't.
"No, that's okay," Elaine replied trying to turn away.
Sherice placed her nipple near Elaine's lips as she turned her head, causing her to graze it.
"Mmm," she purred gently.
Elaine looked at her friend hard.
"Why are you teasing me like this Sherice?" she asked quietly, almost angrily.

Sherice caressed her face, leaned in, and kissed her softly. "Who says I'm teasing?" she replied seductively, kissing her again, and gently probing her mouth with her tongue.
Elaine pushed her away, and continued to look at her.
"You said you didn't want this," she reminded her, scared that her friend was simply toying with her affections once more.

Sherice sighed deeply. She was hurt that Elaine pushed her away, but she understood. Sherice knew Elaine was scared she would reject her again, like before. Sherice took the other strap off her shoulder. The dress fell to the floor, and she stood before Elaine with only her thong.
"I love you," Sherice said simply, looking her friend in the eye, as she kissed her yet again.

Elaine's head was spinning. She'd been waiting since forever to hear Sherice say these words to her, to make love to her, to be her lover.

Now Elaine had someone she had to consider first. As much as she wanted to be with Sherice, it would kill Jaz if she ever found out, and Elaine never wanted to hurt her like that.

Sherice took Elaine's hand, and placed in on her breast. Elaine sighed gently, but didn't take her hand away. Sherice kissed her again, pushing her gently back onto the bed.

"What about Jaz?" Sherice asked quietly after they'd made love.

Elaine sighed deeply. She didn't want to hurt Jaz, but she had to be honest. The woman lying in her arms now was the one she'd always wanted. The one she loved with every fiber of her being.

"I'll handle that," she replied.

Sherice didn't push. She simply smiled and kissed her again. Now she was going to have to live up to her word and handle it, Elaine thought to herself, hearing the car door slam and preparing herself for Jaz's arrival.

"Hey beautiful," he murmured into the phone.

"Hi baby," she replied.

Aidan loved talking to Mariah. She was wonderful, and he loved her with all his heart.

"So you want to get together this evening?" he asked, knowing she already had plans.

"I'd love to baby, but I've got the function at the children's hospital with mommy tonight," Mariah replied.

Aidan feigned forgetfulness when he answered.

"Oh yeah, I forgot," he replied amiably. "How about I stop by for a little while, and see you there?"

Mariah told him that would be great.

Aidan had to make sure every angle of his evening was accounted for. He was going to end the David saga tonight, but he had to make sure there were no loose ends.

"Aidan, are you listening to me?" she asked again, bringing him out of his thoughts.

"I'm sorry baby, my mind was wandering," Aidan replied. "What were you saying?"
Mariah sighed gently. "I'm late Aidan," she said softly.
"Late for what baby," Aidan asked, completely missing what Mariah was trying to tell him.
"I'm almost a month late, Aidan," she told him again.
This time he got it. "You're pregnant?" Aidan breathed into the phone, elated at the possibility.
Mariah sighed gently. "I think so," she replied quietly. "I'm scared."
Aidan was smiling broadly, already thinking ahead to the beautiful child they would have.
"Its OK," he told her. "You don't have to be scared. You know I'll be there for you, and the baby," Aidan told her, his mind already racing ahead to their future.

Aidan had the money Big D sent him from the insurance policy his mother had secretly taken out. He was shocked when he received the two hundred thousand dollars. Aidan hadn't known anything about it. Big D told him Liv made him promise if anything happened, he would send Aidan the money for him to go school. He wanted to send DeSean some of it, but Big D told him she'd made provisions for him too.

At least they wouldn't have to struggle when then got married. They could both finish school, and provide well for their child. Aidan heard her crying softly, bringing him out of his thoughts.
"It's OK Mariah," he told her again. "I ain't trippin," he chuckled lightly. "We kinda shoulda expected it, considering we hadn't been very careful lately."
"I guess you're right," Mariah told him. "I need to make an appointment, and have a test done to be sure," she told Aidan. "Will you take me?"

He smiled, and told Mariah he would cheerfully take her.
"Just make the appointment, and let me know when it is baby," Aidan told her gently. "I love you," he told her again. "I'll see you tonight at the hospital, okay?"

Mariah told him OK as they disconnected.

Aidan sat back and reflected on what he'd just been told. *She's carryin' my seed,* he thought to himself happily. He loved this woman, and she was the beginning of his own legacy. *Damn, I wish my dad was here,* Aidan thought to himself. He wanted the life Big D told him he and Dezi lived back in the day, the power and wealth.

Aidan thought again to David hurting Mariah, and how he might have hurt their child. He began to feel cold all over, his mind clicking and calculating every step he'd planned to take tonight. He wondered if this was one of the traits he'd inherited from his father.

Aidan remembered Big D telling him that his father only killed people when it was necessary. That he only protected what was his. He hadn't really understood then, but he fully understood now. Aidan would do what was necessary to protect Mariah, and their baby. He needed a little help with the details though. Aidan was new at this. Granted, he'd beat down his share of people, but never anything on this level.

He knew there was only one person, outside of his own father, who would understand and help him. Aidan picked up his cell and dialed.

"Wassup youngblood?" Big D answered amiably.

He was glad to hear from the boy. He'd grown genuinely fond of him, and missed their conversations.

"Hey D," Aidan replied, going on to apologize for not calling him sooner.

"No problem," Big D replied smoothly. "You're a young man, with plenty going on," he chuckled.

Aidan smiled and took a deep breath, before beginning.

"I need your help," he said simply.

Big D caught the tone, and called him on it. "A debt you need to pay?" he queried calmly.

Aidan took another breath, and exhaled slowly. He hoped D would help him, and not try to talk him out of it.

"Yeah," he answered evenly.
"OK, so what do you need?" Big D asked without hesitation.

Aidan smiled. He knew he'd made the right call. He'd been thinking since his mom's death, and had come to the conclusion that Big D killed Wallace, as reprise for his mother.

"I need to cancel a contract without fallout," Aidan told him.
Big D smiled. The kid sounded almost exactly like Dezi.
"So what's the set up?" he asked again.
Aidan began to tell him what he had in mind, and Big D listened attentively. Once he'd finished, Aidan waited for a response.
"Hmm," Big D replied. "Its not a bad plan, but you got a few holes," he told him.
"That's why I called you. I'm outta my league here," Aidan replied honestly.
Big D chuckled.
"No, not really," he replied. "You definitely got Dezi in you it just needs to be brought out to the surface," Big D finished, chuckling lightly again.

He went on to shore up the holes Aidan's plan had, telling him exactly when, and how, to accomplish the effect he wanted. Aidan was completely engrossed in what Big D was telling him.

"You and my father were no joke," he said, quietly awestruck from the instruction he'd just received. "OK, I'm going to do just what you said," Aidan told him.
Big D told Aidan that was fine, and he would be all right.
"Remember youngblood," he began. "Whatever heat comes down, you stay cool," he went on. "From what you've told me, your alibi will be airtight," he continued. "So don't let the small stuff sweat you, understand?"
Aidan told him he did.
"Remember who you are man," Big D admonished him again, and Aidan told him he would.

They disconnected, and Aidan headed for his first errand. He had a lot to do, and time was running short.

Big D smiled to himself at how well the young man was coming along. *I knew that Devastator blood would surface sooner or later*, he thought to himself, as he lit the blunt and inhaled deeply. Big D made a mental note to catch up on his letter writing later, as he felt the effects of the weed begin to mellow him out.

He thought briefly of Liv again and the love they shared. His thoughts then shifted to the Clique and the good old days as he closed his eyes and drifted off to sleep the smile still etched on his face.

29

Elaine opened the door and Jaz walked in, barely acknowledging her as she did. *Damn! What is going on with her?* Elaine thought, taking in her mood.

"Why don't you tell me about your morning?" she asked casually, looking directly at Elaine.

Her heart sunk. Elaine knew from the look Jaz was giving her, she'd found out. She didn't know how, but she had.

"I went to Sherice's to see her," she replied, telling half of the truth.

Jaz sighed deeply.

"Why don't you stop lying to me, and tell me the truth?" she told her, still eyeing her distastefully.

Elaine knew she had to tell Jaz, but she honestly didn't want to hurt her.

"Listen Jaz," she began, before Jaz cut her off.

"Did you sleep with her?" she asked point blank.

Elaine's mouth fell open, and she couldn't answer. That was all she needed. Jaz exploded.

"How the hell could you do that to me?!" she screamed. "I asked you didn't I?" Jaz went on raging "I asked you, if you still loved Sherice, to leave me alone!!"

Jaz was crying uncontrollably, and Elaine was at a complete loss of how to comfort her.

"But no, you said you wanted me! You had let that go with her, and you would never hurt me," she continued "That was such bullshit, wasn't it Elaine?!" Jaz screamed again. "Oh, I bet you couldn't wait to go over there when she called, and get inside her panties could you?!!" before abruptly taking a huge breath and becoming deathly quiet for the next few moments.

"I already know you want to be with her," she said quietly finally addressing Elaine again. "I'm leaving now," Jaz told her, turning to leave reaching for the door.

Elaine couldn't let it end like this. She still cared a great deal for Jaz, and felt completely guilty for the devastation she knew the girl was feeling now. Elaine took

her hand off the knob, and turned Jaz toward her. Jaz sighed deeply.
"What Elaine?" she said tiredly, all the fight gone from her.
Elaine took Jaz in her arms and kissed her passionately, which only made Jaz angrier.
"No!" Jaz said, and pushed Elaine away, bolting out of the door.

Elaine tried to grab her, but Jaz managed to get to her car. Elaine was outside, trying to plead with her not to leave like this. Finally after gathering herself, Jaz turned to Elaine and looked her in the eye.
"I hope you and Sherice are happy," she said simply, started the car and backed out.

Jaz felt a little better. She was still hurt, but she knew she would be all right. Her cell rang, and she answered without looking at the ID.
"Hello," she answered softly.
"Hey Jazzy-J," Chase greeted her.

She smiled in spite of herself. *Now what exactly does this joker want?* Jaz thought to herself, chuckling.
"Hey boy, what do you want?" she joked back.
Chase chuckled. "Besides to be your man, you mean?" he answered softly.
She smiled again. *If you only knew,* Jaz thought to herself. She chuckled aloud again.
"Boy, you are so silly," Jaz replied. "What do you really want Chase?" she asked, still smiling.
Chase laughed again.
"I really want to be your man," he replied. "But I called to ask you to bring some playing cards with you tonight."
Jaz laughed again, before replying.
"I can do that," she replied, starting to feel much better.

Jaz didn't like what she was starting to feel right now. She'd just gotten out a situation that had her devastated. She wasn't trying to get wrapped up again, no matter how attracted to Chase she may have been.

"Why do you keep pushing me away Jazzy-J?" he asked her point blank.

She sighed heavily. "Look Chase, I just got out of a situation," Jaz replied.

"Oh, so you and Elaine aren't kickn' it anymore?" he asked casually.

How the hell?! Jaz wondered to herself.

"How did you know about that?" she asked quietly.

Chase was quiet for a moment before he answered.

"I saw the two of you together one night, a couple weeks back," he replied calmly. "I don't think you're gay Jaz," Chase continued. "I think you were curious," he went on. "Especially after the kiss we shared."

Jaz had completely blocked that kiss from her mind. She and Chase had been hanging out and talking. The mood had gotten charged and they'd kissed without really thinking about it. The kiss was really intense, and she'd found herself completely aroused, he'd gently stroked her breast and she'd pushed him away making him stop.

"I don't care about that part of your life Jaz," Chase told her softly, breaking her thought. "I think about kissing you all the time, and how much I want to do it again," he went on, boldly putting himself on the line. "I want very much to be your man," Chase finished waiting for her response.

Jaz was astonished at what she'd just heard. "Chase," she replied gently. "I didn't know you felt like that about me," she replied. "Why don't we just see how it goes, starting with tonight, and go from there, OK?"

Chase smiled brightly. All he wanted was a chance, and she'd just given him that.

"Sure, Jazzy-J," he replied cheerfully. "I can definitely do that. I'll see you tonight," he replied, and disconnected before she could reply.

Jaz smiled to herself and continued her drive home.

Mariah was putting the finishing touches on her outfit for the evening. The children's hospital was one of her mother's pet projects. Kayla absolutely loved going there and spending time with the sick children. She'd arranged this gala, to raise money for the new cancer research wing they were trying to add onto the hospital.

Mariah thought back to her earlier conversation with Aidan. She was glad he wasn't angry. She hadn't intentionally gotten pregnant. Mariah knew Aidan loved her, and he wanted to marry her, she just didn't want him to resent having to do it sooner than the two years they'd planned on.

Mariah chuckled to herself, remembering what he'd told her about them expecting it to happen. They'd gotten caught up a couple of times, and not used protection. They'd both lost their head and he'd stayed inside her. Mariah was almost positive she was pregnant. She'd had a couple bouts with morning sickness, but nothing serious, hoping it would stay that way.

Her mother told her about her own pregnancy, and how pleasant it had been. She hoped her own would be the same way. Mariah also hoped she wouldn't be disappointed that she'd become pregnant.

She was still going to finish college. Mariah was determined, and she knew Aidan would help her.

"Honey are you ready?" Kayla called to her, shaking her from her thoughts.

"Yes mommy, I'm on my way," Mariah replied, grabbing her bag and heading down the stairs.

Kayla looked Mariah over as she arrived by her side. The emerald green evening dress looked absolutely stunning on her. Her face was glowing, and her makeup was flawless.

"You look beautiful tonight honey," Kayla told her, hugging her.

Kayla was so proud of her daughter. She'd been accepted to Duke to follow in her father's footsteps.

"Thanks mommy," Mariah returned. "You look fantastic too," she told her, looking at her mother in the cerulean blue halter dress, she was wearing.

Thomas wouldn't be accompanying them tonight, as he'd been called out of town for an emergency. It would be a girl's night out for them tonight.

"Oh mommy," Mariah began, remembering her earlier conversation. "Aidan said he may stop by the gala tonight."

Kayla smiled warmly, and told her that would be nice.

"Have you told him about the baby?" Kayla asked softly, looking Mariah in the eye.

Mariah gasped, and her eyes filled.

"How did you know?" she asked quietly.

Kayla simply smiled.

"You're my daughter, I know everything about you," she replied casually.

The tears rolled down Mariah's cheeks, as her mother embraced her.

"Honey, it's not the end of the world," Kayla told her gently. "You know I'll help you, and so will Thomas," she told her, as she continued to hold her.

"I know mommy," Mariah replied. "I told Aidan earlier. "He's going to take me to the doctor to confirm it," she continued, completely grateful for her mother's love and understanding.

"Good, I'm glad that you two are handling it," Kayla replied. "Come on, or we're going to be late," she finished, smiling at her daughter again.

Kayla was lost in thought as Mariah drove. She was elated that she was going to be a grandmother, but she was scared, knowing Dezi's son fathered the child. Still, Kayla had to admit she'd never seen any trait of Dezi's irrational behavior in Aidan. The boy was always pleasant and respectful. He treated Mariah like a princess, and she knew her daughter absolutely loved him with her whole heart.

Kayla pushed the bad thoughts out of her mind, and concentrated on making sure her daughter and grandchild were both healthy and happy. The thought of being connected once again to Dezi filled Kayla with a sense of contentment. Whether she wanted to openly admit it or not, part of her missed him still and loved him to this day.

"Are you sure you're not upset with me mommy?" Mariah asked her timidly, once they'd parked.

Kayla looked at her daughter long and hard for a moment, then smiled again.

"Absolutely not," she replied, her own unplanned, paternity complicated, pregnancy flashing into her minds eye.

Mariah sighed with relief, as they headed to the main ballroom.

David was excited about the party. He needed a diversion. Mariah had been on his mind all day, and he was about to lose it. *Shit I miss that damned girl so much,* he thought to himself tiredly, as he dressed.

He knew he was in for a good time at Chase's. There was always plenty of drink and smoke, plus any other drug you may want to indulge in. David was pretty sure there would be a girl or two there he could get his freak on with too. He was horny beyond belief.

Thinking of Mariah all day hadn't helped that one bit either. He thought about Sherice, and that perfect body of hers. Even though she'd taken him through hell, he'd gladly screw her right now if she were willing. *Hell, I'd even do Jaz again right about now,* David thought to himself chuckling.

He sighed and dismissed all the thoughts. He would find some girl willing enough at the party, and get his. David chuckled again and checked his reflection in the mirror. Satisfied that he looked good enough to accomplish his goals for the evening, he headed out.

He thought about taking the gun with him again, but decided against it. He knew Aidan wouldn't be there. Chase and his crew weren't the crowd he hung out with. They weren't enemies or anything, but they weren't friends either.

David stopped at his dresser, and opened the drawer, reaching in and pulling out a few condoms, stuffing them in his pocket. He saw the picture then and stopped. He pulled it out and looked at it. It was a picture of him and Mariah, when they were together.

She was smiling, and David was holding her, as she sat in his lap. *Why did I ever mess around on her,* he thought sadly, as he continued to hold the picture and imagine what if.

Finally he managed to get up, and put the photo back in the drawer. David shook the blues that were threatening to overtake him, and headed for his car. Once inside he began to relax. His car always did that for him.

David absolutely loved the mustang and the speed it afforded him. He'd also had his share of sex in its backseat, which he planned to take full advantage of again tonight if need be.

"Look out tricks, horny ass man on the way!" David said aloud, laughing as he cranked up the CD and peeled out of the driveway.

Aidan watched him leave again, and followed him until he was certain of where David was headed. Aidan heard rumblings about a party, and Jaz confirmed for him that Chase was having one. She'd also been kind enough to inform him of the feelings Chase had for her.

Aidan was secretly pleased she'd found her way back to a guy, and he hoped Chase would be good medicine for her. He even hoped they would sleep together, and get her mind off all the drama she'd just endured with Elaine.

Aidan shook the thoughts, and allowed David to outdistance him. He would catch up with him later and take care of business. He had some other things to do right now. Aidan turned the car toward the hospital and let his mind relax.

30

Chase saw Jaz arrive, and made his way to the door to greet her.
"Hey Jazzy-J," he greeted her cheerfully, taking her in. She was wearing the cutest blue spaghetti strap mini dress. It was thigh length, and sent his imagination spinning as Chase looked at her petite figure in it.

Jaz had nice legs, and a shapely butt. Her breasts were perfect, and he noticed her nipples were hard, letting him know she was braless. Her hair was done in cute flips all over her head, the tips of her hair tinged blue, like her contacts.
"Hey boy," she replied cheerfully.

Chase smiled, and she took him in all over again. Jaz felt her emotions churning. She recognized the dominant one immediately. She was horny, and Chase was sexy as hell. He smelled wonderful. The tank top looked good on him, showing off his muscular chest and powerful arms. The jeans were lying very nicely on that fine butt of his too. Jaz found herself getting very turned on standing here looking at him.
"Come on in," he told her, taking her hand and leading her into the party.

The house was almost full already. There were a lot of people she recognized from school, as well as others she assumed were friends of Chase's, or his brother Malcolm. She saw the usual skanks that were at every party, trying to get hooked up with one of the football, or basketball players. She saw a couple girls rolling their eyes at her, seeing Chase holding her hand.

Jaz smiled to herself, and held his hand tighter. Chase smiled, and continued to lead her to the den. Even though there was a party in full swing, he knew this room would be private. It was his and Malcolm's personal sanctuary. He led her into the room and asked if she wanted something to drink.

"I'll take a coke or something," Jaz replied, as Chase excused himself to get it.

She chuckled looking around the room, and realizing he'd brought her back here to be alone with her. The room itself was very nice. The sofa she was sitting on now was one of the big overstuffed kind, burgundy in color, and very comfortable.

There were also a couple of high back chairs, with matching footrests, also in burgundy. There was a huge projection TV with surround sound, and of course, DVD player. The CD player was really nice too.

He'd turned it on before he left and the romantic R&B was drifting softly out of the speakers. Jaz was surprised at how quiet it was here; compared to the noise and loud music she'd walked through to get here.

Chase returned with her drink, and closed the door. Jaz smiled to herself again, and took the drink from him.

"I thought you wanted to play cards," she told him, as he sat and enjoyed his drink.

He chuckled.

"No, I just wanted you to bring them," Chase replied. "There'll be some folks by later that really love to play," he continued. "I actually just want to spend some time with you," he said softly, as he reached out and caressed her face.

Jaz was having a hard time. She was extremely horny, and Chase's closeness was not helping that. She smiled.

"That's cool," she replied. "It's actually very quiet back here," she remarked.

He smiled, as he moved even closer to her. Chase took her coke can from her hand, and placed it on the table.

"What's going on?" Jaz asked softly, already knowing what he had in mind. He leaned in and kissed her gently on the lips. Jaz absolutely loved it, but she didn't say anything. Chase looked into her eyes. She remained mute. He sighed gently and pulled her to him, kissing her again, this time probing her mouth with his tongue. Jaz found herself completely aroused from his kiss. She had to make him stop. She pulled away.

"Chase, we should stop," Jaz said softly, her mind going back to their first kiss.

He smiled gently. Chase knew Jaz was attracted to him, and he'd aroused her with the kiss. He wouldn't push right now.

"OK Jazzy-J," he replied amiably, handing her the coke back.

Jaz was trying to get her breathing to become even again. He'd really rattled her. She knew if he did that again, she'd end up having sex with him.

Jaz knew Chase really wanted that, she just wasn't sure she was ready for it yet. Chase pulled Jaz to him, and held her as he talked to her. She lay back in his arms, and enjoyed his presence. *This feels so right it's almost scary,* Jaz thought to herself, as Chase continued to talk putting her completely at ease.

"Where's Chase?" David asked one of the guys, as he entered the party.

He'd already snagged himself a beer outside, and was about to grab his second. He wanted to at least say hey to Chase before he got blitzed.

"He's entertaining," Malcolm said laughingly, as he greeted David.

He laughed too. David knew that meant Chase had some girl in the back that he was either going to have sex with, or was already having sex with.

"Who is he entertaining?" David asked jokingly.

Malcolm laughed again.

"That little cute girl," he replied. "What's her name?" he said aloud, trying to recall it. "Jaz, yeah that's it," Malcolm finally said after remembering.

David was careful not to betray his true feelings. *Chase likes Jaz,* he thought to himself. He'd never let on that he felt anything for her. Knowing Chase was in the room with Jaz, David made sure he went in the opposite direction. There was no love lost between the two of them, and he didn't need anything to bring down his high. He spotted TaKari, one of the girls from school who had the reputation of being easy. He was still horny as hell, so he headed over to try and strike up a conversation.

I sure hope this trick is as easy to screw as everyone says, David thought to himself. He didn't want to have to waste too much time talking. Either she was, or she wasn't, and if she wasn't he needed to know early, so he could find one who was.

Mariah was enjoying herself immensely, elated that Aidan had come.

"Mommy knows I'm pregnant," she told him softly, as they took a breather from dancing and talked outside on the balcony.

"You told her?" Aidan asked, his mind reeling.

Kayla had been extremely cordial when he'd arrived. She didn't seem angry or upset.

"No," Mariah replied, chuckling lightly. "She told me."

Aidan was confused. Mariah laughed again.

"She asked me if I'd told you about the baby," she replied. "When I asked her how she knew, she'd laughed and said she knew everything about me," Mariah finished, still chuckling.

Aidan smiled as he looked at Mariah.

"Is she mad?" he asked cautiously.

Mariah smiled, as she caressed his face.

"No, she was very understanding and supportive," she told him.

Aidan breathed a sigh of relief. He didn't want Kayla to be angry with him, or think he'd taken advantage of her daughter.

"She knows I'm going to marry you, right?" he asked; still a little unnerved that Kayla knew.

"Yeah Aidan," Mariah replied, smiling again. "Relax," she told him. "She's not angry," she finished, just as Kayla walked up.
"Hi Mrs. Bradford," Aidan said again.
Kayla chuckled to herself, seeing how nervous he was. She assumed Mariah had informed him she knew about the baby.
"Aidan?" she inquired evenly, deciding she would tease him a bit.
He was alarmed by her tone, and the look Kayla was giving him. Maybe she'd only pretended not to be angry.
"Yes Mrs. Bradford?" he replied nervously.

Kayla laughed. She couldn't do it. The young man was an absolute wreck.
"I'm not angry Aidan," she said gently, as she took his hand.
She saw him visibly relax.
"I'm going to take care of Mariah, and the baby," he told her earnestly.
Kayla chuckled aloud.
"I know you will," she told him again, still smiling, as she left to go and say hello to one of the board members.
Mariah hugged him and kissed his ear.
"You're real funny," she told him, smiling.
Aidan finally relaxed and laughed with her.
"I'm going to go on home baby," he told Mariah softly.

He'd checked his watch. It was time to handle some business.
"OK, thanks for coming," Mariah told him smiling again.
"I love you Mariah," Aidan told her softly.
"I know, and I love you too" she replied.
"I'm so excited about our baby," he told her, as he gently touched her stomach.
Mariah smiled and Aidan kissed her.
"Call me when you get home, OK?" he asked, as he prepared to leave.
Mariah assured him she would, and they said goodbye. She shook her head at his earlier behavior, chuckled to herself,

and went back inside. Aidan checked his mirror, and watched her return to the gala. *Time to go cancel this contract,* he thought malevolently to himself, as he started the engine, ready to put his plan into action.

David had spent the last hour talking to TaKari, and getting drunk. He'd succeeded finally in getting her here in the bathroom. He began kissing her, and she responded.

"I've been wanting to get with you for a long time you know," she told him softly, as he began undressing her. David smiled at her, and kissed her again. *Who cares,* he thought to himself of the girl's declaration; he simply wanted sex.. TaKari was naked now, and he'd taken off his clothes as well.

"You have one fine ass body," he told her honestly, as he took her in.

She giggled and told him thanks. They began to kiss again, and he was getting harder by the moment. David leaned her against the counter, and entered her.

"Mmm, damn you feel good," he murmured, as he thrust into her.

TaKari was moaning and writhing beneath him. He was getting closer, as he continued to thrust deeply into the girl. She was moaning and matching his rhythm.

"Oh shit!" David screamed as he finished.

She came right behind him calling his name. They both were breathing hard trying to recover themselves.

"Damn TaKari" he replied, caressing her face as she smiled at him. "That was fantastic."

TaKari smiled, as she pushed him back onto the closed toilet, and took him into her mouth. David closed his eyes, as he felt himself rising to the occasion once again. *This was the best-damned choice I've made all night,* he thought to himself, already looking forward to the sex that was coming.

Aidan was in place. He'd stopped and spent a couple hours at the Spot. He'd had a long conversation with both the cook, and waitress, before finally paying his tab and declaring he was leaving, headed home.

He surveyed the scene in front of him, and found it exactly as he imagined it would be. There were several people milling around outside, and they were all drunk. Aidan stayed carefully in the shadows, making sure no one saw him.

He made himself comfortable, and waited. He figured David would stay long enough to get good and drunk, and then stumble out to go home. He'd found out from Jaz that no one male was ever allowed to stay the night.

Aidan chuckled lightly at that thought. It helped his plan right along. He was going to make sure David Alston never bothered any of the people he loved, ever again. He found himself unusually calm as he waited.

Aidan smiled to himself again, remembering what Big D said earlier about him having Dezi in his blood, and it surfacing. He supposed that was exactly what was happening now, as he had absolutely no remorse for what he was planning to do.

This was strictly business. Aidan watched a few of the guys outside hook up with some of the drunker girls and take them to various cars and vans they'd obviously set up to have sex in. He wondered how many of these girls would even remember sleeping with these guys in the morning.

Aidan thought about Jaz. He knew enough of Chase to know he was a decent guy. He'd never heard of him doing anything crazy, or taking advantage of a girl like that. He also knew Jaz had enough sense to get out of there, if things got out of hand.

She didn't drink, so he wasn't worried about her getting drunk, and as far as he knew, she only smoked a little weed here and there. Aidan checked his bag once more, and saw that everything was in place. He relaxed his mind and continued to wait.

Chase was thoroughly enjoying his evening. He and Jaz had been here in the den alone all night. They'd talked and laughed, and really gotten to know each other. He'd been into her romantically for the last seven or eight months.

They'd always enjoyed a great friendship, even sharing that one kiss, but she'd always managed to push him away. Not tonight though. Tonight was going to be different. He could feel it. Chase was looking at Jaz as they sat together, and really wanted to kiss her again.

Jaz rose and headed for the restroom. She returned shortly afterward, and sat down beside him again. Chase slid behind her, and moved over to the corner of the sofa.

"Come here," he told her gently.

Jaz moved beside him, and he turned to her, as she found herself pinned in the corner.

"That wasn't fair Chase," Jaz said softly, as he began kissing her gently.

He chuckled.

"I know," he replied, and continued to kiss her.

"Please, stop," she told him, feeling herself becoming aroused again.

"I don't think so," Chase said softly, and kissed Jaz passionately.

His hand gently caressed her breast, and she moaned softly.

"We shouldn't Chase," Jaz told him again, trying to move away.

He kept her pinned in the corner, as he continued to caress her. He gently slid the strap down on her dress.

"Don't," she said quietly.

"Shhh," Chase told her, and kissed her again as he completed his task. "You are absolutely beautiful," he told her, as he looked at her.

Jaz helped him undress, and looked him over lustfully. *Good lord this boy is endowed,* she thought to herself, hoping he knew what to do with it. Chase began kissing her lips again, as he gently lay near her. He kissed her all over, and began with her breasts again.

He found his way down her body, and began to taste her. Jaz cried out in pleasure, as he brought her to orgasm with his tongue. Chase worked his way back up her body, and began kissing her again.

"I want you so much Jaz," he said softly.

"I want you too, Chase," she replied, as he laid her down, and moved on top of her.

Jaz moaned with pleasure from the feel of him inside her, as he began to thrust into her, enjoying and savoring every sensation. Chase concentrated on pleasing her, and soon had her moaning loudly, as she pressed her nails into his back. He began to quicken his pace, as he felt himself getting closer.

They collapsed together breathing hard, and holding each other. After they'd both composed themselves, they began to kiss again.

"That was wonderful Jazzy-J," Chase said softly, still lying next to her.

Jaz smiled.

"Mmm, yes it was," she replied. "I didn't know you had it like that Chase," she teased.

He smiled, and returned to kissing her again, their passion igniting once more.

Chase watched Jaz sleeping soundly, as he held her. He'd gotten them some covers, and was lying beside her. Chase smiled as he lay down beside her, and drifted into his own contented sleep.

31

David was completely blitzed. He'd emerged from the bathroom with TaKari completely satisfied, and looking for more alcohol. He'd found Malcolm in the kitchen, and he'd supplied him with some grain. He could barely stand, but he knew he had to make it home.

David thought about Chase briefly, realizing he hadn't seen him all night. *Damn he musta really been busy with Jaz,* he thought wickedly to himself, wondering if he'd managed to hit it.

"Man, has Chase been MIA all night?" David drunkenly asked Malcolm.

The older brother laughed.

"Yeah, he actually likes this one," he replied. "Wants to make her the girlfriend," Malcolm finished, as he fired up the blunt he'd rolled.

David thought about what he'd just heard. *Well, I guess everyone has their own tastes,* he thought to himself. David hoped Chase knew what he was getting himself into. He pushed it from his mind, as he reached into his pockets for his keys. He told Malcolm goodnight, and headed for the front door.

Aidan saw him stumble out and down the stairs. He immediately scanned the area, and saw there was no one else outside now. *Perfect.* Aidan thought to himself, moving nearer to David's car.

David leaned up against one of the cars parked in the driveway, trying to let the cool night air clear his head. He needed to sober up enough to drive home. It was a pretty good distance, and he needed to be able to get there safely. He supposed he should just call a cab, and come back tomorrow to get his car.

David immediately dismissed the idea. *I'm fine and I can do this,* he told himself, in his drunken delusion of sobriety. He leaned on the car for the next thirty minutes, finally dragging himself to the cars trunk, and pushing off it. He stumbled forward trying to focus. David saw his car finally, parked near the wooded area that sat adjacent the house he'd just left. He began walking toward it.

Aidan saw him stumbling toward him and prepared himself. David reached his car finally and fumbled with his keys, eventually finding the one that would open the door, and start the vehicle. He opened the door and felt his legs get taken out from under him.

Aidan had slipped around the front of the car, and crouched behind the door. He'd reached under and yanked David's footing out from under him. He hit the ground hard bumping his head. David was trying desperately to hang on to consciousness, when he saw the shadowy figure looming over him.

Aidan rolled him into the wooded area next to the car. David was trying to clear the liquor and cobwebs from his head. *What the hell is going on,* he thought to himself, struggling to sit up. Aidan pushed him back down, and David tried to groan in protest.

He looked at the pathetic specimen in front of him, and was disgusted all over again. Aidan thought of David touching Mariah, and trying to rape her. He thought about Jaz and how he'd hurt her. Aidan even thought of Sherice, and how David lied to her and treated her, causing her to lose her baby.

"You're a real piece of shit," Aidan told him coldly. David reacted to the voice.

"What are you doing here?" he managed to get out. It was hard for Aidan to understand him. David was so drunk his speech was extremely slurred.

"I'm here to see you," Aidan replied coldly, continuing to take items from his bag.

He pulled out the ecstasy he'd managed to score from the locker of one of the jocks, when they were all at football practice. Aidan knew they used it when they went to parties, to get girls naked.

He'd heard a few names, and those were the lockers he'd checked first. He'd found it on the second try. Aidan knew the drug was deadly if you took more than one or two. He had six that he was planning to give David.

He pulled out the bottle of vodka he'd planned to have him wash them down with. David was semi conscious, and trying to focus again.

"Why don't you leave me alone man?" he asked Aidan, beginning to blubber. "You already took Mariah from me. What else do you want?" David continued, crying drunkenly.

Aidan was disgusted.

"Here man, have a drink and pull yourself together," he told him, changing his tactic slightly and trying to sound amiable.

David sniffled, and took the bottle from Aidan. He eyed him suspiciously for a moment, and then decided it was OK. He opened the vodka and took a long drag.

"Damn, that's good as hell," he exclaimed.

Aidan chuckled lightly. This wasn't going to be as hard as he thought it would be. Now he just had to get him to take the X.

"You need to get yourself together man, before you try to drive home," Aidan told David.

He nodded thoughtfully.

"You came to keep an eye on Jaz, didn't you?" David asked drunkenly again.

Aidan smiled. A cold, deadly, smile and looked at him again.

"Yes," he lied. "I wanted to make sure she was all right."

David grunted, and nodded his head.

"She's with Chase," he told him again. "He likes her you know," he continued, looking at him slyly.

Aidan was genuinely amused sitting here with this ass, and him talking as if they were best friends.

"Yeah, she told me she thought he had a little crush on her," Aidan replied, still looking at David distastefully.

David chuckled again.

"Man, I need something to mellow this buzz out," he said. "You got any weed?"

Aidan smiled again.
"No, but I've got some pills you can take," he told him. "They usually work for me, when I get a little tipsy."

David jumped at the suggestion. "You got some with you?" he asked.
"Yeah, I got a few I can give you," Aidan replied.
David looked at him expectantly, and Aidan gave him five of the tablets.
"Take all of them," he told him, as David began swallowing the tablets.
He chased them down with a long drag of vodka. Soon he began talking to Aidan again.
"Man I'm sorry for all the drama, you know?" he said, beginning to feel the effects of the drug. "I think the pills are starting to work," David told him.

Aidan knew he was feeling the euphoric high that came from the pills, before they took you on that hard downward spiral. David stumbled to his feet. Aidan didn't stop him.
"Well thanks for everything," David told him, as he once again made it to his car. He opened the door, climbed in and started the car. Aidan went to his own vehicle, and followed.

David began to feel his pulse racing as he drove. He was finding it harder and harder to breathe.
What's happening to me, he thought to himself, alarmed that his vision was blurred and getting worse.
David felt the sudden tightening in his chest, like someone was sitting on it. He couldn't breathe, and everything was starting to get dark. He was trying desperately to breathe, and stay conscious. Aidan saw the mustang begin to weave all over the road, and knew what was happening. He smiled coldly, and continued to follow, watching from a distance.

David was fighting the car now, getting more and more terrified. He was sweating profusely, and couldn't control his body. His arms and legs were convulsing in every direction, and his airway was almost completely

closed. He was gasping hard, trying to catch every ounce of air his lungs would allow in.
His right leg began to convulse wildly, and pressed the accelerator of the mustang to the floor, causing the car to take off like a bullet. Unfortunately for him, it happened at a hairpin curve in the highway, and the car was immediately airborne.

David felt like he was dreaming with everything happening in slow motion. He felt himself floating in the air, hearing the powerful crash of the car, as it hit the large oak tree and burst into flames. He'd fallen hard onto the ground, outside the car. *He poisoned me,* David thought to himself of Aidan.

His life began flashing before him, and he remembered all the heinous things he'd done in the last few months. David thought of Mariah and began to cry, still gasping and clawing for air. His last conscious thought was of the pain his death would bring his parents. David took one last gagging breath, and everything became still.

Aidan watched calmly, as the car was fully engulfed. The bright orange flames danced wildly, igniting the tree the car rested against. He'd seen David ejected from the vehicle as it crashed, falling to the earth like a leaded weight.

Aidan saw him waving wildly in the air for a brief moment, then his arms fell and became still. After watching the flames for a few moments longer, and satisfied that David was dead, Aidan calmly got back into his car and turned around, heading in the opposite direction toward home.

He'd just arrived, and made it to his room when the phone rang.
"Hello," he answered softly.
"Hi baby," Mariah murmured in his ear. "I'm sorry to wake you."
Aidan smiled. *Perfect timing,* He thought to himself.

"Its OK honey, I didn't realize I'd fallen asleep," he told Mariah, continuing to feign sleepiness.
"Well, I just wanted to let you know I'd made it home," she told him, beginning to yawn.
Aidan chuckled lightly. "Well you go ahead and get some rest," he told her.
"Sweet dreams baby," she told him gently, and disconnected.
He smiled, thinking he would actually sleep very well tonight, as he headed for the shower. *I don't know how my father and D did this shit all the time,* Aidan thought to himself, as he ran the water, exhausted.

32

News of David's death spread quickly through the community. The police and investigators concluded the death was an accident, brought on by his driving too fast and being under the influence. They'd tried to press charges against Chase and Malcolm's parents, but couldn't. They were both out of town, and had not authorized any guests at their home. Malcolm was over twenty-one, and was charged with a simple count of contributing to the delinquency of a minor, and serving alcohol to a minor. He would probably get probation for both charges.

Maurice and Sandra Alston were devastated. Mrs. Alston had been admitted to the hospital, and was being kept heavily sedated to avoid her having a complete breakdown. Mr. Alston seemed to have aged overnight.

Aidan was on his way to see Mariah. He'd talked to her earlier, and she was upset. He was taking her to the doctor for her pregnancy test today. Aidan had to get himself together before he arrived, so he could at least pretend to be upset at David's death. He pulled into her driveway and took a deep breath, as he got out and knocked on her door.

"Hi," Mariah greeted Aidan softly, trying to smile. He saw she'd been crying.

"Hi baby," he replied, hugging her tightly. "You okay?" he asked gently.

Mariah shook her head yes, but Aidan saw the tears come again.

"I know you're upset honey," he began. "But you have to think about the baby, OK?" Aidan finished, still holding her.

Mariah sighed gently, and told him she would be all right.

"I just can't believe he's dead, Aidan," she told him, as they rode to the doctors.

He was careful not to show his true emotions, when he replied.

"I know honey, it's just a terrible situation," Aidan replied, agreeably enough.
Mariah sighed gently.
"I don't think I can go to his funeral," she told him quietly. "I just don't think I could take it."

Aidan was glad to hear her say that. He didn't want Mariah there. He didn't want her to grieve for the slime who had done nothing but hurt her.
"I think that's a good idea baby," Aidan told her softly.
Mariah looked up at him, and smiled.
"I'm so glad I have you," she told him earnestly.
He smiled, and squeezed her hand.
"You'll always have me," Aidan replied, as they arrived at their destination. "Come on now. This is a happy occasion," he told her, and she chuckled lightly.
"You're right," Mariah replied, drying her eyes and trying to improve her mood.

They entered the office, and gave the nurse her name. She asked them to have a seat, and they'd be seen shortly. Aidan looked around at the office, and smiled at all the baby photos that lined the large bulletin board they'd posted.

There were ads for various baby related supplies, and cute poems in frames adorning the walls. The wallpaper was a cheerful yellow, with an alphabet building blocks pattern.
He was getting more and more excited as they sat.
"I'm so excited about the baby," Aidan told her, smiling as he held her hand.
Mariah laughed and kissed him.
"I'm glad," she told him, still smiling. "I thought you might be pissed at me," she said quietly.
Aidan was perplexed. "Why would I be?" he asked.
Mariah sighed gently. "I didn't want you to think I was trying to trap you, or hold you back from your dreams and goals," she replied, looking him in the eye.

He kissed her back. "You really spend too much time worrying about crazy stuff. You know that?" Aidan told her.
Mariah smiled again.
"I love you Mariah," he told her honestly. "There is absolutely nothing that could change that, and I want this baby, just as much as I want you," Aidan finished, kissing her again for emphasis.

Mariah giggled, and told him okay. Aidan was glad she feeling better. He knew it was going to be a long week. He'd heard they weren't having David's funeral until the weekend. He didn't care when it was. He was just glad he'd ended all the suffering for the people he loved.

Aidan felt a little bad for David's parents, but he pushed it aside, rationalizing that he'd done what he had to do, to protect his own. Aidan remembered what Big D told him about being who he was. *"A man has got to take care of what's his, or he'll soon find it belonging to someone else," he'd told Aidan when they talked.*

Aidan had already taken the first step toward that when he'd deliberately seduced Mariah, and made love to her unprotected. He knew David was still after her, and he wouldn't take the chance she may go back to him.
He'd been secretly doctoring the condoms they used since those nights they had been together unprotected, hoping for exactly this result. He wasn't going to let anyone take her from him. Aidan absolutely loved Mariah with every fiber of his being. Now he finally had almost everything he wanted.

The nurse came back into the waiting room and interrupted his thought.
"Come on back Mariah," she told her.
Mariah told her she wanted Aidan to come too, and the nurse told her it was fine. He held her hand, and smiled contentedly, as they walked back to the examination room.

"Hello," she answered her cell.
"Hey Jazzy-J," Chase said softly. "You OK?"

They'd found out about David early this morning, when the police had come and awakened them to question them. She'd been visibly upset, and he was worried about her. Jaz smiled in spite of her earlier mood.
"Yeah Chase, I'm cool," she replied gently. "Its just such a shock, and so hard to believe."

He sighed deeply. "I feel sorta responsible," Chase told her, explaining that he'd been the one to invite David to the party.
"Well you didn't make him drink like that and drive, Chase," Jaz told him frankly. "So stop trippin'."
Chase loved talking to Jaz. She always managed to make him feel better.
"Are you going to the funeral?" he asked her.

She'd thought about it. She'd been thinking about David since she heard, revisiting all their old history. Jaz had to be honest and say that outside of the normal grief for loss of human life, she really didn't feel all that bad about him being dead. He'd done nothing but hurt her, and treat her badly. He'd caused her a hurt so deep; she still couldn't bring herself to talk about it.

She'd only told Aidan in a moment of weakness. He'd managed to kill himself before Aidan could get to him. *Probably a good thing,* Jaz thought to herself, not wanting to see her cousin in any trouble.
"No, I don't think so," She replied.
Chase sighed again.
"Well I probably will," he told her. "I mean I know you two didn't really get along, but I wish you would come with me," he told her. "Just for my sake."

Jaz sighed gently. She really liked Chase, and they'd had a wonderful evening last night. She supposed she could do this one thing for him.
"OK," Jaz said softly.
Chase was glad she'd agreed. He couldn't really explain it. He just knew he would need her there with him.
"Thanks baby," he replied, catching them both off guard.
"I'm sorry," Chase told her quickly.

Jaz chuckled. "For what boy?" she asked playfully. He laughed lightly, and changed the subject. They chatted about college for a moment, before she remembered what she wanted to say to him.
"Oh yeah," Jaz started, and Chase heard her tone.
Oh shit, what did I do? He thought to himself.
"Let's talk about you not using a condom last night, Chase," she said.
He took a deep breath, but didn't say anything.
"What if I get pregnant?" Jaz asked softly.
"We'd just decide what to do," Chase replied simply.

Jaz was surprised at how unconcerned he seemed to be. She was definitely scared of that happening. She remembered vividly her last pregnancy, and the hurt was still there.
"Did you even think about using a condom last night?" Jaz asked him again, guardedly.
Chase sighed gently.
"I thought about it, but we were already knee deep, and you felt so good," he told her honestly.
This time she sighed.
"Look Jaz," he began seriously. "I know there's a real possibility you could get pregnant," he went on. "I'm man enough to deal with that if it happens, and you want to keep the baby," Chase continued, "So don't sweat that, and we'll deal with it if, or when, we have to."

Jaz was definitely impressed. Chase continued to surprise her, and she felt better about her choice to be with him intimately, and have a relationship with him.
"Okay, I guess you're right." she replied. "But from now on, we hafta be safe, okay?"
Chase chuckled lightly, and told her scouts honor. They both laughed, and he told her he'd call her later. Jaz was still smiling when she headed downstairs to the kitchen, to make herself some lunch.

33

This was the worst Saturday in her entire life, Sandra thought to herself as she looked out of her window into the heavens.

"Why?" she asked again softly, for what seemed like the hundredth time.

She still couldn't bring herself to say the words. It was hard enough for her to even believe that her only child would never come home again.

Sandra looked at the sky as it hung heavy with thick gray clouds ready to burst with grief of their own over her loss, as the wind blew the trees and they bent majestically in surrender to the power that controlled them.

She sighed gently, and opened the door to David's room. She hadn't been able to come in here for the last week. Sandra felt the tears immediately come, and her heart grow heavy again. She had to do this she told herself, for her own sense of closure.

She sat on his bed, taking his pillow in her arms and inhaling it deeply. It still smelled like him. Sandra looked around the room at the various awards and trophies, the pictures and mementos he kept, and felt his presence again.

"I miss you so much son," Sandra said softly aloud.

She took a deep breath and rose from the bed, knowing she needed to get ready for his service. Sandra stopped at the dresser, seeing one of the drawers askew, and opened it. She saw the photo of David and Mariah lying inside. She began to cry again. This time she cried and asked God's forgiveness for all she'd done.

Sandra felt like David's death was her punishment for the two lives she'd taken, in the form of his unborn children. Now she had absolutely nothing. Mariah and David had never been intimate, nor remained friends. Sandra would never be able to sit and talk with her, and reminisce about David, or their relationship.

She wept deeply, knowing that he was truly gone, and no part of him remained on this earth. The hardest part of that knowledge came from knowing she was responsible for that fact, more so than anyone else on the planet.

Maurice heard her sobbing, and came in to comfort her. "Shh, honey it's going to be all right," he told Sandra gently, as he helped her to her feet.

"Come on, we have to get ready to leave now," Maurice continued, as he guided her out of the room, and gently closed the door.

Kayla and Thomas were getting ready to leave in a few moments. Kayla sighed deeply, thinking how hard this had to be for Maurice and Sandra. She couldn't imagine the pain they were going through, knowing their only child was dead.

It sent a shudder down her spine, and she headed to Mariah's room to check on her. Kayla knocked gently, and heard her say come in.

"Hi honey," she greeted her daughter, who was still in bed.

"Hi mommy," Mariah answered softly, trying to smile.

Kayla knew she was having a rough morning. She'd awakened feeling absolutely horrible this morning. Kayla sighed gently, as she caressed Mariah's face.

"Are you feeling any better?" she asked.

Mariah shook her head no, as she continued to lie still with her eyes closed. Kayla kissed her forehead gently.

"It does get better sweetheart, I promise," she told her, as she rose to leave.

Mariah smiled weakly and told her mother goodbye.

Kayla stopped at the phone on her way downstairs, and called Aidan.

"Hello?" he answered.

"Hi Aidan," Kayla greeted him.

He was immediately alarmed.

"Is something wrong?" he asked apprehensively.

Kayla chuckled lightly.
"No Aidan, calm down," she told him still amused. "Thomas and I are going to David's service, and Mariah is having a really bad morning," she told him. "I don't want to leave her here alone, and I was wondering if you could come and stay with her while we're gone."

Aidan breathed a sigh of relief. He was glad there was nothing wrong with Mariah or the baby, and he was even glad she was sick. He didn't want her to decide at the last minute, out of some sense of displaced obligation, to go to David's funeral.
"Of course, Mrs. Bradford," Aidan replied. "I'll be right there."

Disconnecting, he grabbed his shirt and put it on, then headed for the stairs. He ran into Jaz as she was coming out of her room.
"Where are you going?" he asked, looking her over.
"To the funeral," she replied quietly.
Aidan looked at her hard for a moment.
"Why?" he asked simply.

Jaz was a little frightened, by both the question, and the look he was giving her now. This was a side of her cousin that scared her. It was the side she'd gotten a glimpse of when David attacked Mariah.
"Because Chase asked me to go with him," Jaz replied softly.

Aidan relaxed, he understood then. "Oh, okay," he replied, chuckling a little and giving her a new look.
"What's that mean?" she asked him, smiling slightly herself.
"So are you and Chase together now?" he asked slyly.
She didn't answer, just looked at the floor. Aidan chuckled aloud.
"Did you sleep with him the other night at the party?" he asked, making Jaz blush.
He laughed aloud, and hugged her. "It's OK, lil big head girl," Aidan told Jaz gently, as he released her.

"I'm glad you two worked everything out," he went on. "Chase is a nice guy, try not to corrupt him," he joked. Jaz joined him laughing.

"And where are you going mister?" she asked, seeing Aidan dressed to go.

"Over to Mariah's," he replied. "She's not feeling well."

Jaz was concerned, so she pressed him.

"What's wrong with her? It's nothing serious is it?" she questioned, genuinely concerned.

Aidan smiled. "Morning sickness," he said simply, and turned to walk away.

Jaz grabbed him, and spun him around.

"Morning what?!" she exclaimed, her mouth hanging open.

Aidan chuckled again. "You heard me," he replied.

Jaz was incredulous. "She's pregnant?" Jaz whispered.

Aidan shook his head yes.

"Does Mrs. Bradford know?" she asked again.

Aidan told her Kayla did, and she was fine with it.

"Wow! You really did it this time!" Jaz chuckled.

Aidan told her they were going to go ahead and get married, they just hadn't decided on a date yet.

"Well I'm happy for you guys," she told him "I know Mariah is excited."

Aidan smiled again.

"Yeah, and so am I," he told her, looking wistfully over her shoulder.

Jaz smiled again and told him congratulations.

"Jasmine, Chase is here!" she heard her mother call out.

"OK, I'm on my way," she replied.

"Jaz and Chase, sitting in a tree," Aidan teased, as Jaz walked down the stairs.

He heard her chuckle and tell him to shut up.

Mariah was feeling the full effects of her pregnancy this morning. She'd awakened with a terrible headache and nausea. She couldn't even sit up for the first hour after she'd woken up, because of the dizziness.

Well, I guess this the answer I asked for, Mariah thought to herself, as she lay in bed.

She'd prayed last night, after spending most of the evening going back and forth about David's service. She'd been reminiscing on their past, and their friendship. The relationship they'd had, and even the last few months of his life. Mariah was genuinely hurt that he was dead.

She knew David wasn't a bad person, just confused and out of sync lately. She didn't know if she could take seeing him dead, or even being in the church looking at the coffin knowing he would never come back. Mariah thought of his parents, and how badly they must be hurting right now.

She even wondered if her very presence would cause them even more pain, knowing how much they'd wanted her to be with David. In the end, she'd prayed before crying herself to sleep from her loss, that God give her an answer to go or not.

Mariah took a deep breath and tried to sit up again. This time she actually made it up and out of bed without becoming dizzy.

"What are you doing?" Aidan asked her softly.

Mariah jumped from the sound of his voice; she hadn't heard him come in.

"I'm sorry baby; I didn't mean to scare you," he told her as he walked over to the bed.

Mariah smiled as she looked at him.

"I need to go to the bathroom," she replied.

Aidan told her okay, as she made her way into the room. She emerged moments later, and made her way back to the bed.

"How do you feel now?" he asked, concerned.

Mariah smiled, and told him she felt a little better.

"You want me to make you something to eat?" he asked again.

She thought about it, the thought itself making her nauseous.

"No," Mariah replied. "Just bring me some crackers, and maybe some juice."
Aidan smiled and told her okay, as he headed downstairs to get what she'd asked for. Mariah thought how lucky she was to have Aidan.
"Here you go baby," he told her returning from downstairs, handing the crackers and juice to her.

She managed to eat a few of them, and drink the juice without any ill effects.
"I'll be so glad when this part is over," Mariah told Aidan softly, as they watched TV together.
He continued to hold her as he spoke.
"It will be soon baby, I promise," he told her.
Mariah hugged him tightly, and sighed deeply. Aidan knew she was thinking about David and the funeral. She'd been honest and told him she'd thought about going, until she woke up sick this morning.
He wasn't angry with her. He understood her reasoning, but he was beyond elation that she wasn't able to go. As far as Aidan was concerned, today was a great day.

Here's something I would have never pictured myself doing, Maurice Alston thought to himself, as he sat at the gravesite of his only son. Thomas was saying the final words of internment, and they were preparing to lower the coffin into the ground.
The funeral had been one of the hardest things he'd ever endured. The church was packed, as was the cemetery now, with all David's friends, Maurice's business friends, clients, family and the like.

He was pleased at how well loved his son was. He'd looked for Mariah when he saw Kayla, but she hadn't come. He supposed it was all too much for her. Maurice knew even now, the young woman harbored no ill will against David.
She'd told him as much when they'd talked earlier this week. She'd called while Sandra was sleeping, and they'd gotten a much needed opportunity for closure.

Maurice only wished Mariah and David had been given the chance to reconcile after their last encounter. He looked at his wife, and saw the hurt and pain sketched all over her face.

She'd had a particularly emotional outburst when she saw Jasmine, even going out of her way to hug the young woman. He didn't understand, but evidently the two of them did, as Jasmine returned her hug, and became emotional as well.

The coffin had been placed in the ground, and everyone was starting to leave. Maurice couldn't bring himself to rise yet. Thomas gently touched his shoulder, and told him it was time.

He just couldn't move. All the pain, all the loss, all the grief came pouring out at that moment. Maurice began to cry; deep, painful, racking sobs, thinking of David lying alone and cold, in that grave.

Thinking of all the things he would never see David achieve, never see him discover. Thinking of the grandchildren he would never get to hold, or spoil, the advice he would never get to give.

His son was gone. There was a hole in Maurice now that he didn't think could ever be filled. Thomas stayed with him, and tried to comfort him.

Moments later after finally spending himself, Maurice gathered the strength to leave. He looked at the freshly covered grave once more, read the marker and told his son goodbye. Thomas helped him back to the waiting car.

Sherice walked over to the fresh grave, from the spot where she'd been watching tears of her own flooding her face.

"I'm so sorry David," she said softly. "I never wished you dead," she went on trying to clear the pain she felt in her heart, that she was somehow responsible for this.

"I hope you're at peace now," Sherice whispered, as Elaine came and took her hand to lead her away.

Sandra saw the young woman from the window of the car, and smiled softly to herself. She wanted to apologize to her too for how she'd treated her. She'd gotten that chance with Jasmine today at the service.

Sandra made a mental note to call Sherice later, and talk to her. She felt Maurice take her hand and squeeze it. Sandra looked at her husband and smiled. They embraced and held each other all the way back to their home.

Epilogue

The months passed, and life began to return to normal for the quiet community in Chapel Hill. Jaz and Chase became a serious couple, with the young man proposing marriage to her. She'd told him about her history with David, and why they'd disliked each other.

Jaz was able to move on now that she'd made her peace with his mother and allowed the hurt to go away. All she'd ever wanted was an apology, and Mrs. Alston had given her that. Chase had been understanding, and never brought it up or used it against her, even when they quarreled, which was rarely.

Chase decided to go into the military first, so they would be provided for, and Jaz would have everything she needed. Then Chase would go to college with the money he would get for enlisting. Jackie and Chris approved of Chase, and told her he was a wonderful young man, and would make a good husband and eventually father.

Jaz had seen Elaine once during the summer, and that was to tell her goodbye. She'd heard about her and Sherice leaving for Miami together. They'd parted amiably, and Jaz was good with that. Her life was going well, and she was excited. Chase had been assigned to a base in Arizona, so they were leaving the end of the month.

Sandra and Maurice Alston had a new reason to live again. They'd received a call from a young woman, who said she needed to speak with them. They'd been completely surprised by her call, as they'd never heard her name spoken, or why she would be calling them. They agreed to meet her, and invited her to their home for lunch.

TaKari Stanley arrived at the Alston home and met David's parents. She had a problem, but she thought she'd come up with a solution that would benefit everyone involved. TaKari told them of her involvement with

David, making it seem more than the one night they shared.
She didn't want them to think of his last night that way. "I really cared for David," she told them. "We just got carried away that night," she continued, hanging her head. "I'm pregnant," she said simply.

Sandra and Maurice were stunned. On the one hand, they were delighted that something of David was still left, on the other, how did they know this young woman was telling the truth?
"So what are you proposing?" Maurice asked the girl, trying to see if this was some elaborate con. TaKari took a deep breath before answering.
"I know what I'm about to say may sound cold, but I'm trying to be honest," she replied.

Maurice and Sandra continued to listen.
"I cared for David," TaKari began. "But I don't want any part of this baby," she went on. "The only reason I haven't had an abortion yet, is because I wanted to see if you would take the child," she finished, and waited for their response.

Sandra was ready to say yes immediately. She felt like she was being given a second chance, and she wasn't going to see it walk out of the door. Maurice was elated, but cautious. He asked a few more questions.
"So you're going to give up all rights to the child?" he asked.
TaKari shook her head yes.
"And what do you want in return?" he asked, looking at her intently.
She smiled slightly before answering. "Mr. Alston, I'm not here to try and get anything from you," TaKari replied.
"I just knew that David was your only child, and since this baby is his, I thought you would want it, because honestly, I don't," TaKari relayed sincerely.

Maurice relaxed and believed the young woman. They talked further, with him asking if she was provided

for while she carried the child. TaKari assured him her parents would not throw her out.
She would call them for each doctor visit, and when she went into labor. Once she had the baby it was theirs to take home, and she would sign any documentation they wanted.

Maurice and Sandra thanked TaKari again and again for this special gift she was giving them, and insisted on paying all her medical bills, and providing her money for clothing, and expenses, while she was pregnant. The two women were both in tears by the time TaKari left, and Maurice was a bit misty himself.

Thank you God, he thought to himself of the miracle they'd been given. They both talked at length after the young woman left, agreeing that they would do things so much differently this time. They would be elated to learn months later, that the child TaKari carried was a boy.

Aidan was reflecting on the events of the past few months. He was happier than he'd been in a long time. He and Mariah were married, and their daughter was due soon. They'd agreed to name her after both the women in their lives they loved so much, Olivia Mikayla. He'd been thinking about his father a lot lately. Aidan wished Dezi could be here, as well as his mother, to share this wonderful thing that was happening in his life.

He also thought a lot of his father's activities, and wondered if he were becoming more and more like him. Aidan still felt no remorse for killing David. He'd heard that some girl was having a baby from him, and giving it to his parents. Aidan was glad for their sakes, but he didn't feel he'd done anything wrong in killing him.

He'd talked to DeSean right before his wedding. He'd unfortunately gone back to the streets, and was now serving a fifteen year sentence for second degree murder. He'd been rolling with the Broughton Boys, when they robbed a liquor store and killed the owner. DeSean told

Aidan he still considered himself lucky, because at least he was still alive.

Cameron had been killed in jail, awaiting sentencing. Aidan was saddened that his younger brother ended up incarcerated, but he didn't abandon him. Unfortunately, Shay couldn't take the pressure and left, taking the child without DeSean ever seeing it. He didn't even know if he'd had a son or daughter.

Aidan sighed deeply, and shook himself. This was a happy time. He and Mariah were spending the day choosing things to decorate the baby's nursery. Aidan needed to call Big D later. He'd been on his mind all day. He supposed it was because he wanted to talk about his father again.

Aidan was more curious by the day about the man behind the mystique. *Why couldn't he still be alive,* he thought to himself again, wanting desperately a chance to really know who he was and become a part of the legacy that was still revered even now.

Kayla awakened, bathed in sweat from the dream she'd just had. *What the hell is wrong with me,* she thought to herself. This was the latest in a string of repetitive dreams she'd had over the last month.

She was glad Thomas had already left to begin his day at the church. She'd dreamed they were making love again. Dezi was touching her, and kissing her gently, arousing her to her breaking point, before he entered her, and made passionate love to her.

Kayla could feel his hardness inside her, and his arms encompassing her, as he thrust into her again and again, bringing her pleasure upon pleasure. She felt his lips kissing her breasts, and gently licking her nipples. She heard him moaning gently, calling her name as he enjoyed the warmth of her body.

Kayla felt Dezi's rhythm quicken, and knew he was getting close. She felt her own body begin to respond in kind, and she began softly calling his name too. Kayla felt the immediate rush of warmth from his release, and it brought her to orgasm.

She was screaming his name loudly as her body was rocked with the force of pleasure she'd derived from the act they'd shared. Kayla awoke still trying to gather herself, and steady her breathing. She'd been fortunate that Thomas had never been around when she'd awakened from one of the dreams.

How could she explain it? What could she possibly say to him, waking up, screaming another man's name in ecstasy? The dream had been so vivid, and the memories it stirred, wonderful. It took her back to a time and place where she still believed in the magic that was fairytale love.

Kayla needed the dreams to stop. Surely her luck would run out one day, and she didn't want to have to explain to Thomas why she was having erotic dreams about a man who'd been dead for over twenty years.

He turned the pictures over again, looking at them intently and smiled. They made a lovely couple, the smiling young man, and the beautiful dimpled young woman. He'd sent the money for Aidan, as soon as Big D told him about his mother being killed. He wanted to make sure he was properly taken care of.

They'd come up with the story of a hidden insurance policy, to keep him from being suspicious. Now, looking at his obviously pregnant wife, he was glad they had it. Big D had even told him of the boy's growth in becoming a true legacy. He chuckled, thinking of how he himself had begun early learning to kill, and protect his investments.

There was so much he wanted to share with the boy. There were pictures of Kayla too. She still looked wonderful. He loved her as much today as he did more than twenty years ago. He thought back to that fateful day. He was supposed to be dead, and as far as anyone else knew he was.

"It's amazing what money will buy you," Dezi said wistfully.

He'd called in a favor with the suits, and reached out to the one person he knew he could trust, Big D. He told him all about the government's involvement in hiding him, because of the powerful people he could have brought down. He had to stay out of the states or he would be arrested, and so far he had done just that. He loved island living. He'd been here since he left Virginia.

Kayla had been at his funeral. He'd seen her on the video they'd made for him, weeping. Dezi was amazed at the job they'd done on the corpse they used for him. It had fooled even his mother.

Dezi longed for home now, seeing the son he'd just learned he had, and the daughter he thought was his, joined together. He wanted to see Kayla again too. Big D told him she'd married again after Agent Black was killed.

"Can't say I'm sorry about that loss," Dezi said hatefully. Even after all these years, he still held him personally responsible for losing her. He was never the same without Kayla. True, he'd come here and made a new fortune, but it wasn't fulfilling.

"I needed you here with me baby," Dezi said softly aloud, recalling the past.

He'd had some plastic surgery, and wore contacts now to disguise the true color of his eyes. He'd grown a beard to hide the dimples, but he was tired of hiding. He wanted to meet the grandchild that his son's wife was carrying.

He wanted to meet the son he never knew existed, and he wanted to be with the love of his life one more time. He looked at the ticket in his hand, and headed for his flight.

Dezi Gianni was on his way back from the dead.

LaVergne, TN USA
28 February 2010
174455LV00002B/39/P